PRINCESS OF SHADOWS

Fairy Tale Adventures Book One

A. G. MARSHALL

Avanell Publishing

To my parents.
Thanks for filling my life with
music, stories, adventures, and love.

Air rushed into Lina's lungs. Her eyes snapped open, but she saw only darkness. She pried her arms away from her sides and rubbed an itch on her nose. Something gritty covered her face. Dirt? She brushed it away.

"Luca? Luca, are you there?"

Her voice echoed through the darkness. Lina inhaled again and coughed on the dust. The sound echoed through the cavern.

"Hello?"

No one answered. The echo faded into a silence like the grave.

Lina pushed herself up on her elbows. Her body was stiff, but she managed to swing her legs around to a seated position. She rubbed the diamond in her ring.

"Light," she said. "Illuminate."

A faint glow filled the room. Lina shut her eyes. After the darkness, even the pale light from the diamond overwhelmed her senses.

"Less illumination."

The light faded to a softer glow. Lina squinted at her

surroundings. She had been in the dark too long to see much. She needed time to adjust. When her eyes recovered enough to open them fully, Lina raised her hand so the light from the diamond filled the room.

She was in a small cave. A small, dirty cave. Except for the grime, everything was just as she had ordered it. Just as she and Luca had set it up. Dust coated everything. The tables covered with charms to support her sleep. The scrolls explaining her situation in case a stranger found her. The enchanted mirror.

Lina ran her hand along her stone bed. She traced the swirling vein of silver that ran down the center. Her fingertips tingled with magic.

The seal held.

She stood and walked to a table across the room. Her stiff legs protested, but Lina was too thirsty to care. She had told Luca to keep a pitcher filled with water for her.

The pitcher was empty.

"Just like the donkey to forget something like that," she muttered.

Lina swallowed a few times, trying to relieve her dry throat. The dust that covered the cave had not spared her. She wiped a layer of grime off the enchanted mirror and stared at her reflection.

Her chestnut hair hung down her back in a thick tangled mess. She remembered braiding it before falling under the enchantment. Her bright green eyes twinkled under prominent eyebrows tangled with cobwebs. Lina rubbed them and left a trail of dirt on her face. She licked a finger and wiped her face clean.

Well, cleaner.

Her skin was clear under the dust. No bruises. No sign of a struggle. She looked gray and ghostly in the light of the ring.

Lina smiled sadly to herself. The girl in the mirror smiled back. Lina gathered a bit of shadow magic in her fingertips and touched the glass. She studied her reflection for any sign of change.

Nothing. The enchantment had faded. Lina pushed more shadow magic into the glass, but she couldn't bring it back. She and Luca had enchanted it together. She would need his light magic to fix it completely.

Lina wiped her hands on her skirt. They came away even grimier. Dirt saturated the fabric of her gown. Lina remembered picking her favorite dress to wear for the enchantment. A pale purple silk frock. It was ruined now. She'd need a change of clothes before she met with the Council.

And a bath.

Maybe two baths.

There would be guards stationed at the end of the hallway. Lina pushed on the door. It crumbled at her touch. The falling bits of wood filled the air with even more dust. She ripped the end off her sleeve and covered her mouth with it. The fabric tore in her hand like a spider web.

Lina held her hand through the doorway. Light from her ring illuminated an empty tunnel.

"Luca?"

Her brother's name echoed through the tunnel until silence swallowed it.

Lina's stomach twisted. Luca had promised he would watch her. He might forget to refill a pitcher of water, but even he wouldn't forget something as important as guarding his twin sister while she slept.

Something had gone very wrong. It must have. Had the goblins attacked after all? Had the enchantment failed?

Lina crept down the hallway. One step at a time. Her feet dragged on the rough stone floor. How much time had she spent asleep in the realm of shadows? Everything was easier there. You could fly as easily as you walked. But transitioning back to the realm of light wasn't usually this slow.

Lina reached the end of the tunnel and ran her hand over the smooth stone door. It was just as she remembered. Made from the same stone as the mountain and carved to fit without a single gap.

She studied the door until she found the keyhole. Lina pushed the diamond on her ring into it and turned her wrist. The cavern plunged into darkness as the door swallowed her diamond. Her heart pounded. What if the door was broken? What if she was buried alive?

The latch clicked. Lina pulled her ring out and pushed the door forward. It didn't slide as smoothly as it should have, but at least it didn't crumble like the wood. Gentle white light filled the tunnel. A crisp breeze rustled Lina's hair. She peered around the door and saw stars overhead.

Good, it was night. She wasn't sure she could handle daylight yet. Lina held her ring to her lips.

"Check for danger."

She held her breath. If the light changed to red, there were creatures of darkness nearby. Goblins or worse.

The light stayed white. Its glow matched the moonlight streaming into the cavern. Lina exhaled in relief.

"Extinguish."

Her ring's light faded until it was a normal diamond glittering in the moonlight.

So there was no danger. Luca might be safe after all.

Perhaps the guards were taking a break. Perhaps the danger had passed enough that they didn't need to watch her every second.

Lina slipped around the rock and into the open air. An evening breeze washed over her. She pushed the rock closed and locked it with her ring. The enchantments on the door should keep the seal safe even when she was gone.

The air smelled just as it should. She closed her eyes and savored the scents. Fresh grass and pine trees. The tang of the ocean. The pale sweetness of snowbells. Summer in Aeonia.

Lina opened her eyes and examined her surroundings. Her heart contracted.

She stood in untamed mountain wilderness. Above her, pine forests reached for the mountaintops. Fields of snowbells stretched below her. Their purple blossoms waved in the moonlight like ocean waves.

This was all wrong. They had buried her in the wrong place. She had watched them carve the marble structures around her cave. Helped them weave magic into the stones. There should be a pavilion to her left. And where was the wolf statue?

Maybe they had moved her. A marble pavilion wasn't exactly subtle. Maybe danger had forced them to move her. To dig another cavern in the wilderness.

Maybe things had gone badly after all. Had there been a battle? Had the goblins destroyed the statue? Lina studied the landscape. The hillside bore no signs of a skirmish. She sat on a mossy patch among the snowbells and studied the bottom of the mountain.

Lights of a city nestled at the mountain's base. Yes, that was right. Mias, the capital city of Aeonia, had been visible from the mouth of the cavern. She remembered the view. Moonlight glistened on the ocean waves and white plaster buildings. The view was spectacular. She would know it anywhere. This had been Luca's favorite picnic spot.

So she was in the right place. What had happened to the marble carvings? She understood removing the pavilion, but the wolf statue had been an important part of the protection charms around her.

Lina stood and studied the space around the door. She looked for any hint of difference. Her heart sank.

She didn't remember the moss.

Lina rested her hand on the ground. A faint magical aura permeated it. She dissolved it, crawled to the nearest clump of moss and pulled at it. She threw handful after handful away, praying she wouldn't find anything under it. Please, let it be just earth.

She jammed her finger on something hard. Lina brushed the dirt away, revealing a gleaming rock as white as bone.

"No."

Lina clawed the dirt and moss away. Please, no. It couldn't be.

A worn marble paw took shape as Lina removed its mossy covering. Claws stretched towards her. She swallowed a sob.

She remembered the shape. She had helped make the shape. A fierce guard wolf with sharp claws and green emerald eyes. The claws were dull now. The wolf's teeth rounded at the edges. Worn smooth by rain and moss and time.

Time. How much time would it take to crumble the edges of a marble statue to dust?

Lina wiped the dirt away from the wolf's face. What was left of it, anyway.

Something small and round fell into her hand. The wolf's eye. The round emerald gleamed in the moonlight. Tears filled her eyes and left trails in the dust on her cheeks.

"Luca!"

She screamed into the night. Her voice echoed against the mountains and dissolved in the wind. No one answered.

"Luca."

She clutched the emerald in her fist. The world dissolved in a flash of memory.

"CAREFUL WITH THE PEAS, LINA."

"They're emeralds, Luca."

"Yeah? They look like peas to me. Think we could trick chef into putting them in a stew? I'd love to see the king's face when he swallowed one."

"Luca—"

"Come on, Lina! The King of Gaveron has been giving us trouble for ages. Let's return the favor."

"Luca—"

"One last prank before you go to sleep?"

"Luca, this is serious."

He looked at her with piercing green eyes that matched her own.

"I know. Are you sure you want to do this?"

"Yes."

"You're not afraid?"

"I'm a shadow warrior. I've faced worse. Besides you'll watch over me."

He grinned at her.

"Of course I will."

LINA LOOKED BACK AT THE WOLF'S FACE. HOW LONG would it take to wear marble smooth like that? Decades? Centuries?

Longer than he could live, a small voice in her head whispered. Much longer than Luca could survive.

Lina clutched the pea emerald to her heart and sobbed. She had known this was a possibility. That was the reality of the enchanted sleep. She would wake sometime, but who could say when? Who could say what would be left for her?

Luca had been so confident though. So sure he could find a way to wake her once they had sealed the danger away. They had been a team. Inseparable.

Lina swallowed her tears. Everyone was gone. Not just Luca. Everyone she had fought to protect. Even if they had survived the war, they were gone now.

The lights of Mias twinkled below her. Lina wiped her eyes. Someone had survived. Goblins would not fill a city with light. She leaned on the wolf statue and stood. Her heart pounded.

Lina tore a hole in her sleeve and tucked the pea inside the hem. She clutched the fabric in her fist and walked down the mountain. One step at a time in the moonlight. She would do as she always had. Go forward. Fight to protect her country.

Pale purple snowbells, the same color her dress had once been, swayed around her.

2

"Sit down, son. You're making me tired."

Prince Alaric stopped pacing and rested his hands on his father's desk. His golden hair curled around his head in a tangled mass. He ran his hands through it again. It got more tangled every time he did, but he couldn't help himself. He fixed his dark eyes on his father, opened his mouth, then closed it again. The king shrugged.

Alaric shook his head and resumed pacing.

"I'm not angry," King Noam said.

"But you're not pleased. I thought you'd be pleased."

King Noam chuckled.

"No, I'm far from pleased. We have many important things to discuss at the Council of Kings. I wanted you by my side. Not chatting with princesses."

"The future of Aeonia could depend on those chats."

"Things are rarely that final, Alaric. The Council meets often enough. You will have other opportunities to find a bride. Calling for a Princess Test now could make us seem desperate."

"We are as much a member of the Council as any other

9

country. We have as much right to a Princess Test. I'm more than old enough. We should have called for one at the last Council."

King Noam stroked his beard.

"I considered it, but I thought it would be unnecessary. You were rather taken with a certain member of the royal guard at that time."

Alaric winced. His flirtation with Odette had been foolish. An endangerment to the kingdom.

"That was before I fully understood my responsibilities as crown prince. I understand now I must marry a princess. A true princess."

"Alaric, you know I'll stand by you whatever you decide, but don't let your obsession with your lineage lead you to do something rash."

His obsession? Did no one understand? Alaric pounded his hands against his father's desk. The motioned jarred him. He sank into a chair.

"Forgive me, father. That was uncalled for."

King Noam's features smoothed as he stood and clasped his son's shoulder.

"You take your responsibilities seriously, lad. The whole kingdom appreciates that about you. But is this necessary? Our family has ruled for over a century. No one has questioned our bloodline in all that time."

Alaric frowned.

"There were rumors at the last Council."

"Rumors seldom turn into action. I don't mind a few sneers if you're happy. It is possible to take responsibilities too seriously."

"Hardly. We're talking about the future queen of Aeonia. A queen can cast light or shadows over the land. We've seen both."

"I doubt any of the princesses will be evil enchantresses."

"Father, please. I want to get this right. We have the throne of Aeonia, but we aren't noble. I know our history. If I marry a princess, our legacy will be secure. I don't know yet which countries will come, but if you have a preference, I will abide by it."

King Noam bowed his head.

"The people accept our right to rule. Isn't that enough?"

Alaric shook his head. It was something, certainly, but it wasn't enough. His father watched him with narrowed eyes.

"You say you don't know which girls are coming. Are you sure? Your stepmother has been preparing for months. Hasn't she told you anything?"

"No. I do know she's prepared twenty rooms. She doesn't have their names either."

"Their names. Yes, knowing their names is against the rules. But that didn't stop you from sending spies to find that information, did it?"

King Noam pulled out a packet of parchments. Alaric flinched.

"You weren't supposed to know about that."

He reached for the parchments. King Noam pulled them away.

"Are you sure you want this information, Alaric? Any of these girls will strengthen our position. I hate to be mercenary about your future bride, but that is the truth. Wouldn't you rather get to know them without the pressure of political alliances on your shoulders?"

"I'll only have three days. Hardly enough time to form a real relationship. The Princess Test is all about politics. It always has been."

Alaric leaned on his father's desk and tried to catch a glimpse of the parchments.

"Who is coming?" he asked.

"Of the twenty girls, eight are princesses. The rest are the daughters of high-ranking officials or province governors."

"Only eight? It won't be easy to find the true princesses in the group."

King Noam nodded.

"Yes, it will be challenging. And unnecessary as far as I'm concerned. There may be a few who question our bloodline, but they are not willing to do so openly."

Alaric grimaced.

"They won't dare to question us at all after the test. Who do you think would benefit us the most? Should I look for a country with good exports? Or a strong military? I could secure a trade route."

King Noam sighed.

"It will be harder than you think, Alaric. You aren't allowed to know which country the princesses come from. You won't even know their names. If you are going to do this, try to find someone you actually like."

Alaric smirked.

"As if I would leave something this important up to chance and emotions."

"I know you wouldn't. I read the reports. Your spies were very detailed."

Alaric beamed.

"Were they? Excellent."

He reached for the parchments again. King Noam pulled them back.

"Alaric, assembling this report is a serious violation of the Princess Test. It is supposed to be anonymous."

"No one has to know. Please, father. I sent our best agents. They were not detected."

"If you insist."

King Noam sighed and handed Alaric the parchments.

"For goodness sake don't let on that you know which girl is which. You're supposed to make your decision based on love instead of politics. At least, that was the original intention of the Princess Tests."

Alaric glanced at the first parchment. A pencil sketch of a young woman smiled up at him. Under it, someone had scribbled notes in the margins.

"You added information?" he asked.

"I had our ambassadors supplement what your spies discovered. These reports now contain everything you could want to know about the young ladies."

Alaric's face burst into a smile.

"Father, this is- Thank you!"

"Alaric, you don't have to choose one of these women. It would be traditional, helpful even, but you don't have to. There are many fine ladies on our own shore."

Alaric stared at the packet in his hands. Odette's face flashed into his mind, but he pushed it away. He had given that dream up long ago. He clutched the parchments like a lifeline.

"I will marry one of the princesses, father. I will secure our position. Which would you prefer?"

"Alaric-"

Alaric flipped through the parchments.

"Eldria has a princess coming. Their import system is second to none."

"Alaric-"

"And Santelle! They have an impressive navy. Would a country near our border or across the ocean be better?"

"Alaric, will you please stop thinking of alliances? I want you to be happy!"

"And I want Aeonia to be safe!"

"I'm allowing those profiles so you know what you're walking into. So you can find someone with common interests you can share adventures with! Share life with!"

"Is that what your father did? Handed you a packet of

profiles?"

King Noam frowned.

"No. He handed me one. Your mother's. I had no choice. East and West Aeonia had to be rejoined, and a marriage treaty was the only possible way to do it without bloodshed. But you do have a choice, Alaric."

"I don't want it. I want what's best for the kingdom."

"And a happy king won't benefit the kingdom? Look how happy I've been since I married Marta."

Alaric stood.

"Thank you for this, father. If you'll excuse me, I'm tired."

King Noam lowered his head in defeat.

"The Council of Kings will arrive tomorrow evening. The Princess Test starts the following morning. Good night, Alaric."

Alaric bowed and hurried through the castle. He slammed the door to his room and punched a tapestry.

"Blast!"

His knuckles stung, but the pain helped him focus. He should have known his father would be difficult about this. How long had he kept the parchments from him? Alaric had ordered the reports months ago. These were his lifeline. The only way he could ensure his kingdom's future.

He sighed and spread the parchments over a table. At least he had them now. Late was better than never. He sorted the parchments into two piles. Princesses and everyone else.

The portraits in the smaller pile smiled up at him. Eight princesses. All eligible. All charming.

A happy king. His father had been more than happy since he married his third wife. He had been radiant.

Their love twisted Alaric's heart every time he saw them together. He had dreamed of such a relationship for himself once. He had nearly had it.

But as crown prince, his marriage had more at stake than

love.

He ignored the portraits and sorted the princesses by kingdom. Of the eight princesses, some came from kingdoms with little to offer. Kell, for example, was too small to be a valuable ally.

He paused over Marian of Fletcher's parchment. Fletcher would be a good ally, but Marian was the king's niece. She had the title of princess though. Did that count?

No, he decided. If he were going to marry someone who wasn't a princess beyond a doubt, he might as well have courted Odette.

Alaric stared at the six portraits left. Princesses from the largest kingdoms in Myora. The most powerful families. An alliance with any of these would strengthen Aeonia and silence claims that he was not noble enough to rule. He skimmed the text under each portrait.

His spies had written useful information about each country. The exports. The political situations at the moment. His father's men had crossed out most of it and added personal anecdotes.

What did it matter if Princess Brigitta of Ostenreich fancied horses and chocolate? If her kingdom's main exports were horses and chocolate, Alaric would have found the information much more interesting.

He sighed and turned away from the table.

"Lady troubles?"

"Gah!"

Alaric grabbed the nearest object, a chair cushion, and hurled it towards the voice. The speaker caught it with a thump and laughed.

"I'm always happy when you throw pillows instead of books."

"Go away, Stefan. Or at least knock before you come in."

Prince Stefan picked up the larger stack of parchments,

Alaric's rejects, and thumbed through them. His blue eyes danced. He selected a parchment from the pile and waved it in front of Alaric's face.

"What's wrong with Princess Fiora? She's pretty."

"I don't care about pretty. She's from Kell. We need a powerful country."

"Kell has one of the oldest royal families in Myora. That's something. I bet she's stunning in person. The description says she has bright red hair."

"I don't care how she looks, Stefan."

"Well, I guess pretty isn't the most important thing. Marta isn't pretty, but she and father are happy."

"And Cassandra was gorgeous and nearly ruined the kingdom. This is impossible."

Stefan studied his brother's face. His grin faded.

"This is really bothering you, isn't it?"

"This is an enormous responsibility, Stefan. I am choosing the future queen of Aeonia!"

Stefan coughed.

"Would it take pressure off to think of it as choosing your wife? To ask whom you love?"

Alaric glared at him.

"You know I can't allow my personal feelings to interfere with this sort of thing."

"This is exactly the sort of thing you should allow your personal feelings to interfere with! But you won't, will you? You proved that with Od–"

Another pillow to the face swallowed Stefan's last word.

"You promised not to talk about that," Alaric said.

Stefan set Princess Fiora's parchment back on the pile of rejected girls.

"What can I do to help?"

"Go swim in the moat."

"I'm serious, Alaric."

Alaric sighed.

"I've singled out the princesses from the biggest countries, but I don't know enough about them to make a decision."

Stefan picked up the smaller stack of parchments and read them aloud.

"Colette of Montaigne. I bet she's a snob. Brigitta of Ostenreich. Likes chocolate and horses. Really? That's all they told you about her?"

Alaric shrugged. Stefan continued.

"Merinda of Eldria. She looks decent. Eirwyn of Gaveron. The King of Gaveron is rude, don't choose her. Carina of Santelle apparently isn't interested in anything at all. And Lenora of Darluna likes butterflies. Are they serious? Butterflies? You sent a spy all the way to Darluna, and the only useful information he found is that Lenora likes butterflies?"

"They're not the most useful reports, but they are something. I'm going to the archives tomorrow to research historical alliances and trade records. It's a lot of information to go through. I could use help."

"Wait. I offer to help you with your love life, and you ask me to research trade records?"

Alaric shrugged.

"Welcome to the life of the future king."

"Don't you dare die before you have an heir, brother. I wouldn't deal with this for all the gold in the treasury."

Alaric pulled another pillow from the couch. Stefan raised his hands in defense.

"Fine, I'll help! And not just with picking a princess. I have a surprise planned I know you'll love!"

"Stefan, please tell me you aren't planning anything while the Council is here."

"Would I be me if I didn't?"

The pillow flew towards Stefan's face.

3

L ina made it through the sea of snowbells and walked along the fields at the foot of the mountain. She tried not to think about Luca. Tried not to think about anything.

She needed to get to Mias. That was all. Someone there would have answers. Her feet dragged through the grass. A flock of cashmere goats grazed nearby.

They still raised goats. Lina's breathing eased a little. At least that was the same.

"Hello, there!"

Lina jumped. She lost her grip on her sleeve and panicked as the pea left her hand. She snatched it back and clutched it to her chest. Where had the voice come from?

A young girl lay on the ground. She smiled up at Lina. Her hair shone red gold in the moonlight. Freckles sprinkled over her sharp nose.

Lina stared. A human. An ordinary human. She looked safe. Relaxed and unconcerned about meeting a stranger in the wilderness at night. Her actions were proof that the world had not gone up in flames. Proof that the creatures of darkness had been defeated.

The girl stood and brushed grass off her skirt.

"Sorry if I scared you. I like to watch the stars at night. Is that what you're doing?"

"Um, not exactly. I-"

Lina hesitated. She had no reason to distrust the girl. Her ring had not indicated any danger. But she had no idea how the world was now. No idea what to do next. She simply stood and stared.

"You're traveling, then?" the girl suggested.

"Yes. Traveling."

"I'm Eva."

The girl held her hand out. Lina hesitated. Grasping hands was a gestured reserved for sacred pledges. Surely the girl did not intend to forge a magical bond?

Eva waited. Her green eyes watched Lina without wavering. Lina reached her grimy hand out and took the girl's. She was no longer in her time. She couldn't trust the rules of etiquette that she knew. Apparently grasping hands was commonplace now.

Eva grinned at her.

"I have a cottage not far from here. I herd goats. You can stay the night if you like. My aunt and cousins are in Mias for a few weeks, so there's an extra bed."

Lina considered the offer. What could she do in the city in the middle of the night? She caught herself yawning. She should be wide awake after her long sleep, but she felt exhausted.

"Alright then. If you don't mind, that would be wonderful. I'm Lina."

Eva led Lina through the field to a small cottage surrounded by even more cashmere goats. Lina's throat caught as a memory engulfed her.

. . .

Luca added another bottle of melted gems to the stack in his arms and tottered across the room. Lina gasped as the bottle on top swayed back and forth.

"Watch out, donkey!" she said. "You'll spill the potions!"

Luca stuck out his tongue at her.

"I wouldn't have to carry them like this if you weren't so slow, goat."

"Goat?"

"You call me donkey all the time. I'm allowed an animal based insult."

"So you're saying my hair is soft, right? As soft as cashmere wool?"

Lina grinned at him and tossed her hair over her shoulder.

"No. That's not what I'm saying. You'll notice I didn't call you cashmere goat. I meant an ordinary, plain, wire haired goat.

"You do know I'm a shadow warrior, right?"

"Of course I do, Miss Evangelina Shadow-Storm. That's why it's called an insult. You see, I'm implying that you're stubborn as a goat, smell bad, will eat anything, bleat loudly-"

Lina threw a bolt of shadow magic at Luca. He tossed his head and deflected it with a bolt of light.

Eva watched Lina with wide eyes.

"Are you all right, miss?"

Lina blinked. She turned to Eva.

"Yes. Sorry. I like your cottage."

"Thanks! It's been in my family for generations."

Lina stopped herself from asking how many generations. She didn't want to know. She didn't want to think about it.

"Are you hungry?" Eva asked.

"It's the middle of the night."

"So? Food doesn't disappear from the cupboards after sunset. I've heard traveling is hungry business."

Lina smiled at her.

"Actually, yes. I can't remember the last time I ate."

It had been a picnic with Luca in front of the newly finished wolf statue. Just hours before the enchantment to put her into the enchanted sleep. Lina pushed the memory away.

Eva pulled half a loaf of bread from a shelf. She broke off a hunk for herself and handed the rest to Lina.

"Oh, I don't want to eat all your food."

"Eat it," Eva said. "It will go stale soon. I always bake too much when my cousins are gone."

Lina ate. Eva gave her a glass of water. She drank it in a single gulp.

"I guess traveling is thirsty work as well. I'll get more from the well."

Lina finished the bread before Eva returned. She drank three more glasses of water to wash the dust from her throat. She tried to think of a reasonable question to ask to give her some idea of the date. Ordinary travelers didn't ask what year it was. They didn't ask who was king. They didn't ask-

"Are you here to see the Council of Kings?" Eva asked.

Lina blinked. If the Council of Kings still existed, maybe she hadn't slept as long as she thought. That was excellent. She could report to them just as she had before her enchantment.

"They're meeting soon?" Lina asked.

"The delegations arrive tomorrow night. I'm hoping to get an afternoon away from the goats so I can see some of the Princess Test."

Lina smiled. The Council of Kings. The Princess Test. Things hadn't changed so much after all.

"I didn't come here for the Council, but I'll certainly try to get a glimpse of the Princess Test. Who is choosing a bride?"

"Crown Prince Alaric. I heard at least twenty girls are coming. At least five are princesses."

"Only twenty?"

Eva bristled.

"That's a good number. The main countries and lesser provinces. Kell only had seven come when they hosted the Council."

"Of course. I didn't mean to insult you."

Only twenty, and that a good number. In Lina's time, dozens of princesses had traveled to the Council meetings for a chance to marry into the Aeonian royal family.

Lina sighed. This was going to be a tangle. She needed more information.

"Is the archive still open to the public?" she asked. "I've heard it's the most beautiful building in Aeonia."

"Yes, it's open. But I'd recommend seeing the castle over that."

"Thank you. I'll be sure to see them both."

Lina sighed as she settled into bed. She lay on top of the covers to keep from spreading her dust.

She couldn't fall asleep. Her body was stiff and sore, but her mind wouldn't let her relax. She hovered just on the edge of unconsciousness. Shadows pulled at her, but she brushed them away. Now wasn't the time to visit the realm of shadows. There was nothing to fight. No one to meet. She just wanted to sleep.

Eva's soft snores filled the room. Lina pulled the pea emerald out and twirled it between her fingers. Her heart ached for everything she had lost, but resolve replaced her initial wave of grief. She needed to see the Council. She needed to make sure what she and Luca started had been finished. She owed that to Luca. There would be time for tears later.

Lina slipped into an uneasy sleep filled with dreams of the

war. It was still dark when she awoke, but she couldn't bear to stay still any longer. If they held the same traditions, the archive would open at sunrise. She hesitated for a moment. It seemed ungrateful to leave without saying goodbye to Eva.

The goat herder's soft snores still filled the room. Lina decided against waking the girl and slipped out of the cottage.

❦ 4 ❦

"**W**ake up."

Alaric hit Stefan with the pillow again. Stefan rolled over but didn't open his eyes.

"Go away."

Alaric sighed. He had expected this and come prepared. He poured a vase of water on Stefan's head.

"Hey!"

Stefan sputtered and rolled out of bed.

"What are you doing? It isn't even breakfast time yet!"

"You still wait to get up until breakfast?"

Stefan glanced in a mirror. His short brown hair stuck out from his head like a hedgehog. He smoothed it down, but it popped back up.

"Wear a hat," Alaric said. "Weigh it down with your crown. We're going to the archives."

"It's dark outside!"

"They open at sunrise, and the Council of Kings arrives this evening. We don't have time to waste!"

Stefan rubbed his eyes.

"You were serious. You're going to choose a bride based on trade records."

"Aeonia will benefit from a strong trading partner. Are you helping or not?"

"I will help. After the sun is in the sky, and I've eaten breakfast. Like any normal person would."

"Fine. I'll meet you there."

Alaric wrapped his cloak around his shoulders and left his brother to go back to sleep. He hurried through the city, dodging the early morning crowds as they rushed to start the day. He reached the archive a few moments after the sun slipped over the horizon.

Simon, the archivist, was already up to his elbows in ancient scrolls. Strategically placed windows and mirrors lit the massive building from sunup to sundown. Simon wasn't one to waste daylight.

"You're up very early," Simon said.

Alaric smiled. The white-haired archive keeper returned his grin with a bow. Alaric breathed in the welcome scent of thousands of parchment scrolls stored in the archive.

"The first researcher awake is the first to find his answers."

"Oh, you're not the first today," Simon said. "A young lady was here waiting for me when I unlocked the doors."

"Really? How unusual."

"Not as unusual as she is. Her clothes- well. She must have traveled a long way. Talk about travel dust! I was reluctant to let her in. All that dirt isn't good for our scrolls. She finally agreed to wear an extra smock over her clothes and wash her hands in the courtyard fountain before touching anything."

Alaric smirked. Simon protected the scrolls like they were his children. He took the loose cotton smock the archivist offered him and slipped it over his clothes.

"You think this is a joke?" Simon said. "You know how

long it takes to clean a dirty scroll? The restoration can take months."

"I'm sure. The scrolls of Aeonia are fortunate to be under your watchful eye."

"Humph."

Alaric bowed and walked deeper into the archives. It held historical parchments on every topic imaginable. Shelves bursting with scrolls covered the walls and even the domed ceiling thanks to enchanted glass. The center room held popular topics like royal histories and building records, but that was by no means the extent of the archives.

The trade records were housed in one of the exterior rooms that surrounded the central chamber like spokes on a wagon wheel. Alaric found the parchment he needed and settled into a chair in a corner.

Time to learn about exports. He skimmed the top of the scroll. Ostenreich exported wheat. They had not had a bad crop in fifty years.

Promising.

But was it the best choice? Aeonia grew enough food for the people. Maybe textiles would be better. Alaric read further down the parchment. Two of his top five princesses came from countries with textile imports. Darluna special-ized in silk. Santelle grew cotton.

And Aeonia had goats enough to clothe the country in cashmere. As his stepbrothers often reminded him. He had learned a lot about goats from them.

Alaric rubbed his forehead. This was impossible. Perhaps trade wasn't the best way to choose his bride. Political alliances could be just as powerful. He slid the scroll back into place and wandered across the archive. He was so distracted he almost ran into the only other patron.

"Oh, excuse me, miss."

The young woman nodded and ducked her head. Alaric

stared at her. She wore two oversized white smocks over her clothes. At least, they had been white once. Now they were coated in patches of dirt. How filthy was she to transfer that much dirt to the smock? She was lucky Simon had let her in at all.

"The fault is mine. Please excuse me."

Her voice caught Alaric off guard. It was lower than he expected and lilted like music. She had an aristocratic accent. Both old fashioned and familiar.

She tilted her head up. The intelligence in her green eyes caught Alaric's breath.

"Where are the histories kept?" she asked.

She was a puzzle he couldn't work out. Everything in her manner suggested sophistication and confidence, but her hair was a tangled, filthy mess. Even goat herders weren't this disheveled.

"The histories?" she repeated. "Do you know where they are?"

Alaric gathered his wits and pointed across the archive.

"Histories of royal families are that way."

She smirked.

"You think I'm here to dig up ancient gossip?"

"I- Well, most women-"

She raised an eyebrow.

"Do you have no female scholars here?"

"No. Of course! Yes, we do. Please, forgive me for assuming. The histories of royal families are simply the most popular scrolls."

"With women?"

Was she teasing him? She looked amused under all the dirt. Alaric felt uncomfortable. He wasn't often teased by anyone. Even among his brothers, Stefan was the only one who joked with him.

He took a deep breath and reminded himself he liked the

anonymity of the archive. The smocks covered clothes and jewelry. Any signs of wealth. Everyone was equal here.

If she had traveled as far as her dust suggested, she probably had no idea he was a prince. Alaric smiled at her.

"The royal histories are popular with everyone," he said. "I think because they are more personal. They make the past come alive."

A flash of sadness crossed her face. Tears gathered in her eyes. What had he done now?

"Are you alright?" he asked. "I've hurt you somehow. I meant no offense."

She wiped a tear out of her eye. The moisture left a trail in the dust on her face.

"No, the offense is not yours."

Alaric watched the struggle on her face as she pushed away the emotion and regained focus. His stomach growled. Right, he had skipped breakfast. He reached into his smock and pulled two apples out of his cloak.

It had been wishful thinking to pack one for Stefan, but he was glad he had. He offered one to the girl. She raised an eyebrow.

"We'd better go to the courtyard to eat. The archivist will kick us out for sure if he sees that."

Alaric laughed and followed her to the courtyard in the center of the archive. They sat beneath a tree and ate the apples.

"How did you know about the courtyard?" Alaric asked. "Have you been here before? I haven't seen you around."

The girl swallowed a bite of apple.

"Oh. No, I haven't. Simon made me wash my hands in the fountain. And I studied a blueprint of the building before I came. It has changed since that was made though. The side rooms are new."

"Hardly. They're over seventy-five years old."

The girl choked on her apple. Alaric patted her on the back until she regained her breath.

"What? Really?"

He nodded.

"Oh."

She looked around the courtyard.

"This place hasn't changed at all. The trees are bigger."

Alaric shrugged.

"Yes, I suppose they would be. Speaking of the fountain, we'd better wash our hands before we return."

"Yes, we don't want to bring the wrath of Simon on ourselves."

She scrubbed her hands for a long time under the running water. The water in the basin was a dark gray from her previous washing. They walked back to the archives side by side.

"So what are you looking for?" he said. "Not the royal histories."

"No, I don't need historical gossip today. I'm looking for the histories of countries. Important happenings. Wars and alliances."

"Oh. That will be in the historical archives. They're in one of the side rooms. I'm actually looking there as well."

She walked with him across the archives.

"What are you researching?" she asked.

"Political alliances."

"Ah. For a project? Are you a scholar?"

Alaric shrugged.

"Something like that. What about you? What are you looking for?"

She blinked at him.

"I expect the information I'm looking for will be ancient. Are the scrolls arranged chronologically?"

"Yes, the older scrolls will be in the back. They're pretty

dense reading. Writing styles have changed a lot over the centuries. A lot has changed."

"Yes, I expect it has. Thank you."

She nodded her head and ran to the back of the room. Alaric stared after her. Had he done something else wrong? Maybe she was just in a hurry to find her answers.

He watched her browse the scrolls and realized he didn't know her name. He stopped himself from walking over to ask. It didn't matter. She was intriguing, but he had already wasted too much time. He needed to research his future bride.

Still, he couldn't help glancing her way. What information in Aeonia's history was so important that she would travel that far to find it? That she would feel so passionate about it that just the mention of history brought her to tears?

Alaric shook his head and pulled a scroll from the shelf. That was her business. He needed to mind his own now.

He pushed the girl out of his mind and threw himself into the study of political alliances. Yes, these were much more profitable. An alliance with Santelle would secure the western trade routes and amicable relations with Darluna and Htar. But would it aggravate relations with Gaveron?

"Have you found what you're looking for?" Simon asked.

Alaric shook his head. He needed to look at older records. He slipped further into the side room.

The girl was still there. She pulled scroll after scroll from the shelves, skimmed them, and replaced them. She moved methodically back down the hallway. Back in time to the oldest parchments.

Alaric swallowed. There was no reason he shouldn't go talk to her. She seemed to be looking for something specific. He had read many of the scrolls in this room. It would be only right to offer assistance. What could be more princely than helping a traveler learn about his country?

He smoothed his hair back. Yes, he would walk over to her and-

"Alaric!"

Alaric groaned. Stefan bounded across the main archive room. Simon followed waving a white smock. He caught Stefan and shoved it over his head.

"Stefan, the archive is supposed to be quiet," Alaric hissed.

"Pull the smock over your clothes!" Simon demanded. "You can't be here without a smock! The parchments are delicate!"

Stefan pulled the garment over his torso.

"Have you decided yet?"

"You're still too loud," Alaric said.

He glanced at the girl. She frowned at him and moved deeper into the chamber. No wonder. Those ancient texts were hard enough to read without the distraction of someone yelling. He pulled Stefan back to the main archive to avoid disturbing her further.

"So, have you?" Stefan said. "Have any trade routes won your heart?"

He whispered dramatically and fluttered his eyelashes. Alaric sighed.

"This is a difficult thing. Not to be rushed."

"Yes, but you've been here for hours! You should have found something by now! Don't tell me. They'd all benefit Aeonia. You'll have to marry for love after all."

"I've narrowed it down to the best two," Alaric said through gritted teeth. "But yes, an alliance with any of the nations that are sending true princesses would benefit Aeonia in some way."

"Excellent! You can experience my surprise for you with your new love on your arm."

"Is there really a surprise? I had hoped you were joking about that."

"Never! I talked father and Marta into putting me in charge of the entertainment for the grand ball."

"Stefan. No."

Stefan's smile could have lit the archive without the sun's help.

"Yes. The Aeonian Royal Theater Troupe is producing a new play by our very own crown prince."

"Stefan, you didn't. You can't have. I burned all the copies of that."

"And I found one! It's amazing! The Theater Troupe has been rehearsing for weeks."

"Stefan, I wrote that years ago! That was never meant to be produced."

"That's not what you said when you finished it. You said it was a masterpiece. An artistic triumph! Oh man, Odette's face when you asked her to play Evangelina Shadow-Storm for the premiere. Priceless."

Something crashed deep in the archives. Stefan and Alaric leaned over to look. The green-eyed girl stood motionless. A pile of fallen parchments surrounded her. She stared at them, her jaw dropped.

"See?" Stefan whispered. "The ladies can't resist a playwright."

"Shut up."

Alaric pulled Stefan towards the door. He had done all the research he could today. Simon met them at the front of the archive.

"Did I hear your obnoxiously loud brother correctly, Your Highness? You should have told me you wrote plays."

"I don't. I mean, I did once when I was young. It was nothing. Just a setting of Evangelina Shadow-Storm."

"He loves Evangelina Shadow-Storm," Stefan said. "Loves. Her."

"Shut up. They are not producing that play for the Council of Kings."

"Oh yes they are. I specifically told them not to prepare any backup entertainment."

"What? Stefan! You- Excuse me, Simon."

Alaric pulled his smock off and threw it in Stefan's face. He ran towards the door. Stefan shrugged his smock off, dropped both onto the floor, and chased his brother out of the archive.

L ina stood frozen at the back of the archives. She dropped the handful of parchments. They scattered around her. The men leaned around and looked at her. She should speak to them. Ask them for more information. She tried, but her voice wouldn't work. Her mouth hung open and wouldn't shut.

They had said her name. Surely she hadn't misheard. They had said her full name.

Evangelina Shadow-Storm.

She gathered her wits and shoved the ancient parchments around her back in their places.

They knew of her. Those two men remembered her. She would have to be careful. Who knew who they were? But she could finally find out what had happened!

Lina hesitated. The council had enemies. She shouldn't give herself away. She could ease into the conversation. The blond scholar was friendly. He had shared breakfast with her. He had helped her find the scrolls she needed. She could present the questions as more of her research. As information needed for a project.

Lina rushed to the main room. It was empty. Where were they? She gritted her teeth in frustration and ran to the archivist.

"Those men, where did they go?"

Simon nodded his head to the door.

"Rushed out. Typical."

Lina swallowed her disappointment. It didn't matter. The blond scholar, however charming, couldn't be the only person who knew of her. The archivist would know.

"What were they talking about?"

"Oh, the Council of Kings is meeting here this year. A fascinating opportunity for a scholar. Every country in the Myorian region will be present. They arrive tonight."

Lina shook her head.

"No, the play."

"Ah, yes. It is traditional to provide the Council with entertainment that reflects the culture of the host country."

Was he trying to misunderstand her? Lina forced herself to smile.

"What of the girl they mentioned? Evangelina Shadow-Storm. I didn't see her mentioned in any of your histories."

Simon chuckled.

"No, you wouldn't have. She's a popular local children's tale."

Lina's heart dropped. A lump formed in her throat. A children's tale.

"Are you well, girl?"

"Do you have scrolls about her?"

"Of course not. This archive holds only the most important historical documents."

Lina's heart beat faster and faster. She bit back her anger. Important? Historical?

"Most stories are rooted in truth," she said.

"True, but this is a most implausible tale. You'd have a hard time finding the fact in that fiction."

Tears filled Lina's eyes. She turned and ran from the archive before Simon could see them. Lina left her filthy smocks on the stairs and searched the streets for the men. They were gone. She had wasted too much time speaking to the archivist.

Lina bit back a scream of frustration. A children's tale? It wouldn't have mattered if she had found them. Even the kindest scholar wasn't likely to believe a children's tale had come to life.

Lina stared at the castle. The Council of Kings arrived tonight. They had always had secrets. She had known many of them when she worked for the Council. Rulers had to have secrets to keep the people safe.

Maybe she was one of their secrets now.

Lina trudged through the streets, ignoring the people staring at her tattered gown. A children's tale. Not important. Not historical.

She kept walking until she reached the docks. She could clean off in the ocean before she met with them. At least wash her face. She wasn't sure she trusted the fabric of her dress to hold together if it got wet.

In her day, the docks had been a favorite leisure spot. The crystal blue water had tempted swimmers in every season. She and Luca had often eaten lunch on the white sandy beaches and watched ships sail to far away kingdoms.

No one would consider having a picnic at the docks now. The whole place smelled like fish. Trash floated in the water. Lina gave up on bathing and sank behind a pile of crates. She pulled the pea out from its hiding place in her sleeve hem and twirled it through her fingers. Sailors and fishermen bustled around each other carrying cargo and nets. Lina watched the hubbub and planned her next move.

A children's tale. Perhaps it was a clever ruse to keep enemies from knowing the truth? Maybe the historical documents about her were secret. Hidden away. Something an archivist would not show a stranger. Something even an archivist couldn't access.

A secret of the kings.

The thought comforted her. Yes, that must be it. The Council of Kings would not want people to worry. Would not want their enemies to know that they had a shadow warrior sealing away a horde of dark creatures. They had hidden her. Shrouded her in myth to keep her mission safe.

Lina could only hope that information had survived the years. She was better off waiting to approach anyone until the entire Council of Kings gathered. More kings meant more chance of someone knowing her.

A young boy ran past her crates and ducked into an alley. A group of children ran through the streets after him.

"Get Thaddeus!" the leader screamed. "Down with the tyrant!"

The children ran forward with roars of approval. As soon as they passed, the boy doubled back and jumped behind the pile of crates. His eyes widened when he saw Lina. She smiled at him.

"Do you need help?" she asked. "Are you in trouble?"

He shook his head.

"It's just a game. Who are you?"

"Lina. And you're Thaddeus?"

"Course not. It's the game. Tyrant Topple."

"Oh. I see."

Luca had loved games. He had often bribed Lina into playing them with him. She had never heard of Tyrant Topple.

Lina smiled at the boy.

"Can you tell me who is the head of the Council of Kings?"

He frowned at her.

"King of Gaveron. Everybody knows that."

Lina nodded. It had been the King of Gaveron in her time. As the Council's founding nation, Gaveron held an honorary position as the leader.

The children ran past in the other direction.

"I'd better go," the boy said with a grin. "I've got them confused now."

"Wait! One more thing!" Lina said.

He stuck his hands in his pockets.

"I'm sorry, miss. I don't have any money."

Lina's face turned bright red.

"What? Oh no, I'm not begging. I just wondered if you could tell me the story of Evangelina Shadow-Storm."

"Evangelina Shadow-Storm? What do you want to hear a baby story for? You think I'm a baby?"

"No, of course not. I just-"

The boy shook his head and darted away. Lina slumped back against the crates. A baby story. The boy wasn't that old, and he thought he was too good to recount her story.

Fine. A child wouldn't be privy to royal secrets. She would go straight to the Council. Straight to the King of Gaveron. They would gather for a royal banquet tonight. And she would be there.

Lina tucked the pea back into her sleeve hem and twisted her ring. This world seemed safe. Peaceful. No one was worried about creatures of darkness.

She had succeeded. She just needed to report to the Council. To finish her mission and let them know the goblin hordes were safely sealed away. They might have news of Luca. They might need her for future missions. The goblins were sealed, but had new dangers appeared over the years?

Lina held her ring up to her lips and whispered to it.

"Check for danger."

The diamond flashed white. Lina's smile froze when the light shifted to a pale pink.

❧ 6 ❧

Alaric ran through the village at top speed. He arrived at the castle sweaty and out of breath. Stefan followed him with a grin. Alaric didn't stop when he reached the gate. He nodded to the guards and ran straight to his stepmother's chambers.

"Marta, please tell me you did not put this oaf in charge of the Council's entertainment."

"Hello to you too, Alaric. Stefan."

Queen Marta sat on a small couch in the center of her room. Her lady's maid Hilda bustled around her, arranging the queen's dark brown hair around her silver crown.

"Your Highness has been in the wind again," she said. "If you stayed indoors, your hair would not be so tangled."

Queen Marta waved her hand.

"Someone has to care for the goats, Hilda. A few tangled hairs won't hurt anything."

Hilda's eyes flashed. She ran her hands through Marta's knotted hair. Alaric saw Hilda's point.

"Perhaps a conditioning treatment," Hilda said.

"It's fine, Hilda. Just shove it under the crown."

Hilda gritted her teeth and did just that.

Alaric smiled in spite of himself. He liked his stepmother. The whole kingdom did. She had been a goat herder before she married his father, and she cared little for the frivolities of castle life. Many of the castle maids fretted about the queen's unruly hair and plump, pleasant face. Alaric thought she looked honest.

"My dear brother has taken a dislike to my choice of entertainment for the grand ball," Stefan said.

Alaric glared at him. How could he look so innocent after what he had done?

"What's wrong with the entertainment?" Queen Marta said. "I thought it was a splendid idea. Evangelina Shadow-Storm is one of our most beloved stories. Surely that represents our culture to the Council sufficiently."

"Oh, she's beloved all right," Stefan said.

Alaric elbowed him in the ribs.

"Marta, please. I have no problem with the subject matter, but I'm afraid the quality of the production will be lacking. It would be far better if the troupe had their own playwrights create a script."

"Didn't they?" Queen Marta said.

"No."

"Well, there's no time to change it now. They're performing it in two days. I'm sure it will be fine, Alaric. I trust Stefan to find something entertaining for us."

Stefan's eyes gleamed in victory. Alaric groaned. It would certainly be entertaining. Especially for Stefan.

"I think I'll check on the actors now," Stefan said. "They're fitting costumes today. If you'll excuse me."

He bowed and practically danced out of the room. Alaric sank onto a nearby chair. The costumes. He had designed costumes. Surely they wouldn't actually make the costumes.

Whatever princess he pursued, he needed to win her over

before the ball. Probably have the engagement contract signed. If she could back out, she would after the play.

"The Council's arrival has us all stressed," Queen Marta said. "And as coordinator of the Princess Test, I've had my hands more than full. Stefan has been very helpful. He means well."

Alaric bowed his head.

"I don't mean to create more work for you, Marta."

The queen waved her hand.

"Nonsense. I'm happy to help. Although some of the traditional tests are ridiculous. I think they're more symbolic than anything. I don't see how they'll be any help in choosing a bride."

Alaric groaned.

"That isn't what I want to hear."

"You don't mean to actually choose a bride at the Princess Test? It will be impossible to really get to know someone in three days."

Alaric met his stepmother's gaze. His dark eyes reflected the silver of her crown.

"Oh, Alaric. No one expects this of you. Not at your first Princess Test."

That was the problem with Marta. She had lived the simple life of a goat herder too long before becoming queen. She didn't understand the pressures of ruling.

"I am sure I can find a suitable bride. I must marry a true princess for the sake of Aeonia."

"Not this again. Alaric, your right to rule is secure. Anyone who dares to question it now~"

He raised his hand to stop her. Queen Marta gestured for Hilda to stop arranging her hair and wrapped her callused hands around his smooth ones. He looked into her warm brown eyes.

"I will do what I have to for Aeonia."

Marta sighed and released his hands.

"I know better than trying to talk you out of something once you've decided to do it. Do you have a favorite? I can't be too obvious, but I do make the seating arrangements."

She winked at him.

"Santelle or Eldria," Alaric said. "I must marry a true princess. Not a duchess or someone from a province."

"What do they look like? What are the girl's names? We won't know where they're from, but I can try to guess. I can give you clues."

Alaric clenched his fists. Their names. What were their names? He hadn't bothered to check their names on the parchments. Stefan had read them, but he hadn't been paying attention. He was going to marry one of these princesses, and he didn't know their names.

"It doesn't matter," he said. "I don't want to get you in trouble. I'll find them on my own."

"Of course you will. Is there anything specific you'd like me to test? Our schedule is busy, but I can sneak something in if you want."

Alaric sighed. The tests were meant to show the girls' best qualities and determine compatibility with the prince.

At least, that had been the original purpose. Over time, the matchmaking had become more cynical. More political. Marriages, when they happened, often strengthened alliances with little concern for the feelings of those involved.

The Princess Tests kept the Council of Kings together. Countries were more likely to get along with the possibility of their children marrying in the forefront of their minds.

Alaric liked it better that way. He couldn't imagine trying to truly fall in love in just a few days. His main concern was finding a true princess. If a country didn't have a princess of marriageable age at the time of test, they sent the daughter of a high-ranking nobleman. Politically, such a match still strengthened relationships between the lands.

For Alaric, it would do nothing. He needed a princess. He tried to smile at Marta.

"No, I trust you to choose the proper tests."

"That's not entirely true. You've got something in mind. I can see it in your eyes."

That was the other problem with Marta. She had a knack for knowing what you were thinking. Alaric shrugged.

"I've always imagined proposing to my wife on Mount Evangelina."

Queen Marta beamed.

"Alaric, what a wonderful idea! What about a picnic on the last day of the tests? We can travel to the mountain, and you can propose there."

Alaric hesitated. Yes, that was what he had always pictured. But did he want to share it with a stranger?

He might as well. He'd be sharing everything else with her soon enough.

"A picnic would be perfect. Thank you, Marta."

"It will help make the test more personal. And I've slipped in a few tests of my own. I have to make sure this girl is worthy of my son."

She hugged Alaric and returned to her chair. Hilda secured her hair with more pins.

Alaric didn't like the way she looked at him. He had seen that look before. Marta could be stubborn. She was scheming. Probably planning how to rig the Princess Test to keep him from rushing into a political marriage.

He needed to change the subject. Now.

"Has the jeweler sent any messages? I commissioned a new crown for Cael and- and something else. They should be ready by now."

Queen Marta shook her head.

"I haven't received any. Anyway, Cael and Henry won't be joining us for the Council. There's an emergency with the family goats."

Alaric groaned. He had never understood his stepbrothers' insistence on maintaining the family goat herd.

"What about Benjamin and Marcus? Their session at the Royal Academy ended last week. They should be here soon."

"Didn't Stefan tell you? Everyone at the Academy is ill. They're not well enough to travel."

"What? Are you telling me that out of the six princes of Aeonia, only Stefan and I will be there?"

"It will be fine, Alaric."

"This is the Council of Kings, not a family dinner! Henry and Cael are princes as much as Stefan and I are. They should be at the greeting ceremony. They should be here to help!"

"They're not trying to shirk their duties, Alaric. Sometimes goats need immediate attention. Eva can't handle them on her own all the time. Henry and Cael will be back as soon as they can."

"We can hire someone to take care of the blasted goats!"

Marta fixed him with a reproving glance. Her pleasant face could look very stern.

"Our family has herded goats for generations, Alaric. Longer than your family has ruled. They wouldn't have gone if it wasn't an emergency."

"I should get ready for the welcome ceremony. Please excuse me."

Alaric bowed to Marta and left before he said something he'd regret. Goats. The Council of Kings was arriving tonight, and his stepbrothers were herding goats.

He walked back to his room. He had hours until the greeting ceremony, but he had a lot to do. For one, he needed to learn the girl's names.

❧ 7 ❧

Lina walked the entire perimeter of the city. Twice. She ducked behind trash heaps and into alleyways often to check her ring. It should shine a darker red when she was closer to the danger.

But it didn't. In every part of the city, the ring glowed white and then flashed pink. Lina didn't know what that meant. It should be red or white. Had her enchanted sleep damaged the ring? She didn't sense a change in its magic.

Gathering storm clouds in the sky reflected her mood.

The sun had set by the time Lina gave up on finding the danger. Thunder rumbled overhead as she trudged back to the middle of Mias. She was exhausted. The apple the scholar had given her was the only food she'd eaten all day. But the Council of Kings needed to know about this.

A flash of lightning lit the sky, and raindrops plinked on the cobblestone streets. Lina kept a steady pace while everyone around her rushed to get home. They knew what summer storms in Aeonia could do.

So did Lina. She just didn't care. She didn't have the energy to walk any faster. The scattered raindrops turned to a downpour. They washed the dirt and dust from Lina's dress and plastered her hair to her skin. She clutched her arms around her chest and kept walking. One step at a time. That was all she could do.

The castle lights twinkled in the distance. Lina's stomach growled with the thunder. She gritted her teeth and kept going. The streets were bare now. No one else was crazy enough to be out in the storm. They had secured window shutters and settled in for the night.

Only lightning and the occasional beam of light from a broken shutter lit Lina's way. She kept walking. Kept trudging towards the castle. The council needed to know. They needed to know she was awake. They needed to know they were in danger.

The gates were closed. Of course they were. Even the castle had shuttered to protect against the storm. Lina crossed the bridge and pounded on the gate, but the wind and rain swallowed the sounds.

"Let me in!" she yelled. "I need to speak to the Council of Kings!"

No answer. Lina watched guards patrol the top of the towers, but they couldn't hear her. When the storm quieted, she screamed as loud as she could. She waited for another lull and screamed again. Her fists pounded against the wood. She kicked the gate until her shoe ripped.

"The gate is closed. Go home, girl."

Lina looked up. A small window in the gate slid open. A guard glared down at her. Lina straightened.

"I must speak to the Council of Kings at once."

The guard raised an eyebrow, but he didn't close the window. That was something.

"On what business?"

Lina swallowed.

"I'm reporting back from a secret mission."

The guard raised his other eyebrow.

"You? Who are you?"

Lina shivered. She couldn't tell him her name. The Council clearly wanted her to be a secret. She had only one choice.

"Tell the Council I gave this password: I am a goat."

The guard stared at her. Lina groaned. She should never have let Luca choose her password. Then again, she probably shouldn't have made his password "I have donkey breath."

"We'll reopen the gate in the morning. Go home."

"No! You're in danger! I must speak to the Council of Kings immediately! I am a goat!"

The guard lifted a lantern and examined her. Rain pelted his face and drenched his beard. Lina could only imagine what she looked like. She hadn't looked good before being caught in the rain. And she smelled like fish from her afternoon on the docks. She stood on her tiptoes and screamed into the guard's face.

"I demand to see the Council of Kings! I! Am! A! Goat!"

The guard slid the window shut and clicked the latch. Lina slumped against the gate and shielded her face from the storm with her hands. She would stay here all night if necessary. She had guarded Aeonia for years. What was one more night?

The storm chilled the summer evening. The raindrops were icy. Lina shivered and huddled closer to the gate.

❧ 8 ❧

Alaric examined the princesses at the table across the room. They blurred into a single mass of blue silk gowns and diamond jewelry. Thank goodness he sat with the kings tonight.

It was tradition for the girls to dress in exactly the same outfits. It was supposed to put the focus on the princesses rather than the wealth of their countries. The end result was a bit creepy in Alaric's opinion. The seamstresses had been complaining about making so many identical gowns for months, but he hadn't stopped to consider what that would look like in person.

The princesses chatted with each other, sparing only the occasional glance in his direction. He tried to pick out the girls from Santelle and Eldria, but it was no good. Princess Carina and Princess Merinda looked just like the rest. Hair color was the only thing that separated one girl from another. Why hadn't he memorized their hair colors? He scanned the table. Blond. Various shades of brown. Raven black.

Bright red.

That would be Princess Fiora. He could have guessed that

without the parchments. Her father, the King of Kell, had an enormous beard the same color.

Too bad Kell wasn't his first choice. Fiora was the only girl who stood out from the group. He would have to study the parchments again tonight if he wanted to have a chance of finding a true princess in that crowd.

Alaric stared back into his soup. He wasn't hungry. His stomach churned as the stress of the day caught up with him. If he ate another bite, he might throw up. The princesses giggled, adding to his nausea. He needed to get out of there. Needed fresh air. Needed an excuse to leave.

A guard slipped into the room and stood awkwardly in the corner. He whispered to the head footman. The footman whispered to a waiter. The waiter picked a pitcher of water and approached their table. He walked toward the king, but Alaric gulped the contents of his water glass and lifted it. The waiter came over to fill it.

"Is there a problem?" Alaric whispered.

"A young lady at the gate."

"The gates are closed for the evening. Tell her to go away."

"Yes, Your Highness. They tried, but she refuses to leave. She's raving about being a goat and insists on seeing the council. The guard said normally he would let her stay there and yell, but he thought you might want to take care of it since we have so many guests."

"And they can't open the gates after dark without a royal order."

The waiter nodded. King Noam gestured to Alaric from the head of the table. Alaric stood and whispered to him.

"Trouble at the gate. I can take care of it."

"And leave our guests?"

Everyone at the table stared at him. Alaric smiled back at them. A table full of kings. Their daughters across the room.

Everyone waiting to see who he chose. Yes, he needed to leave.

"Please, let me take care of it. I'm sure it will only take a few moments. I don't want to disturb our guests."

"What's the problem?"

Queen Marta leaned forward to join their whispered conversation.

"A girl at the gate is claiming to be a goat."

Surprise flickered across the queen's face.

"A goat?"

"I know. She must be mad. Enjoy your dinner. I'll see to it."

Alaric bowed to the kings and gestured to the guard in the corner. He heard his father speak as he left the room.

"I've entrusted my son with many duties as he gets older. Such a responsible lad. If you'll be gracious enough to excuse him-"

Alaric ran down the hallway as soon as the dining room door closed. The guard rushed after him.

"Your Highness, I am so sorry to interrupt."

"No, I'm glad you did. Is she really causing that much of a ruckus?"

"Yes, I'm afraid so. She screamed for a while. Then she kicked the gate. We tried to ignore her, but she just won't go away."

Alaric strode into the gate keeper's room. The three guards on duty sighed in relief when they saw him. He slid open the window and peered into the darkness. He could just make out the girl's huddled shape. She lifted her head when she heard the window open.

"The gate is closed," Alaric said. "Go home and come back in the morning."

She stood.

"I will not. I demand to speak to the Council of Kings. I am a goat."

She sounded exhausted, but much calmer than Alaric had expected. He couldn't see much of her through the window. Just green eyes glaring. Alaric glared back.

"The Council is eating and cannot be disturbed. They will not hear citizen requests until the end of the week."

She pounded her fist against the gate with a surprising amount of force. Alaric jumped.

"They're in danger," she said. "Goblins. Wraiths. I don't know. But something is threatening them."

Alaric sighed. She really was mad, speaking of fairy tale creatures as a threat.

"The castle is well guarded. I assure you the Council is safe. Please go home."

"I will not. I will sit here all night. And all day. And the next until you let me see the Council!"

Alaric pulled his head back from the opening. Water ran down his neck and soaked his tunic.

"Open the gate," he said. "We'll have to detain her. Who knows what trouble she'll rile up in the city?"

"Is that a royal order, Sire?"

The guard's hand rested on the latch.

"You've checked the perimeter? She's alone?"

The guard nodded.

"No one else on the streets now."

"Then yes, that's a royal order. Open the gate."

The force of the storm blew the gate open as soon as the guard unfastened the latch. Rain and wind poured into the room. Light gave Alaric his first glance of the girl as she hurried inside.

He stared at her face. Recognition struck him.

"It's you! You were in the archives today."

Her green eyes glittered. A smile lit her face.

"Yes. You're the one who wrote a play about Evangelina Shadow-Storm."

A guard scoffed.

"You wrote a play about Evangelina Shadow-Storm?"

Alaric glared at him.

"Of course not. That would be a ridiculous waste of time."

"Yeah, can you imagine?" the guard said.

The girl's face fell. Her shoulders shook. Compassion stabbed at Alaric's heart. She was obviously unwell. Mentally unstable. He stepped towards her but stopped when she flinched.

She looked terrible. Strands of hair plastered her face. Streaks of dirt covered her arms. How did she still have dirt on her after being out in the downpour?

Her dress was a faded purple. He hadn't seen it earlier. Her smock had covered it.

It might have been stylish when it was new, but the long sleeves were tattered now. One was torn completely off. The fabric had holes that looked as if the rain itself had torn them. Her skirt clung to her legs like a pair of goat herder's leggings after they had chased a goat through a thorn patch. Bits of leather on her feet had been shoes once, but they were a far cry from that now.

The guards worked together to push the gate against the wind. It slammed shut, bringing a sudden calm to the room. The girl took a shuddering breath.

"I need to see the Council of Kings. My name is-"

"That isn't possible," Alaric said. "But we can provide you with shelter for the night. If you'll go with Temus, he'll take care of you."

She put her hands on her hips.

"He'll lock me up, you mean. I'm not mad. The Council is in danger. Look."

She held her ring up to her hand and whispered, "Check for danger."

The gem flashed white, and the light changed to a faint pink before fading away.

The guards gasped. Alaric leaned closer to examine the ring. It was silver forged into an intricate design he couldn't quite make out in the dim light of the guard's room. The gem glittered with the unmistakable brilliance of a white diamond.

Magic. Alaric shivered. He hadn't come face to face with magic since Cassandra's banishment. No good came of magic. He couldn't let this girl anywhere near the council.

"Where did you get that ring?" he demanded. "Who are you?"

The girl brushed her hair away from her face. She seemed surprised by his reaction. She pulled her hand back and buried it in the sopping folds of her skirt.

"What's your name?" he said. "We mean you no harm. We'll find you a safe place to stay, but you can't stay in front of the gate."

"Evangelina Shadow-Storm. The Council."

She swayed, and Alaric grabbed her shoulder to steady her. Beneath her drenched dress, her skin was icy. She shivered.

"Fetch a blanket and a change of clothes," Alaric said. "She can stay with the kitchen staff tonight. Have a guard stationed in case she tries to use more magic. We'll find a place for her tomorrow."

"Princess! Oh, you poor darling!"

Queen Marta burst into the room with the force of a herd of goats. She pushed Alaric aside and wrapped her arms around the stranger.

"You know this girl?" Alaric said.

The girl looked as shocked as Alaric. Her eyes widened as Queen Marta squeezed her.

"Isn't it obvious? She's a princess here for the test! Look at her ring! That's a royal crest in the design."

She held up the girl's hand and flashed the ring around the room too quickly for any of them to really see it.

"Marta, that ring is magic. She's dangerous."

Marta ignored him.

"Poor thing! What happened to your traveling companions, darling?"

"I- The Council-"

"Yes, you've made it in time for the Council," Queen Marta said. "We've just started. You haven't missed a day. Someone fetch food for her! She can have dinner in her room. She needs to rest."

Marta wrapped the girl's arm over her shoulder and led her through a hallway towards the main castle. Alaric followed them.

"Marta, there's been a mistake. I saw this girl earlier today at the archives. She isn't a princess."

"Of course she is."

"She was raving about goblins and being a goat. Her ring-"

"She's traveled a long way and been caught in a rainstorm. That's bound to confuse such a delicate creature."

"All the princesses are here. We aren't expecting anyone else."

"Aren't we? Then why is there an extra room prepared?"

Queen Marta pushed open a doorway in the guest hallway of the castle. The room had clearly been readied for company. A fire roared in the fireplace. Fresh linens covered the bed. Gowns for the Princess Test hung in the wardrobe.

"But-" Alaric stammered. "But she's mad."

"No, she's exhausted. Look at her."

Alaric looked. The girl's eyes drooped, and she slumped against Queen Marta as if she lacked the strength to stand on her own. She might have been asleep on her feet.

"She obviously traveled a long way," Queen Marta said. "Let's put her by the fire so she can dry off."

She pushed the girl towards Alaric. He caught her, lifted her into his arms, and set her in a chair in front of the fireplace. She sank into it, limp as silk.

"She'll need food," Queen Marta said. "And servants to help her ready for bed. She's in no shape to join the Council for dinner."

Alaric had to agree. He studied the girl's face. She had curled into the enormous chair and fallen asleep. She looked peaceful now.

"On second thought perhaps we should let her sleep," Marta said. "But have food ready in case she wakes."

"What country is she from?" Alaric asked. "Who would be stupid enough to send their princess alone? Who is wealthy enough to have an enchanted ring?"

Queen Marta shook her head.

"You know the rules of the Princess Test. You can't know the girls' home countries."

"Marta-"

"No, you had your chance. I offered to help you earlier today. I specifically remember you telling me you preferred to play by the rules."

"Yes, but-"

"Besides, you're only considering big countries. Santelle and Eldria if I remember correctly. Those delegations and their princesses have already arrived. No, it's best if you put her out of your head."

Alaric glanced at his stepmother.

"Are you matchmaking?"

"What? Me? Alaric, I'm a sensible goat herder, not a gossiping courtier. Do you really think I would stoop to matchmaking?"

"Hmm."

"Come on, you should get back to dinner. I'll go to the kitchen and find food for her in case she wakes."

The dinner. That was the last place Alaric wanted to be.

"No, you should go. Father will want you by his side. I'll get the food. Besides, I'm drenched. I can't go back to dinner like this."

"Very well. If that's what you want. Take good care of her."

Queen Marta left before Alaric could say another word. He raised an eyebrow and glanced at the bedraggled princess sleeping in the chair. She sighed and curled into a small ball. Her face contorted into a frown. She shivered and covered her face with her hands. The diamond flashed in the firelight.

Alaric pulled a blanket from the bed and draped it over her.

They were talking about her. Somehow they had the idea she was a princess.

Lina was too exhausted to care. The relative warmth of the guard room took the edge off the chill and lulled her into a trance. Shadows danced before her eyes, calling her to sleep. Her body walked the hallway on its own. Step after step with the queen supporting her weight. By the time Alaric placed her in the chair, the trance was complete.

Trance. Lina had never liked that word for her shadow warrior abilities. It made everything sound mystical and out of control. She resented the idea that shadow travel happened passively.

Lina had spent years honing her natural abilities in the Council's military academy.

It took longer than usual to pull her consciousness to the realm of shadows. The dream world, some called it. The dark parallel of the realm of light that only those gifted in shadow magic could reach.

Lina concentrated on pulling her consciousness from her body into the darkness. The ring focused her energy. There, she was solid now. She hoped they didn't lock her body up in the realm of light while she slept. Usually she had someone to stand guard over her while she used her shadow magic.

Well, there was nothing she could do about that now.

Lina appeared, as she always did, floating in a dark void surrounded by stars. At least, there should have been stars. She counted three faint specks of light on the horizon. Hardly the luminous welcome she was used to. Lina summoned a mirror with a wave of her hand and studied herself.

She wore her usual shadow travel outfit. A black slim cut dress with a cape that flowed behind her in the currents of the shadow realm. Her arms were bare. The diamond ring twinkled in the mirror. It glowed that strange pink color. Danger. But what sort? Whatever it was, it was not immediate.

Lina spun, relishing the weightlessness that came with shadow travel. Like being underwater and in the sky at the same time. She adjusted her hair. Her headband had also appeared, but it had no gems on it. Lina frowned. So the magic really had faded. She closed her eyes and held her palm outstretched. The pea emerald appeared in her hand. She fastened it to her headband. There. She had at least one weapon.

Not that it would be enough if she met a goblin. Lina waved the mirror into the horizon and sank to the ground. Her feet hovered just on the surface like a boat on water. She walked across the smooth plain. Her cape billowed behind her.

It felt so empty. The shadow realm was vast, but it had never seemed this desolate. The geography loosely mirrored that of the realm of light, but everything was more flexible. You couldn't count on things to stay in the same place.

It was dark without the stars, but Lina didn't need to see.

She was a shadow warrior. She sensed everything that happened in this realm. Lina flung her arms into the air. The land around her rippled as she searched.

Yes, it really was that empty. She didn't sense any other shadow warriors. She examined the three stars in the distance. They should be the auras of light wielders, but they were too faint to be anyone with formal training. Certainly too faint to be Luca. Whoever they were, they couldn't help her. They might not even be aware that their light magic shone into the shadow realm.

Lina kept looking.

There. To her left and a little above her head. Something wasn't quite right. The pink light from Lina's ring darkened as she walked towards the disturbance. So, there was danger after all. Nothing too big if the ring was any indication. She might be able to take care of it with the pea.

"Identify yourself," she said.

A deep chuckle echoed through the realm. Lina pointed towards the sound and sent a wave of shadow magic at the sound. A warning shot. The laughter stopped.

"My name is Evangelina Shadow-Storm. I am a shadow warrior of the Council of Kings. A Protector of the Light. Identify yourself."

The ground rumbled beneath Lina's feet.

"I know who you are, shadow wench."

The voice vibrated through her bones and made the ends of her cape flutter.

Lina breathed through her nose. The air smelled clean. No trace of the stench that accompanied creatures of darkness.

What was this thing? She focused her energy in her ring and cast a shadow bolt laced with truth magic towards the voice.

"The truth," she said. "Who are you and what do you want?"

The voice floated through the air, thin with the effects of Lina's spell.

"I am the goblin warrior Nog. I want to devour you and the light you hold dear."

Lina crossed her arms and released the spell.

"You can't. This realm is protected. Your kind has been sealed away."

Nog's laughter boiled the surface of the ground. Lina hovered above it to keep from falling over.

"We have had centuries to break the seal. It will not hold much longer."

"I hold the seal," Lina said. "I will keep you locked away."

"You held the seal," Nog said. "But you're awake now. And you are alone."

A misty shape materialized in front of Lina. She recognized the silhouette. Stocky legs. Massive chest and arms. Horned head with a skull as thick and hard as a marble column. Definitely a goblin warrior.

He was faint. Wispy like smoke. But forming a body that solid through the seal should be impossible. It would take tremendous strength. A combination of light and dark magic.

The shape reached for Lina. She jumped backwards. The tip of a claw brushed her ankle. A chill swept through her bones.

❧ 10 ❧

Lina awoke and jumped out of her chair. She tripped on the blanket covering her lap and nearly fell into the dying fire. She gasped for air by the lungful and shivered.

That shouldn't have been possible. The goblin shouldn't have been there. The creatures of darkness had been sealed away. They shouldn't be able to take a solid form. Not even in the realm of shadows.

And yet Nog had.

Lina lifted the hem of her tattered dress and checked her ankle. A faint bruise colored her skin where Nog had touched her.

She shouldn't panic. He was one goblin. She could defeat one goblin on her own. One on one. She'd won against far greater odds.

Of course, she'd had weapons then. A whole headband of enchanted gems. Now she had a single emerald.

Lina recovered her composure enough to notice her surroundings. She glanced around the room. Judging by the architecture, she was in the castle. A bedroom, not a prison. Good.

Marble columns soared to high ceilings decorated with mosaic tiles. Candlelight gleamed off the white, carved surfaces. Lina studied the pattern on the ceiling. She recognized the designs. She had stayed in the castle whenever she reported to the king.

Lina searched the wall for a keyhole and slipped her diamond into a gap. She turned her hand, and the tiles rearranged to a different pattern.

She smiled. The castle was full of magical details like this. Secrets that members of the royal family could unlock with their signet rings. If the decorative ones had survived, perhaps the secret rooms remained undiscovered.

Lina turned her diamond back, and the tile ceiling returned to its original pattern. The room didn't have a window. She had no way to sneak out. That could be a problem.

Lina examined the furnishings. Ornately carved wooden furniture filled the room. A big chair sat by the fire, but the most impressive piece was an enormous bed with posts and a canopy. A vertical wooden box filled an entire corner of the room. Lina opened the doors and found dresses of every fabric and style imaginable. Cashmere wool, cotton, and silk. She studied the lace. Amazing. She had never seen anything so intricate. Craft had improved while she slept.

They would expect her to change into one of these gowns. Her own dress would not last much longer. She needed to secure the pea. Lina pulled the gem from its spot in the hem of her sleeve and rolled it between her fingers. Her last link to Luca. Her only weapon in the realm of shadows.

Where would it be safe?

Lina searched the room. Everything gleamed. The maids must clean often. If they found it, they might throw it away. Or steal it if they guessed its worth.

If she lost the pea, she'd have to fight Nog and whatever else wandered the realm of shadows empty handed.

Lina rubbed her eyes. There had been multiple weapon store rooms in the castle. Thousands of enchanted gems. If even a few had survived through the ages-

The door handle turned. Someone was coming in! Lina dove for the bed. She shoved the pea under the mattress and jumped on top.

A stocky woman in a plain brown dress entered. She carried a tray laden with food.

"Oh, good, you're awake. I'm Hilda. I'll be your ladies maid while you stay here, Princess."

Lina nodded. So she hadn't dreamed the part where they thought she was royalty. She was, if you got really technical with her genealogy, but she wasn't sure that counted now. Her connection to the royal family had been distant. She might never have seen the inside of the castle if she wasn't a shadow warrior.

Whatever the misunderstanding, she was grateful to be here now. One step closer to the Council.

"We're charmed to have you," Hilda said.

She handed Lina the tray. Lina tried to take princess sized bites of a muffin, but she was too hungry. She stuffed half the pastry in her mouth. Hilda raised an eyebrow.

"I understand you had a difficult journey. The queen asked me to remind you of the rules of the Princess Test since you missed the arrival ceremony. You're not to tell us where you're from. You're not to tell us your name. You will be referred to as princess like all the other girls, even if that is not your actual rank. We will provide a wardrobe from our country to prevent clues in your dress. If Prince Alaric chooses you, you'll be married to him and named Queen of Aeonia. Any questions?"

Lina swallowed the muffin. She had plenty of questions,

but none of them were about the Princess Test. Aeonia had bigger problems than choosing a queen.

"When can I speak with the Council of Kings?"

Hilda chuckled.

"You'll be too busy with the Princess Test to speak with anyone but the prince. The entire Council will attend the Grand Ball the night after tomorrow, so you will have an opportunity to speak to your delegation then. Do you need anything else?"

Lina shook her head and pushed the other half of the muffin into her mouth. However she had gotten in this mess, at least she was near the Council. If she played the part of a princess until the ball, she could talk to them much sooner than otherwise.

In the meantime, maybe she could sneak away and search the castle for enchanted gems.

Hilda watched Lina devour the muffin. Her lips pressed into a thin line.

"Very good then. I'll draw up a bath for you. If you'll come with me, we'll get you cleaned up and into new clothes. The first Princess Test begins soon."

Lina smiled.

"A bath would be very appreciated."

"**Y**our Highness must stop pacing!"

Bastien, Alaric's personal tailor, followed him back and forth across his bedroom. Alaric stopped moving long enough for Bastien to pounce and pin a jeweled brooch to his tunic.

Alaric glimpsed his reflection in the mirror and resumed his pacing. Sapphires covered every part of the enormous brooch. It gleamed like a lighthouse as he moved.

"Nice jewelry!" Stefan said. "I bet the girls will love it."

Alaric glared at him.

"Don't you have somewhere else to be?"

"Nope. As assistant coordinator for the Princess Test, my job is to stay by your side."

"Great."

"Do something with his hair," Stefan said. "Maybe some oil to make it curl more."

"I am not oiling my hair."

"An excellent idea, Prince Stefan!" Bastien said. "I will return. I have some excellent perfume as well."

The tailor bustled out the door. Alaric crossed his arms.

"I hate you."

"Just helping you win your true love's heart. Who did you choose?"

"Still Santelle or Eldria."

Stefan pulled the parchments out of Alaric's desk.

"So that's Princess Merinda or Princess Carina. Oh, Merinda is the one who collects butterflies."

"Really?"

Alaric glanced at Stefan.

"Hmm. That's creepy, right?"

"Depends on if she kills them or not. Just think, you could wake up every morning to a room full of bugs."

Alaric pulled the parchment from Stefan's hands.

"Princess Lenora collects butterflies, genius. Not Merinda. Thanks goodness. My spy didn't say if she kills them. Just that she collects them."

"I can't help it if all these pictures look the same. You need to hire an art teacher for your spies. These drawings are terrible."

Alaric had to agree. The pencil sketches of each princess had little detail.

"There will be plenty of time for royal portraits later."

"Whatever you say. I just hope you can recognize them from these drawings. Carina and Merinda look kind of similar."

Alaric compared the portraits side by side. Blast, Stefan was right. Merinda's expression was a little more pleasant, but the sketches could easily be the same girl. He skimmed the reports.

"Carina has blond hair. Merinda has black. That should help."

"Maybe. This is what you get for trying to cheat," Stefan said.

Alaric spread the rest of the parchments across his desk.

Yes, they should make art lessons mandatory training for spies and ambassadors. These drawings were truly terrible.

He had thought he was being clever having his spies sketch the girls, but these pictures would be no help at all.

"You could run away," Stefan said. "We can take our horses and meet Odette on patrol."

"Please stop talking about her."

Stefan studied Alaric's face.

"We grew up with her. You were close. What happened?"

"She left."

"What do you mean she left?"

Alaric sighed. Stefan wasn't going to be satisfied until he heard the whole story.

"She tried to joke with me while submitting a report. I told her we should start keeping our relationship more professional since I was crown prince and would be king one day. I said I had responsibilities to fulfill, and I couldn't let my personal feelings interfere with my duties to Aeonia."

Stefan dropped a parchment.

"You didn't. Alaric, you idiot! What did she say?"

"She apologized for being too casual with her commanding officer and requested a transfer. Then she saluted and walked out. I haven't seen her since. There, now you know. Does that make you happy?"

"No, it doesn't. When did this happen?"

"Over a year ago. Before I sent the couriers to request the Princess Test. I sent a formal invitation for her to rejoin the castle guard under a different commander, but she declined. I know I hurt her, but what else could I do? It really is over, Stefan."

"And you're really going to marry one of these girls?"

Stefan waved the parchments. Alaric picked up the parchment Stefan had dropped and tucked them back into his desk.

"Yes. I am. Will you help me figure out which girls are the princesses? Preferably Merinda and Carina?"

"I'll try, but it won't be easy. All the girls know the rules. They'll notice if I break them. It could cause an international incident."

Bastien burst through the door with an armful of bottles.

"I have the perfumes and oils! If Your Highness will sit here."

Alaric groaned, but his tailor wouldn't take no for an answer. Bastien poured half a bottle of oil over Alaric's head and worked it through his hair. He spritzed scent over Alaric's clothes until the prince gagged on the smell.

"Bastien," he choked. "Bastien, please stop."

Across the room, Stefan waved the cloud of perfume away from his face.

"I think that will do, Bastien," he said. "We don't want the princesses to be jealous that Alaric smells better than them."

Bastien closed the perfume bottle with a click.

"Humph. How am I supposed to help you win a bride if you won't listen to me? This whole family is impossible. Hilda comes home upset every night because your mother refuses to dress the part of queen."

Alaric took a deep breath and grimaced at the taste of perfume in the air.

"I am sorry if we cause trouble for you. You and Hilda are very appreciated."

Bastien set aside the perfume bottles. He rummaged through his cloak.

"Of course we're appreciated. You would be lost without us. But you'll understand better when you're married. When your wife is upset-"

He shuddered and pulled a bulging velvet bag from his cloak. Alaric shuddered just as much as Bastien had.

"Bastien, what is that?"

"Your Highness didn't think I would let you meet the princesses dressed so plainly?"

Alaric's eyes widened in horror as Bastien pulled more brooches from the bag.

"Bastien-"

The reproach in his tailor's eyes stopped him. Alaric bit his lip and allowed Bastien to pin more gems to his clothes.

By the time Stefan led him to the first Princess Test, Alaric barely recognized his reflection.

His chest glittered with a rainbow of gems. The oil made his hair hang in perfect ringlets. He smelled like a field of snowbells. Princess Lenora's butterflies would probably flock to him.

Stefan gave him a sympathetic glance before he opened the door.

"You look nice."

Alaric glared. Stefan's sympathy turned to a smirk. They both knew he looked ridiculous.

"Prince Alaric of Aeonia," the herald announced.

The trumpeter stationed at the door blasted a note. Alaric rubbed his ear and stepped through the door.

The line of girls blinked as his chest caught the light and flashed in their eyes. They all wore pale pink gowns and pearl necklaces. They watched Alaric with expectant eyes. He cleared his throat.

"Um, ladies."

Stefan coughed and elbowed him in the back. Alaric took another step forward. He wished he had prepared a speech.

"Welcome to Aeonia, Princesses. I am honored to have you here."

There, that was better. He bowed. The princesses curt-sied in unison. It really was creepy. He scanned the line. Six were blond. Four had black hair. Many of the girls looked similar. Especially since they wore identical outfits. And expressions. They had the same sweet smiles.

Blast.

Queen Marta stepped in front of the group.

"Welcome, Princesses. You all know the procedures. You are here to be tested. To prove your charms and worth. If Alaric chooses one of you, you will be queen of Aeonia after me."

The princesses curtsied in unison again. They looked expectantly at Alaric. He turned to Queen Marta. Please, let something happen. Let the ground swallow him whole.

The door flew open, and the trumpet blared. The princesses gasped. Hilda led a girl dressed in the same pink dress and pearl necklace into the room.

"Sorry we're late," she said. "It took a while to get her hairstyle right."

The late princess stood tall and examined her surroundings. Alaric's breath caught in recognition. She was the girl who had been at the gate last night. The girl from the archive.

She didn't look crazy now. She looked beautiful. The pink gown made her skin glow. The hair that had given Hilda such trouble was a rich chestnut brown. Lighter than Alaric had thought it was, but then she had been soaked last night.

She caught Alaric's eye and curtsied.

"Thank you for your assistance last night."

Her voice was just as he remembered it. Low and musical.

"What's the meaning of this?"

A princess stepped out of the line. She had bright red hair and a lilting accent. Fiora of Kell. Her words were shrill with indignation. She turned an accusing gaze on Alaric.

"Why does he know her? We're not supposed to have met yet. And why does she get to come in late? I didn't see her at the table last night. She should be disqualified."

The other princesses muttered in agreement. Queen Marta stepped forward.

"I am sorry you feel unfairly treated, Princess. This Princess had an unfortunate travel mishap and arrived later than intended. After the gate closed for the evening. Prince Alaric is one of the few people authorized to open the gate after sunset. He gave the order to let her in."

"So he did meet her," the red haired princess said. "That is a clear violation of the rules. Not to mention she's wearing personal jewelry! No one else was given a diamond ring."

Her voice was icy with disdain.

Fiora stepped forward and addressed the group of girls.

"I call for the disqualification of that princess. She should be ejected from the Princess Test immediately."

Lina eyed the red-haired princess. The princess met her gaze with a raised eyebrow and a challenge. The gauntlet had been thrown. How would she respond?

Lina glanced at the prince. He had seemed normal when she met him at the archive. Nice, even. Now he looked like a ridiculous fashion portrait. She should have known someone so handsome would be vain. He was wearing more jewels than the princesses!

She glanced back to the group of princesses. They glared at her. Right, she was their competition. And in their eyes, she had cheated and gained an unfair advantage.

Lina sighed. She didn't care about the Princess Test. She didn't want to marry the vain prince.

But she couldn't afford to be tossed out of the castle now. She had to warn the Council.

So, she'd have to be a princess.

Lina put her hand over her heart and curtsied to the floor. She wobbled and almost lost her balance in the enormous pink skirt. She stayed bent over. A gesture of humility and apology.

She hoped. If curtsy trends had changed, who knew what she was actually conveying?

"Forgive my lateness, Princesses," she said. "My travel misfortunes have been great indeed. I did not intend to gain an advantage through them. The circumstances were beyond my control. In my haste to get ready, I forgot to remove my ring."

She pulled the ring from her finger and tucked it into her sash. Her finger felt bare without it.

Queen Marta grabbed her shoulder and pulled her up.

"Of course you didn't mean to gain an advantage, Princess. We can afford to be generous, can't we, Princesses?"

She looked down the line, making eye contact with each girl. Most of them nodded at her. Princess Fiora glared daggers at Lina, but she stepped back into line.

"Go stand with the others," Queen Marta said. "You are late, but I have not yet officially announced the start of the Princess Test."

Lina joined the line of girls. The whole situation reminded her of being at the military academy. This was just another line of cadets in uniform.

Itchy, stuffy, starched pink uniforms.

The red-haired princess rejoined the line, but she looked anything but happy about it. Lina would have to watch out for her.

Queen Marta clapped her hands.

"Well, now that we're settled, I'd like to declare the official beginning of the Princess Test. Please allow me the honor of introducing my stepson, Crown Prince Alaric."

Prince Alaric bowed. The gems pinned to his tunic caught the light and nearly blinded Lina. She examined the jewels. None of them seemed to be enchanted.

Of course it wouldn't be so easy.

"The first test is simple," Queen Marta said. "We will give

the prince a chance to see your grace and wit in conversation. Each of you will have fifteen minutes to converse with the prince. Who would like to go first?"

The red haired princess stepped forward. Lina smirked at the expression on Prince Alaric's face. It served him right for being such a dandy.

Queen Marta nodded.

"Very well. Prince Stefan, please escort this charming Princess and Prince Alaric to the conversation parlor. The rest of us will wait here."

The girls formed small groups and chatted with each other after Prince Alaric left. Lina stood awkwardly. Everyone seemed to know each other. They had probably gone through many Princess Tests together.

"Won't you join us?"

Lina looked up. A girl with blond hair and sweet blue eyes smiled at her.

"Yes, thank you."

The girl pulled Lina into a circle with a princess with dark black hair.

"Is this your first Princess Test?" the black haired princess asked.

"Yes."

"I thought so. I haven't seen you before. I'm Eirwyn Blanche. You can call me Eirwyn."

"Quiet!" the blond princess hissed. "Not so loud. We'll be in real trouble if they hear you say your name."

"Are they really that strict about all this?" Lina asked.

"Oh, yes," Eirwyn said. "Especially when the prince really is looking for a bride. If they catch you saying where you're from, they'll kick you out. Sometimes these tests are just for show or to provide an official way for a couple to get engaged. But I've heard Prince Alaric isn't attached to anyone."

"Really?" Lina said. "I'm surprised he hasn't been snatched up. He certainly stands out with all those jewels."

The blond princess chuckled.

"It is awful, isn't it? They always try to show off their wealth at these things. Just don't say things like that too loud. I'm Carina."

"I'm Lina. So you really would marry him if he asked?"

Carina shrugged.

"My father has made me attend every princess test since I came of age. I'm not ready to get married yet, though. I'd rather stay at home. I've mastered the art of blending in."

"She really has," Eirwyn said. "Just watch. She's an expert at being mediocre. She won't be good enough or bad enough for anyone to remember her."

"And you're not mediocre?" Lina said.

Eirwyn's face fell.

"My father doesn't care much about me one way or the other. He said if I don't marry Prince Alaric, he has someone else in mind. He definitely wants me to make a political match. Everyone says it would solve a lot of our problems."

"Eirwyn, careful!" Carina hissed.

"What? There's more than one country in Myora with problems. So no, my family doesn't care. I wouldn't mind getting away though. It would be nice to be queen somewhere. To have some freedom."

Carina patted her friend's arm.

"Things will get better."

Eirwyn smiled at her.

"You'll just have to catch Prince Alaric's eye," Lina said. "Maybe if he falls in love with you, he'll let you wear some of his jewelry."

"Or share his hair oil," Carina giggled.

"I don't think there's any left in the bottle!" Lina said.

"Quiet," Eirwyn said. "So you're not looking to make a match, Lina?"

Lina shook her head.

"No. I think I'll follow Carina's strategy. So, what's the best way to be mediocre at conversation?"

Carina's eyes lit up.

"Oh, there are so many ways! First, don't say anything for the first minute or so. Make them feel awkward."

"They'll do their best to forget you after that," Eirwyn said.

"And then talk about the most boring thing you can think of," Carina said.

"Like what?"

Carina grinned.

"The Prince of Eldria loves architecture. When I went to the Princess Test there, he kept trying to tell me about the room. He said the stone was really expensive. So I counted all the stones in the wall out loud."

"You what?"

It came out louder than Lina had meant to speak. The other princesses glared at her.

"Careful," Eirwyn said. "Some of these girls take these things very seriously."

"Like the red head?"

Both girls shuddered.

"Watch out for Fiora," Carina said. "She's on a mission to get married, and she'll pummel anything that stands in her way."

"Right. I didn't mean to have an advantage."

"But you did meet him last night?" Eirwyn said. "He let you in the gate?"

"Yes."

Yes, he had let her in the gate. Lina was pretty sure he had done more than that. She had a vague memory of him picking her up. But she had probably imagined it.

"What was he like?" Eirwyn said. "I've heard he's unfit to rule. Father said he's bound to be either stupid or vicious."

Lina blinked at her.

"Vicious?"

"You know, because of his ancestors. The war."

Carina nudged her friend with her elbow.

"Quiet. They'll hear you."

"So? I'm just repeating history."

Lina's heart sank. History. Carina studied her face.

"Your family didn't warn you, did they? The nerve. Sending you here unprepared."

"It isn't like it's a secret," Eirwyn said. "I heard they don't try to hide it. Any of it. They have scrolls about it in the archive!"

"Not in the history section, though," Carina said. "Our court scholar visited a few years ago. He said all the records are in the histories of royal families. They had to explain the family tree somehow."

Lina swallowed.

"So what exactly happened?"

"Hush!" Eirwyn said. "Prince Stefan is coming this way."

Lina looked up. She recognized Prince Stefan as the other man from the archive. So they were brothers. He had been the one to mention her name.

Prince Stefan bowed. The three girls curtsied. Lina watched Carina and Eirwyn carefully so she could move in unison with them.

"It is your turn, Princess," Stefan said.

He held his hand out to Lina. She nodded and followed him.

"Be average!" Carina whispered in her ear as she passed.

❧ 13 ❧

Alaric stared at Princess Fiora. How long had he been talking to her? One minute? Five? Seven?

Please let it be seven. Let it be eight. It took every bit of his self-control to stay seated and smiling.

Fiora sat on the edge of her chair, ready to pounce. Her blue eyes glinted, and strands of her red hair stuck out around her head.

"Well," she said. "Do you prefer rubies or sapphires?"

Alaric cleared his throat.

"Actually, I-"

Fiora laughed, a shrill sound like a wagon wheel scraping against a gate.

"Forgive my banter, Prince Alaric. Your preference is clear from your shirt. That is a lovely sapphire brooch."

Alaric straightened the brooch. Its weight kept pulling his tunic down

"Thank you, Princess."

They stared at each other.

"Your whole outfit is tasteful," she said. "A wonderful representation of Aeonian culture."

She batted her eyes at him. Alaric straightened the brooch again.

"You are too kind, Princess."

"I've always been fond of Aeonian culture."

This was unbearable. She smiled at him. The corner of her eye twitched.

"I am glad you enjoy our fair land. Have you visited before, Princess?"

He knew she hadn't. The people of Kell rarely left their island. Fiora flushed.

"Such a question! One might think you were trying to discover my country of origin, Prince Alaric. I would of course remember meeting you. Everything about you stands out. Your sense of style. Your chivalry. Your-"

She kept talking. And talking. And talking. She listed Alaric's positive qualities like she was reading from a dictionary.

Alaric stared out the window. How long had it been now? At least five minutes, surely. Maybe even ten? Fifteen minutes, Queen Marta had said. That hadn't seemed like a long time when she said it. A fifteen minute conversation.

It felt like an hour.

"-and of course your artistic talents."

Alaric jumped back to the present.

"My what?"

"Surely Your Highness is aware that your reputation as an author precedes you?"

"No. I have no idea what you're talking about. As crown prince, I have very little time for hobbies."

"Ah, but you found time to write a play for our amusement. I am so looking forward to it."

She bent her head down and gazed up at him through her long lashes. Doubtless she meant to look flirtatious, but the overall effect was more predatory than anything. Alaric's heart beat faster from sheer panic.

The play. She knew about the play. That meant others knew as well. At least the whole Kell delegation.

He wouldn't be able to cancel it. It would have to be produced. The show must go on.

He broke out in a cold sweat. Fiora fluttered her eyelashes at him.

"I wonder if Your Highness would be so kind as to give me a preview of your work? I would love to hear you recite something."

"I-"

Alaric's mouth had gone dry. Conversation. No good. If this were a Prince Test, he definitely would fail.

"Your Highness? Is it too soon to be so forward? I apologize if I am overstepping any boundaries. I've never felt such a connection with someone."

Fiora leaned forward. Please, no. She seemed to have mistaken his silence for passion. Alaric leaned back in his chair.

The door opened, and Princess Fiora leaned back into her seat. She glared daggers at Stefan as he approached them.

"Princess, please come with me. Your time for conversation is over."

Stefan took Fiora's arm and led her away. She brushed Alaric's shoulder with her hand as she passed. Stefan looked back at Alaric and raised an eyebrow.

Alaric wiped the sweat from his forehead with his sleeve. It left dark patches on the velvet.

Please, don't let every conversation be like this.

Stefan entered the room again. Empty handed, thank goodness.

"That bad?"

"Stefan, that woman is a harpy."

Stefan laughed.

"I'm sure they won't all be like that. Who would you like me to bring in next?"

Alaric thought for a moment.

"The one who came in late."

"Ah, so her strategy is working. She is standing out."

"No, it's not that. I met her yesterday at the archives before you came."

Stefan raised an eyebrow.

"You remember," Alaric said. "She was in the back. She dropped a bunch of parchments on the floor."

Stefan shrugged.

"Not really. I don't pay much attention to anything in the archives. So she's a researcher? She sounds like your perfect match."

"Stefan-"

Stefan winked and left the room before Alaric could respond. He returned with a girl on his arm.

The girl from the archive. The late princess.

"Princess, may I present my brother, Prince Alaric."

The princess curtsied far lower than was necessary. Alaric met her gaze. Her green eyes sparkled as much as the gems on his tunic.

She smiled at him and sat on the chair. She folded her hands in her lap.

And said nothing.

Stefan left. Alaric smiled at the girl. She smiled back.

They smiled at each other until it grew awkward. Then they frowned at each other. Alaric cleared his throat. His mouth still felt dry, but he could speak now.

"I'm glad you've recovered from your ordeal."

More than recovered. She was glowing. Alaric had never

seen anyone so pretty. It wasn't just her features. There was something alive in her expression. Some secret dancing in her eyes.

"Thank you for your help."

And then she was silent again. What kind of game was she playing? Was she angry with him?

"I'm sorry if I got you in trouble," he said. "I didn't know you were a princess. I didn't mean to meet you early."

"So you would have left me outside if you'd known who I was?"

"What? No, of course not!"

"You would have sent guards to look after me instead?"

"No, I-"

"So, you would have acted just the same even if you had known I was a princess."

"I suppose."

The girl stared at him. She wrinkled her skirt in her fists and smoothed them out.

"May I ask you a question?"

Alaric blinked.

"Of course."

"Tell me about Evangelina Shadow-Storm."

Alaric groaned. Not this again. Please, let her talk about anything but that blasted play! The girl frowned.

"Is something wrong? I understand she is a figure in a- a children's story from your country."

Alaric nodded.

"And she is popular? Well liked?"

"Well enough."

"Does anyone know the origin of the story? Where it came from?"

Alaric leaned forward in spite of himself. This was a conversation he could contribute to.

"No. When I was young I searched the entire archive for a mention of her. I wanted her to be real. But she isn't. She's just a myth."

"What does she do in this myth?"

"She defeats a horde of dark creatures. Goblins."

The princess shivered and glanced down. At her shoe? Her ankle? She composed herself and met Alaric's gaze.

"And they stay defeated?"

He nodded. The princess took a deep breath. She frowned. She clearly had something else to say. Alaric waited, but she didn't say it. Just as she had in the archive, she mastered her emotions and smoothed her features into a serene expression.

"You can ask me," Alaric said. "Whatever you're thinking, you can say it."

She frowned.

"Is it that obvious?"

He shrugged.

"Alright then. I've heard, um, rumors. About your family."

"We've ruled Aeonia for over a century. I don't need to prove my bloodline."

The princess flinched at the venom in his tone. Alaric bit his lip. He wasn't helping his family's reputation by snapping at everyone who asked about it.

"You don't have to pretend it was rumors," he said, fighting to keep a civil tone. "My family's history is common knowledge. Everything is in the History of Royal Families in the archive. We're not trying to hide anything."

"Apparently the historical gossip is more interesting than I thought. I should have read it while I had the chance."

"I'm happy to answer any questions."

Alaric tried to look relaxed. The last thing he wanted to do was discuss his family's past, but he would if necessary. He realized he was clutching the edge of the chair and loosened his grip.

The princess studied him but said nothing.

❧ 14 ❧

Lina watched the prince. She had a hundred questions, but she didn't dare to ask any of them. His temper had flared when she hinted at his past.

She was supposed to be a charming princess. She should be making mindless small talk. Asking about flowers or something.

A century. He said his family had ruled for a century.

She had slept for at least a hundred years.

How had his family come to power? Had they invaded? Was that the war Eirwyn had mentioned?

Then what had happened to Lina's family? The original rulers of Aeonia?

Nothing good if Eirwyn expected the prince to be vicious.

Lina swallowed. No, she didn't dare ask Alaric about any of this. She already stood out too much. She should have sat for fifteen minutes and not said a word.

"Truly, ask me any questions you like," Alaric said. "Is there anything you'd like to know about Aeonia?"

Yes. So many things.

"No."

"Oh."

It was his turn to stare at her, stunned into silence. Lina wished she had a way to track the time. Surely most of the fifteen minutes had passed.

"What happened to your traveling companions?" he asked. "Did your ship crash?"

Her traveling companions. That was the last thing Lina wanted to talk about. Time to play the part of a princess. She fluttered her eyelashes.

At least, she tried. She had never been good at flirting. She probably looked like a goat with dust stuck in its eye.

"Your Highness! Asking about my travel accommodations? Are you trying to discover where I'm from?"

The prince leaned back in his chair. Lina swallowed a laugh. He looked terrified. If anything, he was worse at flirting than she was. Some men would enjoy an endless parade of women focused on them, but Prince Alaric did not seem to be that type.

That was going to make the Princess Test a miserable experience for him.

Lina leaned forward and fluttered her lashes more. If this was what it took to shut him up, she could manage it for fifteen minutes. She would flutter her eyelashes until they cramped.

Alaric leaned further back in his chair. Lina took a deep breath so she could sigh dramatically. She choked on a bitter taste.

"Are you wearing snowbell perfume?"

Her lips curved into a smile in spite of everything. Maybe fashions had changed, but she doubted it. Snowbells were a decidedly feminine scent. The prince glared at her.

"How do you know what snowbells smell like?"

"Oh- I-"

Blast! Of course a visiting princess wouldn't recognize the scent. Lina's mind churned. There had to be some reason.

Someone tapped her shoulder. She jumped and looked up. Prince Stefan smiled at her.

"Excuse me, Princess. Your time for conversation has passed."

Lina nodded. She took Stefan's arm and walked out of the room.

She couldn't resist a backwards glance at Alaric. He watched her leave with far too much interest.

She needed to have Carina give her more lessons in blending in.

"So, is my brother being charming?" Stefan asked.

Lina shrugged.

"Were you this quiet during the conversation?"

A true princess would be more interested in the prince. She would use opportunities like this to gain useful information. Lina reminded herself that she needed to play the part.

"The conversation was-"

She searched for the proper description, but nothing proper came to mind.

"Is it going that badly?"

Stefan stopped walking. Lina looked up at him. He looked concerned.

"Is my brother really that miserable?"

The concern in his face broke Lina's heart. How many times had Luca looked at her that way? She patted Stefan's hand.

"I'm sure I'll find your brother charming as I get to know him."

Stefan looked like he wanted to say more. A shrill voice interrupted him.

"It has been well over fifteen minutes! Is the second princess still with him? I demand to know!"

Stefan grimaced.

"Have fun with her."

He showed her to the door and hurried away. Princess Fiora glared at Lina as she entered.

"I should have known you would cause trouble. Some people are so desperate they'll do anything to gain an advantage! What did you and the prince talk about?"

Lina shrugged.

"Don't ignore me. I could report you to the Council for your behavior. What country are you from, anyway? Who had the nerve to try to rig the test?"

"Do you really want me to tell you? We're not supposed to reveal that. You're the one worried about upholding rules."

"Don't turn this around on me. Prince Alaric and I had a very stimulating conversation. I'm sure I impressed him."

Lina yawned. Last night's shadow travel was catching up with her. Fiora's nostrils flared.

"How dare you!"

She stomped to the window and stared outside.

"Surveying your domain?" Lina asked.

Fiora ignored her.

Lina studied the room. It looked much like others in the castle. The original marble structure was decorated with wooden furnishings.

She sat in a chair in the opposite corner from Fiora and closed her eyes. She hadn't slept well last night. A rest would do her good. Just for a few moments.

She considered traveling to the realm of shadows to check on the seal. No, it was too risky to sink into a trance with Fiora glaring at her from across the room. And she had no power in the realm of shadows in the daytime. It would be better to wait for night. Lina pushed the shadows away as she dozed. It was far easier to resist them when the sun was up.

The sound of a door slamming woke her. Lina sat up and

glanced around. Several more princesses milled around the room. Most gathered with Fiora around the window. They all whispered and glared at Lina.

The nap renewed Lina's energy. She studied the room. There had to be a way to escape. She couldn't afford to spend her day being glared at. She didn't have time to fight over a prince she didn't want. There were goblins breaking through the seal!

Escape from this room would be difficult. There was one window and one door. She could have climbed out the window if she was alone, but Fiora would definitely see her. And she would definitely get her disqualified from the Princess Test.

Stefan had led her down a hallway. If she sneaked through that, she could search the castle for gems to help her fight Nog.

Lina stood and paced around the room. The other princesses watched her every move. She rested her hand on the doorknob and tried to turn it.

Locked.

Across the room, Fiora raised an eyebrow. Lina turned from the door and examined the fireplace.

"This seems to be a quality castle," she said. "I wouldn't want to be queen in a place with shoddy workmanship."

Fiora crossed her arms and glared. The other princesses followed her lead. They didn't stop watching.

Sneaking out would not be possible. She needed another way.

Stefan led Carina into the room. Lina fought the urge to run through the open door. That would do her no good. She needed to be a princess until tomorrow night. She needed to go to that ball.

Carina smiled at Lina. Lina smiled back. Thank goodness at least some of the princesses were nice.

"How did it go?" Lina whispered.

"I think I was sufficiently bland, but it was hard. He was even blander than me. How about you?"

"Frustrating. He certainly isn't a charming prince. Carina, what would happen if a princess sneaked away from the group?"

Carina's eyes widened.

"I'm not sure. Talking to the prince outside of the tests would get you disqualified, but I'm not sure about sneaking away. Why?"

"I need to look for something in the castle."

"Ooh, an adventure! What is it?"

Lina bit her lip. She didn't dare tell Carina the whole truth. But maybe part of it.

"I'm looking something I lost."

"Can't you ask the servants to look for it?"

Lina shook her head.

"I'd rather look for it myself."

"Hmm. What's really going on, Lina?"

Lina swallowed. She couldn't afford to give away her identity before the ball. She had to keep them thinking she was a princess. But maybe Carina could help her. And right now, she needed help.

"The Council is in danger, but no one believes me. I need to search the castle to look for threats."

Carina pulled Lina to a corner of the room.

"What's the danger?"

"I'm not sure, but it's definitely there. Watch this."

She pulled her ring from her sash and held it to her lips.

"Check for danger."

Carina gasped as the diamond flashed pink.

"Is that ring magic?"

"Yes. I showed the prince last night, but he didn't believe me. No one does."

"You showed the Crown Prince of Aeonia a magic ring? Lina, what were you thinking?"

"What's wrong? Aeonia is a magical country."

"No, Lina, they're not. The queen- Lina, don't you know anything about Aeonia?"

"What's wrong with Marta?"

Carina's eyes widened.

"Not Marta. The other one. Lina, keep that ring to yourself. Please. It could cause trouble."

"Why? What other queen?"

Lina waited for Carina to say more, but she didn't.

"Carina, we're in danger. If they won't believe me, I need to look for myself."

Carina swallowed.

"You trust that ring?"

Lina nodded.

"And you're willing to risk disqualification?"

Lina hesitated, then nodded again. If she found the danger, she'd have proof to bring the Council. If she found enchanted gems, she'd have a way to fight any creatures that came through the seal.

Carina winked at her

"As long as you're sure. Follow my lead."

Carina grabbed Lina's sleeve. She pulled down as hard as she could. The fabric ripped.

"Carina, what are you doing?"

Carina grabbed the fabric at the tear and pulled until the sleeve hung off Lina's arm.

Stefan entered the room with another princess. Carina grabbed Lina and pushed her towards the prince.

"Her dress is torn," she said. "She's trying to stand out again. I insist she change into a new gown."

Fiora left her place by the window and examined the dress. Stefan stared at Lina.

"How did that happen?" he said.

"Does it matter?" Fiora asked. "She's trying to cheat. She must have her dress mended or be disqualified."

Stefan sighed.

"Fine. Come with me please, Princess."

"Don't lead her through the prince's room!" Fiora said. "He can't see her a second more than the rest of us."

Stefan bowed.

"I will make sure he does not see her, Princess."

Stefan led Lina down the hallway. He ducked through a side door and found a servant.

"Take this Princess to Bastien, please. He should be free since Alaric is in the Princess Test all day. Keep her out of sight until the sleeve is fixed."

Lina followed the servant through the castle. The structure had changed since her time. Hallways had disappeared. There were more windows. Once, she had known every hiding place for enchanted gems and weapons.

She could only hope the secret passageways were still there.

Bastien gasped when Lina entered.

"What in the world happened to you?"

Lina shrugged.

"I'm a bit clumsy. I caught it on a door."

Bastien examined the sleeve. He clucked the whole time.

"Lucky for us it ripped at the seam. It won't take much time to repair. You'll be back with the prince in no time."

"Is there a place to rest while you work? I am tired from my travels. Perhaps a place with a window? I would enjoy some fresh air."

Bastien nodded.

"I understand. Prince Alaric often requests a place to rest while I sew. There's a spare fitting room through that door. It has a window and a couch. Trina will help you change."

A short blond maid led Lina to a small side room. Lina slipped her ring onto her finger before letting the maid help her out of the pink gown. Lina stood in her undergarment. A loose fitting white slip.

Much more practical for sneaking around than the pink gown. She closed the fitting room door and examined the room. It would be a nice place to rest. There was a couch and several chairs.

But what really interested her was the window.

Perhaps respecting her request for fresh air, someone had already opened it. The window wasn't large, but she would be able to fit through.

It was a little unorthodox, sneaking out a window in her undergarments, but she didn't really have a choice. Lina pulled a curtain down and tied it around her waist. She would need it to carry whatever she found.

She climbed out the window. Thank goodness this part of the castle was stone rather than smooth plaster. It was easy enough to climb along the wall.

Lina climbed sideways around the castle. The breeze pulled her hair loose and rustled the curtain around her waist. There had been a secret storage place for enchanted gems in the tallest tower. No one went up there without a reason. Too many stairs. It seemed the most likely place to have remained undisturbed. She froze every time someone walked by on the ground, but no one saw her.

Finally she reached the tower. Lina climbed in the window. The tower was empty except for a pile of spinning wheels in the corner. She pushed them aside and felt for the indentation in the rock. There.

Lina pushed her ring into the hole and turned her hand. The latch in the wall clicked. A trap door in the floor fell open.

Lina fell against the rock wall with relief. The room was still there!

She climbed into the trap door. The room smelled musty. She held her ring to her lips.

"Light. Illuminate."

The diamond glowed white. Lina gasped.

The room was empty. Absolutely empty. Even the shelves had been removed. Lina sank to her knees.

"Oh, Luca."

She searched the floor, checked every crack, but it was no use. Everything was gone.

❧ 15 ❧

Alaric smiled at the princess across from him. She smiled back.

"I-"

"Do you-"

"I'm sorry-"

"No, what were you saying-"

They had been interrupting each other like this for the whole conversation. Alaric took the high road and waited. So did the princess. They sat in silence and stared at each other.

"Do you like horses?" the princess blurted out.

"Yes!"

Silence. Alaric picked at the fabric on his chair. The princess did the same. Was she Brigitta? The parchment had said Brigitta liked horses.

"Did you have a pleasant journey?" he asked.

"Yes."

He waited for her to say more. She didn't. Alaric bit back a sigh of relief when Stefan opened the door and escorted the princess out.

His legs were stiff from sitting so long. He walked to the

window and stuck his head outside. Maybe fresh air would clear his head. The conversations hadn't helped him figure out the princess's identities at all. They ran together more than ever.

Except for Fiora with her militant flirting. And the late princess. It bothered him that he didn't know her name.

Alaric turned his head in a stretch and nearly fell out the window. A lone figure clung to the highest castle tower. Someone was climbing the wall!

Stefan joined Alaric at the window.

"That was the last princess. You don't have to climb out the window to escape. Do you have a favorite yet?"

"Stefan, do you see that?"

Stefan looked.

"The girl climbing the tower wall in her undergarments? Yes. Yes, I do."

"Should we call the guards?"

"If she's trying to rob us, she picked the wrong tower. I think that one is used to store junk. No one ever goes up there."

"But she's breaking and entering. Besides, she might fall."

The girl reached the top of the tower and pulled herself inside. They caught a glimpse of her face as she turned.

"Stefan, that's one of the princesses! The one who came late!"

The princess disappeared into the tower. When she didn't reappear, Stefan shrugged and sank into one a chair. Alaric paced around the room.

"We can't call the guards," he said. "It could cause an international incident if we arrested a princess for robbery during the Princess Test."

"There isn't anything to steal in that tower. Maybe she just wanted some fresh air."

Alaric could understand that. He'd considered jumping out a window more than once that day.

"How did she get out of the room? Aren't they supposed to stay together?"

Stefan rubbed his chin.

"Right. She tore her dress. I sent her to Bastien to have it fixed."

"She tore her dress? She's been sitting in a chair all day."

"I think she got in a fight with one of the other princesses."

"What? What in the world happened in there?"

Stefan winked.

"Wouldn't you like to know?"

"Stefan, this is serious."

"Fine. Maybe she's just scouting out the castle. Trying to decide if you're rich enough to marry. She'll be disappointed if she does manage to find the treasury. I'm not sure there's a jewel left there."

He gestured to the array of gems pinned to Alaric's chest.

"Shut up."

"You look nice."

"Stop smirking, Stefan."

"I'm not smirking."

"Yes you are."

"I can't help it. My brother just looks so handsome!"

Alaric caught his reflection in the mirror and groaned. He looked more ridiculous than he remembered.

"Why don't you have to wear jewels?" he asked. "You're a prince. Maybe I should speak with Heinrich. I can't have my brother being dressed below his station."

Stefan bristled.

"Leave my tailor out of this! He understands my simple taste perfectly."

Alaric compared Stefan's short hair and non-jeweled outfit to his own ringlets and brooches.

"Want to trade? I'm sure Bastien would enjoy a challenge."

Stefan snorted.

"Definitely not. I'm sticking with Heinrich. You've got bigger problems than your hair, Alaric."

Alaric glanced out the window again. The princess was still in the tower. Should he tell someone?

He decided against it. If she was trying to cause trouble, she wouldn't be able to cause much up there. Hopefully she could find her way back to wherever she was supposed to be without causing problems.

He left the window and turned to Stefan.

"So, what test is next?"

"You're on break for a few hours. The princesses are having lunch in their rooms and preparing for the next test. You're having lunch with the kings."

"Great."

Alaric tried to ignore his father's amused expression when he entered the dining room. He didn't need a reminder that he looked ridiculous.

"Your son is very handsome," the King of Darluna said.

"The Princess Test is going well?" King Noam said.

Alaric nodded. He sat by his father and sipped wine from a crystal chalice.

"I'm glad you're having a true Princess Test," the King of Gaveron said. "It will help legitimize your rule."

Alaric nearly spit wine out of his nose. He managed to swallow the mouthful, but it left him coughing too much to respond.

He had known the other kings felt this way, but they had never discussed it openly. Alaric turned to his father for an explanation.

"It is nothing," King Noam said. "We have been discussing our family's lineage in the council meetings. The fact that we are the youngest ruling family in Myora."

"Young doesn't cover it. There are peasants in Kell with more claim to a throne in their lineage," the King of Kell said.

He stroked his bright red beard.

After his conversation with Fiora, Alaric hadn't thought it was possible to dislike Kell more. The king proved him wrong. Alaric sat taller and wished Bastien had given him a crown to wear for the day.

"The people accept our rule. Aeonia is flourishing."

"Oh, no one questions your prosperity," the King of Gaveron said. "But Aeonia would flourish even more with a true noble on the throne. I find the trend of romances between nobility and citizens disturbing."

Alaric inhaled and glanced at his father. King Noam gritted his teeth, but he seemed willing to let the slight on his marriage to a goat herder pass.

After hours of conversations with the princesses, Alaric was not in such a generous mood.

"I find having a citizen on the throne helps us keep the citizens in mind," he said.

He glared at the King of Gaveron. The king returned his gaze.

"And I find ancient bloodlines and centuries of ruling experience to be invaluable."

"No one made that claim while we were at war. Only now that we prosper do you question our lineage."

"I question nothing. I am only observing that noble families have a right to rule. I am sure you are very aware of that as you consider the princesses."

"Gentlemen, please," the King of Darluna said. "All of us have daughters and nieces in the Princess Test. No one refused to participate. Clearly we do not hold the royal family of Aeonia's questionable origins against them."

"Questionable origins?"

Alaric slammed his chalice on the table. Wine sloshed onto the tablecloth. The King of Darluna put his hands in the air in a gesture of surrender.

"You must admit your family came to power under difficult circumstances. Forgive me if I have offended you, Prince Alaric. I meant no disrespect."

Alaric glanced around the table in dismay. If the kings were willing to discuss the matter so casually, it was worse than he thought.

"Please, let us not discuss business over lunch," King Noam said. "We will have plenty of time for debate later. If Your Majesties approve, our court musicians will provide us with entertainment while we eat."

The kings nodded. Alaric fell silent and ate little. The lute player's plaintive tune did nothing to help his mood. He glared into his soup until lunch ended.

"A word, Alaric," his father said as the kings left the dining room.

Alaric followed him into his study. King Noam shut the door.

"Are you trying to start a war?" the king demanded.

"I'm sorry, father. I've never had my legitimacy as a ruler questioned in my presence."

The king's face fell.

"The King of Gaveron has spoken of little else since he arrived. He hints that he will make sure a noble is seated on Aeonia's throne before he leaves."

"Father, I won't allow them to bully us! They're just jealous that Aeonia is united again. That you united us. We're thriving, and they can't stand it."

"There may be something to that. It certainly seems that

the older families would like more control here. Some whisper that we should be annexed into Gaveron so Aeonia can be ruled by a true noble family."

"We've ruled for a century! They had over a hundred years to raise such claims! They did nothing!"

"Alaric, they aren't wrong about our family's rise to power. Blood was spilled."

"Blood is always spilled in a war! We have ruled in peace since then."

"People remember violence more than peace. The Council of Kings accepted us because there were no members of the original royal family left. Have you ever wondered why?"

Alaric's face fell.

"They died in battle. That's what the scrolls in the archive say."

"I've read the scrolls, Alaric. But I have a hard time believing every single member of such a large family was killed in battle. What about those away on diplomatic missions? What about the children?"

"Father, what are you implying?"

King Noam shrugged.

"History written by the victors is often skewed. My guess is that assassins were hired to hunt down the remaining members of the royal family. It is the only way to explain such a complete disappearance."

Alaric stared at his father.

"You really believe that?"

"Some version of it, yes. Certainly the other countries think the same."

"Even if that were true, you and I had nothing to do with that. We are good rulers. Aeonia is at peace thanks to you."

"Yes. Thanks to my marriage to your mother, Aeonia was united once again."

Alaric sighed. King Noam smiled.

"How is the Princess Test going? Have you picked one yet? Found a true princess?"

"I've only had one conversation with each of them."

Except for the gate princess. He couldn't admit that though. It might get her disqualified. He considered mentioning her climb up the tower, but decided against it. His father had enough worries.

King Noam sighed.

"More may depend on this than I originally thought. As much as I hate to admit it, adding a true princess to our lineage would silence many of their protests. Choose wisely, son."

"Those kings are despicable. How dare they insult Marta?"

King Noam shook his head.

"It isn't the first time. Many of them objected to sharing a table with a former goat herder. Prejudices run deep in the old families."

Alaric clasped his father's shoulder.

"I won't let you down, father. I will make a good match."

King Noam smiled sadly.

"I hoped this would be unnecessary. I thought I could negotiate my way to better relations. But you were right all along. You showed rare insight in requesting this Princess Test. I'm proud of you."

Alaric nodded. Winning his father's approval usually made him feel proud. Now he felt more trapped than ever.

"I think it would be best not to delay the results of the test," Alaric said. "The more time the kings have, the more trouble they can cause. I'll announce my choice on the third evening as soon as the test ends."

"Are you sure? You are allowed a few days after the test to consider your choice."

"Yes, I'm sure. I won't give them extra time to undermine us."

"It is a good idea, but I'm sorry it's necessary. I'll tell the kings of your decision tomorrow."

Alaric smiled, but he didn't feel happy. He left his father and walked towards his room.

He had underestimated how difficult it would be to identify the princesses. They dressed alike. They moved in unison. Most of the conversations had been similar.

Picking a girl out of the crowd would be difficult even if you knew her. The different hair colors helped a little, but everyone's hair was styled exactly the same.

He ran through the king's faces in his mind. Would their daughters resemble them? The royal family of Kell had the same bright red hair. Others might share hair color or other traits. That could be helpful. It was difficult to keep the princesses straight without knowing their names. He would search for identifying characteristics at the next test.

Servants scurried out of his way as he walked. He knew he looked fierce. He couldn't help it. Yes, his family had come to power under questionable circumstances. They had not originally been nobility. But his country was at peace now. Aeonia thrived. How dare the kings question them after a century of silence?

He reached his room and slammed the door. Twenty girls. Eight princesses. Did they share their father's views? Did they despise him for his origins?

Alaric had known he wouldn't be able to marry for love, but he hadn't considered the possibility that his new wife would hate him. That she would consider him an impostor. The latest in a line of pretenders with blood on their hands.

Alaric pulled the parchments from his desk and studied the portraits. Was Brigitta the princess who asked if he liked horses? Or was that Colette? They looked similar in the sketches.

Alaric spread the parchments over the desk and studied them side by side. Something was wrong.

Where was the gate princess? He would recognize her even in a poorly drawn pencil sketch. Alaric flipped through the parchments one by one. He pulled the larger pile out of his desk and studied it as well.

She wasn't there. She was not one of the princesses who had agreed to attend the Princess Test. Twenty princesses agreed to come. He had twenty parchments from his spies.

But twenty-one princesses arrived. How had Marta been expecting her? Had she simply sent her acceptance late?

She traveled alone. She arrived with none of the finery of a princess except for her ring.

Her magic ring.

Alaric shuddered.

Whoever she was, she was up to something. Climbing towers. Working magic. She was here for more than the Princess Test

He shoved the parchments into his desk and pulled a cloak over his ridiculous clothes and hair. He needed to do some research.

She should go back to the fitting room. Lina knew that. But she couldn't bring herself to do it. She hadn't found any gems, but maybe she could find some answers.

She wrapped the curtain around her shoulders. Lina hoped it looked enough like a cloak to keep people from getting suspicious. She couldn't afford to draw attention to herself by running around town in her undergarments.

Lina climbed down the tower. She found a tree that stretched across the moat and climbed through the branches until she was clear of the castle.

She jogged to the archives. Royal histories. She hoped she could find the information she needed in those scrolls.

She took a smock from Simon and slipped it over the curtain cloak. Now she looked just like everyone else. Simon didn't recognize her. She had been covered in dust last time, so that was fair.

The archives were busier in the afternoon. Lina walked towards the shelves with the most people around them. To be fair to Alaric, most of them were women.

"Is this the royal history section?" Lina asked.

The women giggled.

"Yes, of course! Are you checking your genealogy?"

Lina blinked.

"My what?"

"To see if you qualify for the Princess Test!"

One of the women clutched her hands over her heart.

"I'd give anything to be up there. They're so lucky to have a chance at Prince Alaric!"

The other girls swooned. Lina watched them in confusion.

"You don't think he's vicious?"

The women gasped in unison.

"Vicious? What gave you that idea?"

Lina swallowed.

"I-"

"He's a darling. And so responsible. I needed help with trade negotiations for my cashmere weaving business last year, and he handled it himself. Some merchants from Gaveron tried to charge me extra import duties. Prince Alaric changed the terms of a trade agreement to prevent it."

"My brother's in his army unit. He said he's the best commander he's ever had."

Other women added their defenses. Whatever the princesses thought of Prince Alaric, the Aeonian citizens clearly adored him. Lina held up her hands in surrender.

"Actually, you're right. I am here to see if I qualify for the Princess Test. A girl can dream, right?"

"I knew it! What years do you want to check?"

Lina bit her lip. She hoped she wouldn't incriminate herself by naming a specific year.

"Maybe 1215 or so?"

The women gasped.

"You realize that's the old royal family, right? Before King Thaddeus?"

Lina nodded. Her heart beat faster, but she kept her expression calm.

"Well, you're certainly ambitious! If you proved you were descended from them, you might find yourself queen without marrying a prince."

One of the women offered Lina a scroll. She unrolled it and glanced at the dates. Yes, that looked about right.

"Aren't there any members left? What happened to them?"

The woman put her hands on her hips.

"Who can say? Most of the cowards disappeared at the first sign of trouble. The rest were none too prepared to fight."

"And you don't mind being ruled by invaders?"

"Invaders? What scrolls have you been reading? Alaric's family is from Aeonia. They defended the people from the king."

Lina took the scroll to a quiet corner of the archive. She unrolled it until she found names she recognized. There. King Dacian had ruled during her time. Lina checked the dates. Dacian had died ten years after she went to sleep. His son Thaddeus took the throne at sixteen.

The genealogy ended with Thaddeus. Someone had drawn a thick black line across the parchment.

Lina stared at the line. It seemed so final. Like the whole family had ceased to exist. Was it because of the war?

Lina traced the branches of the family tree back. Her family would be in a remote corner of Dacian's line. There. She found her grandparents and traced their names on the parchment. At last, she had some kind of record. Proof that her family had existed.

She traced the line to her parents. More proof. She and Luca should be right next to them.

Lina frowned. An ink blot covered the place where she

and Luca should have been listed. She held the parchment up to the light, but she couldn't read anything through the blot.

They had erased her. She examined the rest of the parchment for ink blots. There weren't any. Scribes were too careful to spill ink by accident. Even if it had happened, they would have rewritten the parchment. Or written her name beside the blot.

Someone had removed her and Luca from history with a single drop of ink.

Lina returned to the line. She wasn't the only one who had been blotted out. If there were future generations of the royal family, they had never been recorded. Did the line show death? Or did it simply mean that the royal line had ended because they lost the war?

She rolled the scroll up. She needed to get back to the castle before they missed her. How long did it take to sew a sleeve back on?

She sighed. All her searches had led to nothing. No enchanted gems. No answers about the past.

She would have to rely on the Council for help.

"I knew you'd enjoy the royal histories."

Lina jumped. A hooded figure stood in front of her.

Prince Alaric.

Lina's heart beat faster. What was he doing here?

"Did you find some interesting gossip?" he asked.

Lina scowled at him. She was not in the mood for banter. She and her entire family had been erased from history, and his family was responsible.

"What can you tell me about this?"

She opened the scroll and pointed to the thick black line that marked the end of the royal family.

Her family.

Alaric ran his hands through his hair, ruining his perfect ringlets. Lina shoved the scroll closer to his face.

"What happened here?"

She tried to keep her tone light, but it sounded like an accusation. Alaric answered her steadily.

"The royal family disappeared. My family has ruled ever since."

"An entire family disappeared? You expect me to believe that?"

"That is what the records say. Some died in battle. We know King Thaddeus did. The rest disappeared."

"Disappeared. The whole family just disappeared."

"I wasn't there. I don't know any more than you."

Now he sounded angry. Lina rolled the scroll shut. She hadn't been there either, but she could have been. This would have happened in her lifetime if she hadn't been asleep.

In Luca's lifetime, if he hadn't been erased from history by an inkblot.

Had her brother been killed in battle?

Would she have been able to protect him if she had been awake?

Guilt washed over Lina. She had thought she was protecting Aeonia. That her country would be safe while she slept.

That hadn't been the case.

She gripped the scroll too hard and crushed it. Prince Alaric pulled it from her hand and smoothed the crumpled edges.

"What are you doing here?" he asked.

"Looking up royal gossip. Isn't that what princesses do?"

"Not at the archives. At the Princess Test."

Lina opened and closed her mouth a few times. Of course he was suspicious of her behavior. She was doing a terrible job impersonating a princess.

She had to get away. Lina couldn't be exposed as a fraud now. She had to speak to the Council.

Lina leaned closer as if to tell the prince a secret. He bent over so he could hear. She grabbed his hood and pulled it away from his face. His blond hair gleamed in the sunlight.

"Prince Alaric!" she said.

Her voice echoed through the quiet building. Across the room, the group of women snapped their heads up.

"What are you-"

Alaric didn't have a chance to finish. He didn't have a chance, period. The group of women ran towards him calling his name. They surrounded him, speaking all at once and so loudly that Simon left his desk to tell them to hush.

Lina slipped out of the crowd and ran from the archive. She made it through the town without a problem, climbed the tree over the moat, and scaled the castle wall.

She pulled herself through the window and crawled to the couch. A light sheen of sweat coated her skin. Lina panted from the exertion of the climb. Voices echoed from the room next door.

"What do you mean she isn't there? Of course she's there!"

"She isn't! I sent her in there while I mended her sleeve, but she's disappeared!"

Lina replaced the curtain and crawled into a chair in the corner of the room.

Hilda burst through the door. She glanced at Lina and nodded.

"Bastien, she's in the corner. Why do you always call me to do things you are perfectly capable of doing yourself?"

Bastien peeked through the door. He nodded at Lina and slipped back out.

"I'm sorry, my love. Truly, I did not see her."

"As if I didn't have enough to do today. I'll take care of her. You go help Alaric prepare for dinner."

"Of course."

Hilda glared at Lina.

"You've managed to muss your hair. And you're sweaty. We have less than an hour to prepare for dinner."

Lina nodded. Hilda's frown could have soured goat's milk.

"Why do I always get stuck with the difficult ones?" she muttered. "Maids, wipe her skin clean! I'll fix her hair."

The maids patted the sweat off Lina's skin with soft towels and helped her into the pink gown. Hilda gathered supplies and shook her head when they finished.

"We'll have to start from scratch," she said. "Pull her hair down and brush it."

The maids rushed to do Hilda's bidding. Lina winced as they brushed knots out of her hair. A page came into the room.

"If you please," he said. "We're ready for the next princess test. Queen Marta would like–"

"You'll have to delay it," Hilda snapped. "She isn't ready yet."

"But you've had all afternoon–"

"I'll send her when she's ready. Not a moment before."

The page looked at Hilda, decided it wasn't worth questioning her, and bowed before leaving the room.

Hilda attacked Lina's hair with the strength of a goblin warrior. Lina suspected she set a new record for fastest hairstyle completion.

"Try not to take any more naps," Hilda said.

Lina curtsied.

"I apologize for the inconvenience. Your skill and speed are admirable. I've never seen anything like it."

Hilda flushed with pleasure.

"Well, at least you're polite. Trina will lead you to the next test."

Lina nodded to the maid. They hurried through the castle. Lina took note of each turn they made. As far as she could tell, they were headed for the armory. This particular one had never held magical weapons, but maybe that had changed?

Her jaw dropped when the maid opened the door. The armory had been transformed into an elegant dining room. Crystal chandeliers hung from the ceiling. A long wooden table held dishes and silverware for a formal dinner. The plates and glasses gleamed in the candlelight.

The princesses stood in a line at the back of the room behind Queen Marta and Stefan. Fiora was in the front. She glared as Lina entered. Queen Marta smiled at her.

"Excellent, your dress has been repaired just in time. The next Princess Test is a test of manners. How do you dine in elegant company? Prince Alaric will seat each of you. He will sit at one end of the table. I will take the other."

Lina hurried to the back of the line. She caught Carina's eye as she walked past. Carina stood in the exact middle of the line. She raised an eyebrow in a questioning glance. Lina shook her head.

Prince Alaric entered the room to a trumpet fanfare. Lina smirked. He looked even more ridiculous than he had for the conversation test. His chest glittered with even more gems. They spilled over onto his sleeves. A plume ornamented his oiled hair.

Prince Alaric bowed to the princesses. They curtsied in unison. Alaric walked to Fiora and took her hand. He looked to the queen. Stefan rolled a set of dice and gestured to a chair in the middle of the long table.

"What is this?" Fiora demanded.

"The seating will be determined randomly," Queen Marta said. "It is the best way to keep things fair."

Fiora frowned but followed Alaric to her chair. He pulled it out for her and went back to fetch the next princess.

Lina studied the place settings. There were at least four

forks and two spoons. So manners had become more complicated over the years. Well, she was a trained shadow warrior.
If she could mimic enemy fighting styles in the heat of
battle, she could figure out how to eat dinner in another
century.

A roll of the dice landed Carina the chair to the left of the
prince's throne. She shot a panicked look at Lina. That seat
would make blending in difficult. Fiora tapped her finger
against the table in an agitated gesture.

The middle of the table filled with princesses. By the time
Lina reached the front of the line, there was only one seat
left. The chair across from Carina, to the right of Alaric.
Blast. He was bound to ask her about her activities that
afternoon.

She took Alaric's arm and followed him to the seat. Carina
beamed at her. It was good to have an ally. Perhaps together
they could be sufficiently bland to avoid being the prince's
choice.

At some unseen signal, a team of waiters surrounded the
table. They placed silver bowls of soup in front of each diner
in perfect unison. Lina watched Carina to see which spoon
she used. She mimicked the graceful swoop of her arm as she
moved the spoon to her mouth.

"Did you have a restful afternoon?"

Prince Alaric's face was calm, but his eyes gleamed as he
stared at Lina.

"Yes, quite," she said. "Our conversation and my travels
left me quite exhausted. I took a nap."

"Did you?"

Carina looked from Alaric to Lina. She cleared her throat.

"Are there always so many seagulls in the harbor, Prince
Alaric?"

Alaric blinked.

"I beg your pardon?"

Carina repeated her question in a bubbly voice. Alaric sighed.

"Um, yes. It is the sea after all."

"Fascinating. Tell me more about them."

"Um."

"Yes, they're such fascinating creatures," Lina added. "Tell us all about them."

The two girls leaned in towards Alaric. He cleared his throat.

"Well, they're birds that gather near oceans."

Carina laughed as if Alaric had told the most amusing joke in the world. A sweet, tinkling laugh that filled the room and made Fiora frown into her soup.

"How droll! Why do they prefer to live near water?"

Lina and Carina ate a spoonful of soup in perfect sync, even swallowing together. They kept their eyes on Alaric. He took a deep drink of his wine.

"I believe they live by the sea because they eat fish."

Carina gasped.

"Birds that eat fish? I thought they all ate seeds!"

She and Lina smiled at each other in shared amazement, then looked away before they burst out laughing. It was too easy, diverting his attention.

Alaric narrowed his eyes at Lina.

"Princess, about this afternoon-"

"What kind of fish do they prefer?" Carina said. "I've always been partial to snapper. Do they eat snapper? I can't imagine a bird eating snapper."

As if on cue, the waiters cleared the soup and set a baked fish in front of all the diners. Lina watched Carina for the proper motions to eat it. They moved in unison, breaking the skin with a small silver fork and taking dainty bites.

"After our conversation-" Alaric began.

Carina interrupted him.

"For example, if we were to set this fish out on the harbor, do you think those charming birds would eat it?"

Lina clapped her hands with delight.

"Oh, what an experiment!"

Thank goodness for Carina. She made this almost too easy.

"Do you really not have seagulls at your home?" Alaric asked.

Carina gasped.

"Your Highness! Asking questions about my home country? You're fishing as much as those wonderful birds!"

She giggled. Lina joined her. At the other end of the table, Fiora stabbed her fish with enough force to bend the fork.

❧ 17 ❧

Alaric watched the fork bend under Fiora's grip. He swallowed and fell silent. The princesses next to him shared a look of triumph and ate their fish in unison.

The way they moved was eerie. It was difficult to tell who was leading the motions, but he suspected the blond. Strange. He had pegged the brunette as the mastermind of the operation.

He had no idea what that operation was, but something was going on. Ordinary princesses didn't climb castle towers when they were supposed to be showing their powers of conversation. They didn't sneak out of the castle to read archive scrolls about the original royal family of Aeonia.

At the other end of the table, Queen Marta gestured at Alaric. He pretended not to understand although her meaning was perfectly clear. She wanted him to talk. To get to know the girls.

Alaric set down his fork and swallowed. He tried to think of something, anything to say. The princesses watched him with predatory gazes. As if daring him to say something they couldn't turn around on him.

Alaric picked up his fork and took another bite of fish. No. It wasn't worth it. Those girls were merciless. He wouldn't get any useful information out of them here. He didn't say another word during the dinner. Not even when the waiter asked him if he would like more wine.

Thank goodness the dinner was the last Princess Test of the day. Alaric sprinted back to his room as soon as Queen Marta dismissed him. He didn't know what the girls were doing the rest of the evening. He didn't care. He just needed to get out of there.

Alaric slammed the door behind him and sank into a chair.

"Going that well?"

"Stefan! How many times do I have to tell you to knock?"

"More than you have. Did you figure out what the princess was doing climbing the tower? She sat next to you at dinner. You had a chance to talk to her. What a stroke of luck."

Stefan grinned in a way that made Alaric suspicious.

"You rigged the dice?"

"All too easy. I was nice, wasn't I? I almost put Fiora next to you."

Alaric grimaced. If he never spoke to Fiora again, it would be too soon.

"So, what was she doing on the side of the tower?"

"She did more than climb the tower. I saw her at the archives this afternoon."

"So you had plenty of opportunity to find out what she's doing."

"Not exactly."

"Do tell."

Alaric shook his head. Stefan didn't need to hear how the princess had escaped by surrounding him with a mob of peasant women. And he certainly didn't want to relive the experience.

"Come on, Alaric! You saw her this afternoon and ate dinner with her! You should have answers by now!"

"It isn't exactly dinner conversation, Stefan. So, Princess, I noticed you climbing the tower in your undergarments this afternoon. Would you care to explain?"

Stefan shrugged.

"I'm sure you could have figured something out."

"I tried! The blond one kept asking me about seagulls."

Stefan raised an eyebrow.

"You were thwarted by Princess Carina asking about seagulls?"

"That girl is Princess Carina?"

Stefan nodded.

"Didn't I tell you? I've been listening to their conversations when I get the chance. I've picked up a few names."

"And you forgot to tell me that?"

Stefan shrugged.

"I have to be careful. If anyone knew–"

"Yes, yes, I know. Apparently everyone wants to cancel this test or disqualify the other girls. They think I'm a blood-thirsty barbarian, Stefan."

"Maybe it's your hair. You should oil it more."

"Stefan, this is serious! You should have seen the way she looked at me."

"Who?"

Stefan's eyes gleamed. He looked entirely too interested. Alaric picked up Princess Carina's parchment.

"You're sure that girl is Carina? This portrait doesn't look much like her."

"Yes, I'm sure. The portraits don't look much like any of the girls."

Alaric slumped deeper in his chair.

"Blast. She was at the top of my list. A treaty with Santelle would unite trade routes and give us military support."

"She's that bad?"

"She's a merciless bore. Still, I have to consider her. Do you know which one is from Eldria?"

Stefan shook his head.

"Still working on it."

"Well, let's hope she's better than Carina. A treaty with Eldria would be acceptable. And their princess isn't likely to be obsessed with seagulls. Keep listening. You're in the best position to research them right now."

"Again, when I offered to help you with your love life, I didn't really have research in mind."

Alaric raised an eyebrow.

"What exactly did you have in mind?"

"Not important. But I could use some backup. I sent for Cael and Henry."

"And?"

"They insist they're too busy with their goats to leave the mountain."

"Blasted goats."

Alaric stood and pulled a heavy cloak over his jeweled tunic.

"Where are you going?"

"To the archives. I'm going to ask Simon about the gate princess."

"Lina."

"What?"

"I overheard her talking with Carina. Her name is Lina."

Lina. Alaric glanced at the parchments to make sure. No, Lina wasn't listed there. He shoved the parchments back into the drawer.

"Have you ever heard of a Princess Lina?"

"She might not be a princess," Stefan said. "Maybe she's a

duke's daughter from a small province. Or maybe Lina is a nickname. Marta trusts her. That counts for something."

"Marta didn't see her climbing the castle. Or researching the original royal family. Are you coming with me to the archives or not?"

"Fine."

They made it to the archives just as the sun set. Simon stood outside the building with a ring of keys, fastening the intricate locks that protected his precious parchments.

"We're closed for the night, Your Highness," he said. "I can't make exceptions, even for royalty."

"That's fine, Simon. We're actually here to talk to you. Do you mind if we walk home with you?"

Simon bowed.

"My home is humble, but you are welcome."

Alaric and Stefan fell into step beside the archivist.

"I was wondering about that girl," Alaric said. "The dirty one who came to the archives."

"Ah, yes. I had to burn those smocks. That was a touch more than travel grime."

"Do you know where she came from? Did she say anything that might have been a clue?"

Simon shook his head.

"She was here when I arrived, and she went straight to the historical records. She left soon after you did."

Alaric's face fell.

"I see."

"She did ask me about Evangelina Shadow-Storm."

The two brothers shared a glance.

"Really?" Stefan said.

"Yes. She overheard you talking about the play and was very interested. She seemed almost angry that we didn't have scrolls about the legend. As if we would house such fanciful tales in our historical archives."

"She asked me about Evangelina Shadow-Storm in our conversation today," Alaric said. "I thought it was because of the play."

"An attempt to impress you?" Stefan said. "To win your heart by showing an interest in your favorite story?"

Alaric elbowed him in the ribs. He bowed to Simon.

"Thank you for your assistance."

They left the archivist. Alaric turned towards the castle. Stefan turned to the docks.

"Where are you going?"

"To see if seagulls really eat fish."

"Ha. Very funny."

"She came from another country, right? We don't know which one, but if her ship wrecked or her travel party ran into trouble on the mountains, someone will have heard of it. Surely someone saw her arrive."

"Stefan, that's genius."

Alaric immediately regretted his words. A smug smile spread across Stefan's face. They walked to the docks.

"You'll never catch me!"

A boy ran past them. A group of children chased close behind.

"Down with the tyrant!"

"Down with King Thaddeus!"

Alaric watched them run down the streets.

"I wish they wouldn't play that game."

"What's wrong with Tyrant Topple?"

He shrugged.

"It brings up the past. Reminds everyone of what happened."

"We used to play it. Those kids aren't really thinking about war. It's just a game, Alaric."

"Sure."

They reached the docks. Most of the piers were empty,

but a few sailors loaded crates onto ships in the moonlight. Alaric approached the nearest one.

"Excuse me. Have there been any shipwrecks recently?"

The sailor stopped loading crates and wiped his brow.

"Of course not. The summer seas are fair as fair can be. You'd have to be an idiot to wreck in this weather."

Alaric narrowed his eyes in Stefan's direction.

"I'm sure some people could manage it. You haven't heard of any travel misfortunes in mountain expeditions? Everyone expected at the harbor has arrived safely?"

The man grunted.

"No. Haven't heard of anything."

"I see. Have you seen a girl wandering around? In a purple dress? Chestnut hair? She would have looked disheveled."

The sailor leaned on the crates and looked at Alaric with sympathy.

"Lost your sweetheart, have you? Lads! You seen a girl around? Anyone come by ship?"

All the sailors stopped working and turned to Alaric.

"She met misfortune on her travels," Alaric said. "I think her escort was lost."

One of the younger men scratched his beard.

"Did you say she had a purple dress? I might have seen someone like that. She was hiding behind a stack of crates this morning."

The oldest sailor guffawed.

"Don't listen to Timon. He thinks he sees mermaids when we sail."

"I don't think anything, Gruff! There are mermaids! They probably hide from you because you're so ugly."

Alaric cleared his throat.

"She would have traveled with a large party. At least, I think so. Something dreadful must have happened to them."

Gruff ran his hands through his wild gray hair.

"That's what they always say, lad. There's always a misfortune. Always a need for more money before they can come to you."

"No, she really was in trouble! You haven't heard anything about a ship sinking or a party running into trouble crossing the mountains?"

"The travel conditions have never been better," Gruff said. "Nobody's run into trouble. Gossip about travel spreads through the docks like wildfire. We'd know if something had happened."

"Oh. Well, thank you."

The old sailor nodded in sympathy.

"It's happened to us all, lad. You get sweet on a girl in a foreign port. You send her money to come to you. She says the ship sank. We've all fallen for the story."

The sailors nodded one by one.

"She ain't coming, lad," Timon said. "You'd have better luck courting a mermaid."

Stefan clapped his brother on the back.

"You'd best forget about Gladiola," he said. "I told you not to send her your life savings."

Alaric glared at him from beneath his hood. The sailors murmured in sympathy.

"He saved for three years to bring her here," Stefan said.

He waved his hands from side to side, working the crowd. The sailors watched in rapt attention.

"He worked as a goat herder. As a harvester. Any work he could get to bring her back to his side."

Alaric stomped on Stefan's foot. Stefan patted him on the shoulder. The comforting gesture felt more like a punch.

"That's too bad, lad," Gruff said. "But don't you let that get you down. There's other lasses out there. If you ever need work, you come see me. Men down on their luck have to stick together."

The sailors nodded their agreement. Alaric thanked them and walked away, careful to keep his hood pulled down over his face.

"Don't worry," Stefan said. "You'll get over Gladiola."

Alaric glanced behind him to make sure they were far enough away from the sailors.

"You're despicable, Stefan."

Stefan grinned.

"What? I thought it was funny."

"It wasn't. And we still don't know where she came from."

Stefan shrugged. Alaric was in no mood to talk, so they walked back to the castle in silence.

Alaric thought of Lina the whole time.

❧ 18 ❧

L ina lifted the mattress and reached under it. Her heart swelled with relief. The pea was still there. She tucked it back into its hiding place.

Hilda helped Lina out of the pink dress and into a white nightgown. Lina examined the room. There was no window. No secret passageways to unlock with her ring in this part of the castle. No way to get out except the door.

She waited a few moments, giving Hilda time to make it out of the hallway. Then she stuck her head out.

"Can I help you, Princess?"

A guard walked towards her. Lina glanced down the hall. Guards stood by each princess's door.

"No, thank you. I thought I heard something."

She ducked back into her room and leaned against the door. She listened to the guard walk back to his post.

Of course there were guards. The Council of Kings wouldn't risk the safety of the princesses.

And they certainly wouldn't allow any chance for cheating. The guards kept the princesses in and visitors out.

Lina hoped Prince Alaric wouldn't tell anyone they had

spoken at the archive. She couldn't afford to be disqualified now.

She sank onto the bed and pulled the covers around her. The mattress was soft and inviting, but she fought sleep.

Did Prince Alaric suspect her? He had seen her at the archive and the gate. Lina couldn't imagine what he thought about it. The rest of the castle accepted her without question, but Alaric had seen her doing things normal princesses wouldn't. He would have to be an idiot not to suspect something.

And he wasn't an idiot. He had been trying to question her at dinner. Searching for answers. Thank goodness Carina was a master at awkward conversations.

And thank goodness for the guards. Depending on what he suspected, Prince Alaric might have tried to gain a private audience with her. He knew she was up to something, but he couldn't question her in front of everyone. Admitting he had seen her multiple times outside the test would lead to scandal.

She needed to stay away from him. Speak with him as little as possible. The ball was tomorrow night. She would check in with the Council and complete her mission. The King of Gaveron could take care of the rest with whatever special forces the Council commanded in this century.

Lina's eyes closed. She breathed in the clean scent of the linens. The fire crackled. Shadows pulled at her until she fell into a trance.

Lina woke in the realm of shadows. Her white nightgown had disappeared. She wore her black gown and cape. She searched the sky. Three stars twinkled on the horizon. She considered reaching out to them, but they were too faint to do much good. And if they were searching for her, she wasn't sure she wanted to be found.

Lina studied the emptiness. In her time, Aeonia had been

a center of magical education. The shadow realm had been filled with shadow warriors and the stars of light wielders.

Now it was empty. Lina closed her eyes and inhaled. It was more than the emptiness. Something had shifted. Her ankle throbbed as she walked. The ground was too solid. The world was more gray than black. Vast emptiness stretched as far as she could see in all directions. It felt more like a barren wasteland than the shadow world rich with magic she remembered.

Lina pulled the pea emerald from her headband and held it flat in her palm.

"Dagger."

The jewel stretched into a solid beam of green light. Lina imagined the shape of her favorite dagger until the light became it. A sleek blade decorated with swirling etches. The pea settled into the hilt, and green light swirled around her hand and up her arm. The magic strengthened Lina's senses.

She smelled it before she saw it. Decay, rot, fear, chaos. Whatever you wanted to call it, it was a stench she recognized all too well.

Lina tightened her grip on the dagger and jumped. She landed halfway across the realm of shadows. Right in front of a shimmering scar that floated in the air. The seal.

"Show yourself, Nog."

The goblin's hulking form materialized behind the shimmer. Lina reached her senses out. Yes, he was alone.

That was something, at least.

"Welcome back, goat girl."

Lina clenched her teeth.

"What did you say?"

"You're a pathetic goat. Too stubborn to know when you're beaten."

"No one calls me a goat and lives."

"Your brother did. Well, I guess not."

Lina stepped closer.

"What do you know about Luca?"

Nog grinned. The stench of his breath made Lina gag.

"Nothing I'm telling you. Nothing you don't already know. He's gone. You're alone."

"There are still stars."

Nog's laugh echoed through the vast landscape. The bruise on Lina's ankle pulsed.

"Stars? Those pricks of light? Stars indeed. All the true stars died years ago."

"It doesn't matter. You're trapped."

Nog's eyes flashed red.

"Am I?"

Dark magic curled around Lina's dagger. She reached her hand out to strengthen the seal, but it wasn't coming from Nog. It didn't feel like goblin magic. It wasn't strong enough.

But it had been enough to distract her.

A gnarled hand shot through the shimmering shield. Nog wrapped his claws around Lina's arm. Pain shot through her wrist as he scraped down her skin. Her hand went numb. She almost dropped the pea.

"Shadow bolt!" she screamed.

The pea emerald crackled with green lightning. Nog roared with pain as the light crawled across his skin, but he didn't let go of Lina's arm. He pulled her towards him.

Towards the shield. Lina gulped. If Nog escaped, he might be able to pull her in. Trap her behind the shield. She could only guess the consequences of that. She likely would die. The shield would probably collapse.

An image flashed through Lina's mind. Aeonia overrun with goblins and other creatures of darkness. Houses on fire. People screaming and fleeing for their lives.

No.

It couldn't happen again.

Lina twisted her wrist and stabbed Nog with the dagger. He squeezed her arm until it felt like the bone would shatter. She bit her lip to distract from the pain and pressed the dagger into his skin.

Nog roared and kept squeezing.

Lina studied the shield. There was a tiny crack. Easily closed.

If she could concentrate. Pain roared through her arm. She inhaled and concentrated her energy on a single burst.

"Seal!" she screamed.

The pea's green light intensified. It transformed from a dagger to a single lightning bolt. The magic energy crawled over the seal. It found the crack and wove it shut.

"No!"

Nog pulled on Lina's arm with all his strength. She jerked backwards. Her shoulder wrenched, but the goblin lost his grip. Both fell backwards. Lina landed on her cape. It hovered in the air and held her upright.

Nog landed on the other side of the seal. He pounded against it and roared, but the seal contained the sound and stench. Lina hugged her injured arm to her side and smiled.

That should hold him.

She tucked the pea back into her headband and held her diamond ring to her lips.

"Heal," she whispered.

White light bathed her right arm. The pain eased some, but it didn't disappear. Lina massaged the bruises. Her healing magic had never been as good as Luca's.

It had never needed to be.

She closed her eyes and slipped into a restless sleep.

She awoke back in the castle. The fire hadn't died yet. She hadn't been gone long. Lina sighed and tried to get comfortable. Her arm hurt no matter how she positioned it. It would be bruised. Her shoulder throbbed, but she could wiggle her fingers.

Nothing broken, thank goodness. She wouldn't be climbing castle walls for a while, but hopefully she wouldn't need to. She just needed to make it through the Princess Tests tomorrow. To stay in the castle until the ball. The Council of Kings would take care of everything once they knew about Nog. They probably even had healers to mend her arm.

Lina focused on breathing. In and out. It distracted her from the pain. She doubted she could sleep, but she'd need rest to get through whatever ridiculous tests the princesses were doing tomorrow.

19

Alaric watched Lina during breakfast. She didn't eat much and yawned a lot. She tucked her right arm into her skirt. What was she hiding? A weapon? A secret message?

Her yawning made everyone else yawn. Fiora in particular seemed to be fighting it.

"Didn't you sleep well, Princess?" she asked.

Lina raised her dark rimmed eyes and smiled at Fiora.

"I'm afraid not. The mattress is much harder than I'm used to."

"Hmmph."

"That is a shame," Queen Marta said. "Perhaps I can take you to select a different mattress later today. I want all our guests to be comfortable."

"Absolutely not," Fiora said. "We stay together as a group. We get the same treatment. If you or anyone else talks to her separately, she might reveal her identity."

Some of the princesses rolled their eyes. Some nodded in agreement. Lina yawned.

"I wouldn't dream of demanding an unfair advantage.

Thank you for your consideration, Your Highness, but I will make do with the mattress I have."

"Delicacy is the mark of a true princess," Queen Marta said with approval.

Alaric stared at her. The Princess Tests were going to his stepmother's head. This was a woman whose idea of fun was chasing goats around a mountain. Delicacy? It was probably the quality she valued least in a person.

"Our first princess test this morning is music," Queen Marta said.

Alaric looked up.

"Music?"

"A queen is often called upon to entertain guests. She should possess talents necessary to do so. All the princesses have prepared a song for you. Your favorite will perform it at the ball tonight."

Yes, the Princess Tests had definitely gone to Marta's head. Alaric had heard her sing. She sounded worse than her goats. She usually entertained dignitaries by stuffing them with food and taking them on mountain hikes.

The princesses around the table chatted about the next test while they finished eating. Alaric downed his glass of goat milk in a single gulp and leaned back into his chair. At least he wouldn't have to talk to them. This should be less painful than the other tests.

The princesses needed time to get ready. Alaric watched them as they left. Yes, Lina definitely had something hidden in her sleeve. It was a perfect dress for hiding something. Long and flowing. She kept her right arm glued to her side.

Was she limping? Yes, her steps were uneven. Alaric frowned. Had she injured herself climbing the tower? He had tried to check on her last night, but the stationed guards had shooed him away.

"Looking forward to music?" Stefan asked.

Alaric shrugged.

"Still worried about the mystery girl?"

"Of course I am. I think she's a spy."

"A spy for what? All the countries are here."

"Maybe she is here to assassinate someone. Or to influence my choice."

Stefan laughed.

"I think she's definitely influencing your choice."

"What do you mean?"

"You like her."

Alaric recoiled.

"That's ridiculous. I don't know anything about her."

"You know she likes history. You know she's clever. You know she's bold enough to climb a castle tower."

"I know she's accused me of being a bloodthirsty impostor. I know she's devious. I know she's sneaking around my castle."

"Sure."

"Stefan, this is serious. She could be dangerous."

"Dangerous to your heart."

"Shut up! The Council of Kings is questioning our right to rule. I can't let anything interfere with the Princess Test. And I certainly can't fall for someone with an unknown lineage."

Stefan's face paled.

"The Council is doing what?"

Alaric sighed.

"Some have questioned our right to rule. They say we have no right to this land since we aren't from a noble family."

"Alaric, I had no idea. Our ancestors conquered this land a century ago. That has nothing to do with us. The Council must see that."

Alaric shrugged.

"They'll see it more once a princess with noble blood sits on the throne."

"Oh. Oh, I see. This Princess Test is about more than trade agreements then. Alaric, why didn't you tell me? I could have helped you. I could have-"

"Not prepared my terrible play to be performed as entertainment?"

"It isn't terrible. The guests will be entertained."

Alaric shook his head.

"Evangelina Shadow-Storm. Why can't the princesses be like that, Stefan? I'd marry a girl like that in a heartbeat."

"You know she isn't real, right? No one is that brave."

"Maybe not in that way, but there must be people willing to fight for what they believe in."

"Odette was."

Alaric glared at his brother.

"Why do you keep talking about her?"

"Because I want you to be happy! And she made you happy!"

"She didn't! She was all wrong for me. We were wrong for each other."

"But you ended your relationship with her so recently. I want to make sure your rebound isn't an arranged marriage to a princess who collects butterflies."

"Things between us ended years ago. We were just both too stubborn to admit it."

Stefan stared at his brother. Studied the lines in his face. He had always carried too much responsibility. Tried too hard to be the perfect ruler. Stefan half wished Evangelina Shadow-Storm was real. Someone that strong could share the load his brother carried. Help him find himself under all the responsibilities.

He shook his head and smiled at Alaric.

"What can I do to help?"

"Keep an eye on Lina. Keep listening for princess names. Watch for signs of trouble. We can't afford for anything to go wrong."

"The princesses should be ready now. You can watch them yourself for a bit. I wonder what song Lina the mystery princess has prepared?"

Alaric smacked his brother's shoulder, but a spark lit his eyes. He was curious in spite of himself.

20

"Carina, I don't know this song."

Carina smiled at her.

"Of course you do. Everyone knows The Snowbell Song. They sent us the sheet music last year!"

She hummed a tune Lina didn't recognize.

"Nope. Don't know it."

Fiora walked to their side.

"Trying to stand out again? Everyone must sing the same song. Anything else could give a clue as to your country of origin. If you sing one note that's different, I'll call for your disqualification."

Carina sighed.

"Fiora, at this point I'd be more surprised if you didn't call for someone's disqualification. Do you really want this dandy prince so badly?"

"Don't use my name," Fiora snapped. "We're not supposed to know each other's names."

"Or countries," Carina said. "But everyone knows yours."

Fiora ran a hand through her bright red hair.

"It can't be helped. Changing your appearance–"

"Is against the rules," Lina said. "Yes, we know."

Fiora glared at her and walked away. Carina waved to Eirwyn.

"Eirwyn, Lina has stage fright and can't remember how The Snowbell Song goes. Help me teach it to her?"

Eirwyn smiled at Lina.

"I don't blame you. I'm nervous to. Try to find a spot at the back of the line. By the time it's your turn, you'll have heard it so many times you won't be able to get it out of your head."

Carina clasped her friend's hand.

"Eirwyn, you're a genius!"

Eirwyn smiled.

"Carina told me about your secret mission. That we might be in danger?"

Lina raised an eyebrow.

"She can keep a secret," Carina said. "She helped me cover for you while the tailor sewed your sleeve."

"Are we still in danger?" Eirwyn asked.

Lina slipped her ring from her sash and raised it to her lips.

"Check for danger."

The ring flashed red. Lina's heart sank. Not pink. Red. Whatever the danger was, it was getting worse. It hadn't ended when she sealed Nog away.

Eirwyn studied Lina's ring with interest.

"Where did you get that? Magic gems are so rare! It looks ancient."

"We have a magic sapphire," Carina said. "My father keeps it in the deepest vault in a golden case. No one knows how to use it, but he insists it is magic and valuable."

Lina frowned.

"You don't have a court enchanter?"

"Heavens, no," Carina said. "We don't have any magic users. Not many people have the gift."

"I've heard there are enchanters in Kell," Eirwyn said. "And there are rumors about the dwarfs in Gaveron."

"Magic isn't a gift," Lina said. "Magic is a skill. Something you learn."

The princesses watched her skeptically.

"I know I'm not supposed to ask, but where are you from?" Carina said. "I haven't heard of any countries with magic schools."

"That would be amazing!" Eirwyn said. "I'd love to learn magic."

Queen Marta interrupted their conversation.

"We're beginning, Princesses. Please form a line."

"Go to the back," Carina whispered. "I'm staying in the middle."

She jostled her way to the middle of the group. Lina and Eirwyn walked towards the back. Fiora got there first.

"No way," she said. "I'm going last. I want to be the last thing he sees."

Lina shrugged and took the second to last place in line. Eirwyn stood in front of her. They walked through a corridor to a small theater. From her place backstage, Lina peeked through the curtains. The audience was small. Queen Marta, Prince Stefan, and Prince Alaric sat in a middle row. The rest of the seats were empty.

A lute player sat on the stage. The first princess nodded to him, and he began a haunting tune. She sang, and Lina listened carefully. Thank goodness the song was simple. She hummed along. Yes, she would be able to sing this.

The first princess finished. The audience of three clapped for her. Only Queen Marta looked enthusiastic. Prince Alaric looked bored. Prince Stefan looked worried.

It was an unusual look for him. Lina watched him until the next singer began.

Yes, he was worried about something. Probably his brother, judging from the way he kept glancing in his direction.

The next princess sang, and Lina focused on learning the lyrics. They described snowbells on the mountainside. Not complicated. By the end of the fourth princess's performance, Lina knew the song well enough to sing it.

By the end of the tenth, she knew it well enough to hate it.

❧ 21 ❧

Alaric's jaw dropped in horror.

The same song.

They were all going to sing the same song.

He lost count after ten. The performances blurred together. The sappy lute introduction that had seemed sweet and sensitive at first. The lilting tune sung to perfection each time.

And by perfection, he meant exactly the same way. He turned to Stefan.

"Did you know about this?"

"That they were all singing the same song? No. I wouldn't have come if I had known."

"Hush," Queen Marta said. "It is the next princess's turn."

Alaric recognized her. The seagull princess. Carina of Santelle. He studied her as she sang. There was nothing remarkable about her. The flowing blue gown that looked beautiful on many of the princesses hung loosely on her shoulders and swallowed her shape.

She sang the song simply. With just enough feeling to keep it from being boring, but not enough to draw him in.

He looked at her and felt absolutely nothing. It cleared his head. Made him see things straight.

Santelle was the obvious choice for a marriage treaty. Aeonia grew enough food. They had enough wool. They didn't need a trading partner.

They did need a navy for protection in case anyone contested Alaric's claim to the throne. And they needed a true princess. Alaric suspected that would be enough to silence those with objections. They might question him, but they wouldn't question a Princess of Santelle.

No one would risk a fight with Santelle. No matter how much they wanted to attack Aeonia.

He looked back at Princess Carina and winced. Could he really spend his life with her by his side? Maybe it wouldn't be so bad. He could take her to the docks and feed fish to seagulls.

Did he have a choice? He hadn't identified any other princesses besides Fiora, and an alliance with Kell would help Aeonia much less than one with Santelle.

If he married Carina, he would bury his heart completely. She was too bland to inspire passion either way. He didn't love her or hate her.

He could rule without feelings clouding his judgment.

Carina finished her song and curtsied. Even her curtsy was boring. But as she walked off the stage, Alaric made his decision.

He chose his future bride.

The next few princesses passed in a blur. Now that he had made his choice, he just wanted it to be over. He would announce Carina as the winner of the singing competition. That was a clear enough sign of favoritism given her lack-luster performance. The rest of the Princess Test would be a formality.

Then Lina walked onstage.

Alaric's heart skipped a beat. The blue dress suited her. It flowed around her as she walked. She still kept her right arm glued to her side. Her hand stayed buried in the skirt. She limped slightly.

Was this it? Would she attack them here and now?

No. She nodded to the lute player and breathed deeply while he played the introduction. Alaric leaned forward. He caught Stefan and Marta sharing a look, but he didn't care. Lina made eye contact and held it.

She sang, and Alaric didn't know how to describe it. It went beyond her voice. She wasn't the best singer. Not even close. Her voice, if he was honest, sounded scratchy and tired.

But it captured him completely. She sang without artifice. Without pretensions. She made him see the words in a completely different way. Made him feel like he was in the field of snowbells with her.

She sang like magic.

Alaric gripped the edge of his seat. He wanted to stand. Wanted to run to her. To ask her for all her secrets and be brave and strong enough that she could trust him. That she would tell him the truth.

Lina finished the song and curtsied. She had to move her right arm to do it properly. Pain flashed across her face when she did.

Alaric's heart leaped. She was hurt! He needed to help her! Needed to-

Fiora entered the stage as Lina left it. She stood in the center, demanding everyone's attention with her posture. It occurred to Alaric that Kell's royal family was even older than Santelle's.

Fiora's singing broke the spell. Alaric leaned back in his seat. He couldn't afford to be so foolish. The piercing voice cleared his head.

He could not make this choice with his heart. He had to

unite his lineage with a noble family. Aeonia needed protection. Needed Santelle's navy.

He needed magic. Needed to see the sparkle in Lina's green eyes again.

Magic. Alaric's heart froze. Had Lina enchanted him with her magic ring? Was this how his father felt when Cassandra had him under her spell?

He couldn't trust feelings. Couldn't trust magic.

Couldn't trust Lina.

Alaric gritted his teeth as Queen Marta called all the princesses back to the stage. They watched him. Waited for him. He stood and walked to the stage. This was it. Time to declare his favorite.

Time to make a choice.

Lina had given the best performance. Everyone knew it. The princesses glared at her. If he chose anyone but Lina, he would show enough favoritism to announce his intentions.

Choosing another girl meant choosing his future bride.

Fiora stood on the end of the stage. She stared at him, her mouth set in a grim line. Had she realized her advantage? That she was the easiest princess to identify? That Kell had the oldest royal family?

Lina stood next to her. She met his gaze, even smiled a little, but something haunted her eyes. She looked exhausted. As if the performance had drained her strength.

Carina stood in the middle. Alaric's eyes passed her a few times, even though he was looking for her. She caught his eye then looked down at the floor. Probably thinking about fish.

"Your Highness," Queen Marta said. "We are waiting for your decision."

She and Stefan glanced at Lina. It was obvious what they expected him to do.

It was obvious what Alaric wanted to do.

But he couldn't. Lina was a mystery. Dangerous. Whatever

her reason for infiltrating the Princess Test, he couldn't let her ruin it. He couldn't let her magic ensnare him.

Alaric walked past Fiora. Past Lina. He swallowed, buried his emotions beneath a cool facade, and stopped in front of Princess Carina. He took her hand. Alarm flashed through her eyes so quickly Alaric thought he might have imagined it. He blinked, and her face became passive. Inexpressive.

She curtsied.

"You honor me," she said.

Whatever honor she felt didn't reach her voice. Alaric swallowed.

"I choose this Princess."

He ignored Marta's horrified face. Stefan's wrinkled brow. Alaric stiffened his back, bowed from the waist, and kissed Carina's hand.

🐿 22 🐿

"I don't understand what I did wrong!"

Carina paced across the dressing room. Lina and Eirwyn watched her from a couch.

"I was bland, right? Please tell me I was bland!"

Lina and Eirwyn nodded.

"I don't understand. Was it the seagulls? Did he find that interesting? Lina, you were there. He was bored, right?"

Lina stood and wrapped her good arm around her friend.

"Extremely bored. You were marvelously boring."

"Then why? How? Why did he choose me?"

Eirwyn led Carina to the couch and helped her sink into it.

"He must have guessed where you're from. Santelle is an obvious political choice."

Lina flinched. Santelle? Carina was from that nation of bullies? Was Aeonia so desperate for protection that they needed to marry into military might?

Tears filled Carina's eyes.

"I don't want him," she whispered. "I don't like him. I don't like it here. I want to go home."

Lina sat next to Carina and patted her shoulder.

"It isn't official yet, is it? He only chose you as the winner of the singing test."

Carina tried to answer, but the sound caught in her throat. Eirwyn tapped her foot.

"It might as well be official. Carina was by no means the best singer in the test. In fact, I think that honor belongs to you."

"Me?"

Carina nodded.

"He couldn't take his eyes off you while you were singing. Did you use magic to help?"

She gestured to Lina's ring.

"Of course not. I just sang. I- I've had an emotional few days. I needed a way to express it."

"Hmm," Eirwyn said. "I guess he hasn't figured out what country you're from yet. Neither have I."

"That doesn't matter. There are still several tests before Prince Alaric declares a bride."

Eirwyn glared at Lina.

"Don't you understand? By choosing Carina even though she wasn't the best singer, Prince Alaric has marked her as his favorite. It would be difficult to back out of the arrangement now."

"It would be impossible," Carina sobbed. "My father would take it as an insult. He already thinks Aeonia is over-confident and weak."

"Will he want you marrying Prince Alaric then?" Lina asked. "Aren't you allowed to say no?"

Both girls dropped their heads to the floor.

"Technically, we are," Eirwyn admitted.

"Technically," Carina said.

"What do you mean?"

Eirwyn huffed.

"How are you ignorant of all this? You're a princess! You should know these things!"

"I'm just trying to help!"

"Please, don't shout," Carina said.

She took a shaky breath and turned to Lina.

"It would be even more insulting for me to refuse Prince Alaric than it would be for him to back out of choosing me as his favorite. It would be seen as more than a personal choice. I act for all of Santelle. If I reject Alaric, Santelle rejects Aeonia. Father would have grounds to reject treaties and trade agreements. Other nations would see it as a precedent."

"It could lead to war," Eirwyn said. "Not directly, but it would start the ripples. Relations between the Myorian countries are strained right now. One false move could destroy our peace."

"That's stupid!" Lina said. "I'll talk to them at the ball tonight. I'll get you out of this, Carina."

Carina paled.

"Please, don't. Your home country would suffer horrible consequences. I'm not even sure you should tell anyone about the suspected danger."

Lina stared at her.

"Why not? They need to know."

"I don't think they'll believe you. They might think you're trying to manipulate them."

"But you believe me."

"Yes, of course."

"Because you saw my ring."

Carina shook her head.

"No. I believe you because I trust you. Magic isn't common in most countries, Lina. The Council will see it as a parlor trick designed to scare them."

Lina turned to Eirwyn. The girl shrugged.

"She's right. For all we know, a red glowing light on your ring means safety. Or nothing at all."

"Why would a red glowing light mean safety?"

"Just be careful, Lina. And don't try to interfere on my behalf. If I have to get married to keep the peace, then I will."

Lina studied her friend. Carina's bland facade slipped away. She met Lina's gaze with calm bravery. Lina clasped her hands.

"You're too good for him."

"I hope not. I hope he improves once I know him better."

The door clicked open, and the girls fell silent. Hilda walked in carrying a bundle of gowns. She examined Carina's tear-stained face.

"Queen Marta thought you all might like to get ready for the ball together. Some of the other princesses are doing the same."

Carina stood, but her shoulders shook. Lina and Eirwyn stood on either side and supported her.

"We'd like that very much," Lina said. "Please thank Queen Marta for her kindness."

"I bet Fiora's group is plotting how to disqualify me," Carina said. "She was furious."

They all laughed.

The princesses prepared for the ball without saying much. What could they say that the maids wouldn't carry away as incriminating gossip? Still it was nice to have companionship.

Hilda led an army of servants as they styled the princess's hair in identical curls. They placed wreaths of snowbells over their heads.

Lina flushed when they brought in the gowns. They were lovely. Light purple lace in a simple silhouette. But the sleeves were short. That would show her injury. She risked pulling up her sleeve to glance at her wrist. Bruises curved around her arm. Each of Nog's claws had left a mark.

Carina glimpsed the bruises and raised an eyebrow.

"How?" she whispered.

"Danger," Lina whispered back.

She gestured toward the dresses across the room.

"What lovely gowns," she said loud enough for everyone to hear. "Are those short sleeves an Aeonian style?"

Carina's eyes widened with understanding. A princess arriving at the ball with bruises around her wrist would be more than enough to cast suspicion on the Princess Test. It could destroy faith in Aeonia.

"Yes," Carina said just as loudly. "They are far shorter than anyone in my kingdom would feel comfortable wearing."

She nudged Eirwyn.

"Oh, yes," Eirwyn said. "So very short!"

She looked questioningly at Carina. Hilda sighed.

"There is something wrong with the gowns, Princesses?"

Carina smiled at Hilda. Her face was radiant when she wasn't trying to blend.

"The gowns are lovely, but those sleeves are shockingly short! Does everyone in Aeonia show their wrists so freely?"

Hilda stiffened.

"This evening wear is hardly scandalous, Princess. I designed these gowns myself."

Carina blushed.

"I would feel so much more comfortable if I could wear gloves."

Hilda bristled.

"Gloves?"

"Yes, gloves that cover me at least to the-"

She looked at Lina. Lina tapped her elbow.

"Elbow-length gloves," Carina said. "If I can't wear them, I'm afraid I won't be comfortable wearing that gown."

Hilda rolled her eyes to the ceiling.

"Very well. I'm sure I can find one pair of elbow-length gloves."

"One!" Lina said. "Oh no, that won't do. She's trying to stand out! If she wears gloves, we all must wear gloves."

"That's only fair," Eirwyn said. "I don't want anyone getting an unfair advantage. Think of the scandal."

Hilda studied each girl's face, clearly suspicious.

"Evening gloves went out of fashion decades ago. It will be impossible to find twenty identical pairs on such short notice."

Carina sank into the couch in a huff.

"Then it will be impossible for me to attend the ball tonight."

Hilda's lips pursed together in a thin line. Lina almost laughed aloud. The lady's maid clearly wanted to scold Carina for being so spoiled.

But she didn't dare, and Carina knew it. Carina crossed her arms and pouted. Hilda looked ready to explode.

"I will see about the gloves," she said through gritted teeth.

❦ 23 ❦

Alaric examined his reflection in the mirror. He had managed to rein Bastien in tonight. He looked almost like himself. His hair was pulled back away from his face. It had only the tiniest bit of oil in it, and the oil was unscented.

Bastien had insisted on securing his hair with a velvet ribbon. Honestly. A ribbon? How was he supposed to convince the nations of Myora that he was a competent ruler when his hair was tied back with a velvet ribbon?

He ran his fingers over the ribbon, debating if he should pull it out.

"Your lady will love it," Bastien said.

Alaric sighed and dropped his hands.

"The jeweler is here," Bastien said.

"No," Alaric said. "No brooches. No gems."

The jeweler bowed.

"Not quite what I had in mind. The item you ordered is ready. I thought you might need it for tonight."

He handed Alaric a small velvet bag. Alaric bounced the pouch in his hands. With all that had happened, he had forgotten about his order. The jeweler bowed again.

"Would His Highness like to examine the item? To make sure it is satisfactory?"

His Highness would not, but Alaric opened the bag and shook the ring into his palm. His throat tightened.

"It looks perfect," he said. "Thank you."

The jeweler beamed.

"It was a challenge, but of course Your Highness would want something unique."

Alaric examined the ring.

It wasn't flashy. Not nearly flashy enough for a princess. Just a round stone set in a gold filigree band. Maybe he should have asked for a ring from the castle treasury. There were plenty down there to choose from.

But he wanted the ring to mean something. To be special.

He raised the ring to the light. The round, green stone shimmered but didn't sparkle.

"It is not too late for me to re-cut it," the jeweler said. "The emerald will shine more if it is faceted instead of round."

"No, I don't want to cut it."

"It is a most unusual stone. Where did Your Highness acquire it?"

"Mount Evangelina. I've had it since I was a child."

The jeweler's eyes widened.

"Your Highness found an emerald on the mountain? I wasn't aware there are mines there."

"I found it buried in moss. I thought it was a marble for many years."

The jeweler laughed.

"Certainly not! This is an emerald of the finest quality. It would shine like the sun if you let me re-cut it."

"No, I want to keep it in its original form. Thank you for such excellent work."

The jeweler bowed and left.

Alaric slid the ring onto the tip of his finger and stared at it. The ring certainly was unusual. A perfectly round emerald. Maybe he should let the jeweler re-cut it. It would still be the same gem.

Well, it was too late for that now.

"Are you ready for the ball?"

"Gah! Stefan! Knock!"

Alaric dropped the ring. Stefan snatched it off the floor.

"You're giving her the Evangelina stone?"

"Give me the ring, Stefan."

"Your most prized possession?"

"Stefan-"

"Proof that Evangelina Shadow-Storm exists? You're giving the seagull princess that gem?"

"It isn't proof that she exists. It's just an emerald. Someone dropped it on the mountain, and I found it. That's all."

Alaric snatched the ring away. Stefan shrugged.

"That's not what you said when you found it. You said you'd found proof that Evangelina Shadow-Storm was real. You said-"

Alaric threw a pillow at him. It hit Stefan in the face. He put the ring back in the bag and tucked it into his pocket.

"I had a wild imagination as a child. Don't you forget anything?"

"Nope. Why not give her a ring from the treasury?"

"Because I want this to mean something, Stefan. I want to give her something special."

"Like definitive proof that Evangelina Shadow-Storm exists?"

"Shut up."

"Fine. I came here to tell you not to come into the ballroom before you're announced."

"Don't tell me. Trumpets?"

Stefan nodded.

"All of them. See you soon."

As soon as the door closed behind Stefan, Alaric pulled the ring out and studied it again. The jeweler had done an excellent job. The gold filigree curled around the gem in elegant swirls. Alaric liked the ring a lot. Which probably meant Carina wouldn't. Someone that bland would probably prefer a simple silver band.

Lina would like it. The emerald would match her eyes.

Alaric pushed the thought away and secured the ring in his jacket pocket. There was still time to get a ring from the treasury if he needed one. Maybe Carina would improve upon closer acquaintance.

Maybe she would refuse to wed him after she saw the play.

Alaric checked the mirror one last time before going to the ball. He frowned. The person in the mirror looked dejected. Heartbroken. Not like a prince about to secure his right to rule and his country's future.

He straightened and forced the emotion from his face. There. Impassive arrogance was the best he could do tonight. In many ways, it was just what the situation called for.

He stood tall as he walked to the ballroom. Tonight wasn't about him. He needed to act for Aeonia. Alaric patted his pocket several times to make sure the ring was still there. Its presence was strangely comforting. Like carrying a piece of the mountain with him.

Alaric reached the ballroom and hesitated outside the door. He took a deep breath and nodded to the musicians. All six of them put their trumpets to their lips and blew three long blasts. He winced. Did they have to be so loud?

The doors opened, and he walked through. He had everyone's attention. Kings, queens, and princesses stared at him.

He walked towards the princesses. It was easy enough to

find them. They stood in a group dressed in identical light purple gowns. They had wreaths of snowbells in their hair.

And they wore gloves.

Alaric blinked. Yes, every princess wore elbow length white gloves. What was Hilda thinking? Was this part of the test?

He found Carina in the group. She stood in the middle. Lina stood beside her. He took Carina's gloved hand and kissed it. The glove smelled musty, and he swallowed a cough.

Carina curtsied. He caught the tiniest smirk on her face.

"Will you honor me with a dance, Princess?" he asked.

She nodded, her face blank again. He led her to the center of the dance floor, aware of everyone watching them.

Carina was an average dance partner. She followed his lead but nothing more. No extra flourishes. No smiles. No conversation. She didn't seem aware of the music, but she didn't miss a beat.

Alaric's hands sweat. He was sure Carina could feel the moisture through her gloves. They were damp by the end of the first dance. Yes, surely she noticed, but she said nothing.

Alaric did his best to match her disinterested expression. This was politics. Royal children doing their duties.

Nothing more.

The dance finished. Other couples joined them on the floor. Carina didn't move away, so they continued dancing.

Alaric wanted to talk, but what could he say? They were as good as engaged. They both knew it. But he hadn't officially asked. She hadn't said yes.

He studied her face. She would say yes, wouldn't she? Maybe he shouldn't have been so ambitious with his choice. Santelle was powerful enough to refuse Aeonia if they wanted to, but that would have severe consequences.

Maybe he should have settled for Kell.

"Prince Alaric."

He looked at her. Carina stopped dancing. Couples swirled around them.

"I won't refuse you."

Alaric's face brightened with relief. How had she known? Maybe she wasn't as dull as she appeared.

People were starting to stare. Alaric pulled her back into the dance.

"Thank you."

She nodded.

"I won't risk war. You were clever to pick me out of the crowd."

The dance ended, and she pulled her gloved hand from his.

"I believe it is tradition for the prince to dance with each princess," she said. "If you will excuse me."

She disappeared into the crowd. Alaric caught a glimpse of her walking towards the Santelle delegation.

Towards her father.

Blast. He would have to speak to her father. He hoped the King of Santelle wouldn't ask too many questions. He just wanted this to be over.

A flash of red caught his eye. Fiora curtsied and offered her hand. He took it and led her to the dance floor before he realized what he was doing.

"Reconsider," Fiora said.

Alaric blinked at her.

"She doesn't want you. Reconsider. Choose someone else. Choose me."

She watched him, waiting for a reaction. Alaric didn't give one. He was beyond caring. Fiora glared at him. Alaric swept her towards the corner of the room.

"She has already accepted. It is too late to change anything now."

"We would welcome you into the family," Fiora said. "We would welcome you as one of our own. Please."

"Princess, this conversation is over. I have made my choice."

"You chose wrong."

Fiora slipped her hands out of Alaric's. It was easy with the gloves on. Alaric watched her walk away with a mixture of amusement and disgust. He spotted Stefan across the room and walked to him.

"Are you having a good time with your lady love?" Stefan asked.

"Yes."

"I can tell. Something in the heaviness of your step. The droop in your eyes."

"Stefan, please."

"Why her, Alaric? There are nineteen girls more interesting than her."

"Twenty. And you know why."

Stefan shrugged.

"Your other lady has been busy."

He gestured across the room. Alaric stared in horror as Lina approached the King of Gaveron. He caught a gleam over her gloves. The magic ring! She might attack him!

"We have to stop her. She'll ruin everything. Stefan, help me stop her."

"How?"

"Dance with her. Show her the architecture. Give her food. Keep her busy."

"Do it yourself."

"Stefan—"

"I do have official duties tonight, Alaric."

"Stefan, if this is about that blasted play—"

"This ball is still part of the Princess Test. I'm co-host

with Marta. Go stop your lady from making a spectacle of herself. I'll help you when I can."

Alaric eyed Stefan suspiciously.

"Stefan, I've made my choice."

"Of course you have."

Alaric sighed and hurried towards Lina. He doubled his pace when he saw her diamond ring flash red.

❦ 24 ❦

Lina's ring flashed red. The King of Gaveron watched with raised eyebrows.

"Honestly, Princess. You are too old to find amusement in such tricks."

Lina's eyes reflected the light of her diamond. This was bad. The King of Gaveron was the leader of the Council of Kings. In her century, she had reported to the King of Gaveron as much as the King of Aeonia. He commanded the Council's secret troops.

If anyone had access to classified reports about shadow warriors and creatures of darkness, it would be the King of Gaveron.

But he didn't believe her. He didn't believe the ring's magic. That much was obvious.

There was only one thing left to try. Her password. Lina took a deep breath and looked the King of Gaveron straight in the eyes.

"I am a goat."

He blinked.

"I beg your pardon?"

Was that recognition or disgust in his eyes? He took a step backwards. Lina's throat tightened, but she tried again.

"Your Highness, I know it has been a long time, but I'm here to report for duty. I am Evangelina Shadow-Storm. I am a goat. Do you have donkey breath?"

"What nonsense is this? Do you know who I am, girl?"

The king took another step back. There was no mistaking the disdain in his eyes now.

He thought she was crazy. He didn't know who she was. He didn't know the truth about the seal.

The Council of Kings had forgotten her.

Tears pooled in Lina's eyes. She winced when someone put a hand on her injured shoulder.

"Playing your tricks again?" Prince Alaric said.

He pushed Lina aside and bowed to the King of Gaveron.

"Please pardon her, Your Majesty. I think the stress of the Princess Tests has stretched her sense of humor."

The king bowed.

"It is a stressful time for all of us. That is no reason to play jokes with magic rings."

"Of course not, Your Majesty. Please excuse us."

The king walked away. Lina's shoulder throbbed. She pushed Alaric's hand off her arm.

"He doesn't believe me."

She said it more to herself than to Alaric. Her heart was broken. She and Luca had been completely forgotten. Everyone here would call her insane if she tried to tell them the truth.

Lina pushed away the tears with her good hand. She would only be able to protect them so much without help. She had sealed Nog away, but the ring still glowed red. Another threat lurked somewhere, and no one cared.

"Dance with me," Prince Alaric said.

Lina had forgotten he was standing there. She shook her head.

"I don't feel like dancing."

"It is tradition for the prince to dance with every princess."

"I don't care."

Tradition. How dare he lecture her about tradition? Lina didn't want to dance. Her shoulder hurt. Her ankle ached.

But she couldn't afford to leave. A mysterious danger threatened Aeonia, and all the royal families of Myora were here. If something attacked them, it could lead to disaster. Chaos. War. She needed to stay here to guard them.

Lina rested her right hand lightly in Alaric's. Thank goodness Carina had convinced Hilda to make everyone wear gloves. She gripped the prince's shoulder with her left hand. If he wanted to dance with her, he could support her weight.

Alaric didn't comment. They floated across the floor. He danced well. Under other circumstances, she would have enjoyed it. But her injuries still ached. And her heart hurt worse. The king's rejection stung.

"Tell me about your magic."

Lina flinched.

"What?"

"The magic you used when you sang. Tell me about it. Was it from your ring?"

"I didn't use magic when I sang. I didn't use my ring."

She met Alaric's gaze. He looked confused.

"But you sang with such expression. I felt– Are you sure you didn't use magic?"

Lina smiled in spite of everything.

"Is it so hard to believe I'm a decent singer? That I am capable of expressing feeling through song?"

Alaric studied her face. He shook his head.

"Forgive me. I did not mean to imply anything. But you have used magic in the past. I thought you had done it again."

"My magic is fairly specific. I couldn't use it for music if I wanted to."

"Why are you here?" he said. "Why are you trying to stir up trouble?"

"I'm trying to protect you."

He studied her face more closely. He should know every inch of it by now, Lina thought. She knew every inch of his. In fact, she was becoming fond of looking at it.

He looked much nicer tonight without the oiled hair and jeweled chest. He was handsome without being obnoxious about it. And his dark eyes were kind.

"I believe you," Alaric said.

"What?"

"That is, I believe you're sincere about wanting to help. But riling up the kings won't do any good. Especially the King of Gaveron."

She snorted.

"Riling them up. Is that how you see me? Some sort of troublemaker?"

"Isn't that what you are? Normal princesses don't climb castle towers."

Lina missed a step. Alaric caught her. The motion jerked her shoulder. She winced.

"Is that how you hurt yourself?" Alaric asked. "What are you doing here?"

"Trying to win your heart."

Lina said it with as much venom as she could muster. Alaric laughed.

"As if anyone believes that. Who are you really?"

Lina opened her mouth to say she was a princess, but Alaric's expression stopped her.

"You came early," he said. "You stopped by the archive.

You were filthy. You claim you had trouble traveling, but none of the delegations had travel difficulties. I checked."

Lina clamped her mouth shut.

"You're either in trouble or you're causing trouble. Either situation needs my attention."

Lina studied his face. Of course looks could be deceiving, but he looked trustworthy. And he hadn't had her thrown out. She had given him multiple opportunities to do so, but he hadn't reported her yet. Hadn't had her disqualified. He had given her chance after chance to prove herself.

Could she trust him? Clearly he wouldn't believe the whole truth. But maybe a part of it?

Maybe.

"I'm a protector," she said slowly. "I guard Aeonia from the shadows."

"Not a princess then?"

"I am noble. I'm not deceiving anyone by being here."

She watched Alaric's reaction. He nodded.

"Are you one of the Society of Evangelina?"

Lina missed another step.

"The what?"

He laughed.

"I guess not. It's a local organization. They do good. Watch out for people. My stepmother is a member. I thought maybe she planted you here to keep an eye on me."

Lina glanced at the queen across the room.

"The Society of Evangelina," she repeated. "Named after the legend?"

Alaric nodded.

"She's popular among the people?" Lina asked.

Alaric nodded again.

"Our most popular story. The closest mountain to the city is named after her. They say that's where she sleeps."

Lina's heart beat faster.

"Sleeps?"

Alaric smiled at her.

"You protect Aeonia, but you don't know the story of Evangelina Shadow-Storm. Who are you?"

Lina gasped for breath. She wanted to tell him. She wanted to trust him. But what could she say? He might believe her intentions, but how could he possibly believe her origins?

It was impossible to explain one without the other.

Her anguish must have played out across her face. Alaric led her to a chair at the edge of the room and helped her sit.

"Lina, you can tell me. Let me help you."

"You know my name?"

He looked chagrined.

"Sorry, I know I'm not supposed to. Please don't tell anyone. Stefan overheard it."

Lina swallowed. She had to try. One last time. She looked up at him. He watched her with a serious expression. She studied his eyes. She had thought they were black, but actually they were a dark blue. Like the sky in the realm of shadows.

"Alright," she said. "If you really want to hear it. My name is Lina. But that isn't the whole story. I-"

The trumpets blared. She jumped.

"Ladies and gentlemen! Kings and queens! Princes and Princesses! If you will follow me through to the next room, we are ready for the entertainment to begin!"

Prince Stefan stood on a small podium gesturing towards a door. Alaric's jaw tightened.

"Blast. Please excuse me. I'm so sorry."

He hurried away. Lina pushed herself out of the chair and limped across the ballroom alone.

❧ 25 ❧

"**W**hat are you doing, Stefan?"

Stefan smiled at Alaric.

"Saving the Princess Test. That girl is a loose cannon, right? There's no telling what she'll say to the kings. So I arranged for the entertainment to start early."

"Early? Stefan, this is beyond early. The ball started less than an hour ago!"

"Yeah, it took some convincing. But here we are."

Stefan gestured to the door that led to the theater. Alaric's heart sank. The stage was decorated with sets he recognized all too well. He had designed them. It was all there. The enchanted pavilion with the wolf statue. The dark curtains to represent the shadow realm.

This was really going to happen.

Queen Marta approached them.

"I've arranged for you to sit next to your princess," she said. "She'll join you after she sings."

She gestured to two seats marked with gold ribbons. Alaric sighed as he sat in his place. He didn't actually remember much of the play. He had written it years ago. But he had a feeling it would be a disaster.

The kings and nobles found their seats, and the lights lowered. Carina and the lute player walked onstage. She curtsied and stood still as a statue through the lute introduction. She sang the song just as she had at the Princess Test. Alaric sank deeper into his seat. There was no way anyone would think he chose her because she was the best singer.

Carina curtsied to the nobles' mild applause and walked backstage. She joined Alaric a few moments later.

"You were marvelous," he said without enthusiasm.

She nodded, keeping her attention focused on the stage.

Alaric searched for Lina. He couldn't help himself. There she was. Near the front of the theater. He had a perfect view of her face.

Blast Stefan. She had been about to tell him the truth. He was sure of it. And now they were separated. Who knew when they would have more time alone?

The stage lights came on with alarming brightness. The lute player stayed on the stage. With a twist to his stomach, Alaric remembered that he had written a musical number to start the show. Please, please, please let that have been lost.

A cellist joined the lute player. They played a repetitive tune over and over again. The narrator joined them. He wore a black suit with silver sparkle accents, just as Alaric had requested in the script. Alaric watched, helpless, as the actor took a deep breath and opened his mouth.

"Evangelina. Evangelina.
Won't you be my queen-ah? Be my queen-ah?"

THE NARRATOR KEPT SINGING. THREE ACTORS DRESSED AS goblins joined him. They waved their claws in time with the music and shook their horns. They mimed putting crowns on their heads every time the narrator said "queen-ah."

No wonder Odette had refused to play any part in this production. It was worse than he remembered. Alaric glanced down at Lina. She stared at the stage in undisguised horror.

Well, he couldn't blame her.

The song continued.

> "She fought through forests and shadows deep.
> She saved the land through eternal sleep."

THE GOBLINS MIMED GOING TO SLEEP. ETERNAL SLEEP. That sounded pretty good to Alaric at the moment. He glanced over at Carina. She looked bored enough to go to sleep herself.

That was something. At least she didn't look horrified like Lina.

The goblins danced off the stage, and the narrator took his place in the right hand corner. He cleared his throat and stared out at the audience.

> "I'll tell you a tale of sorrow and woe.
> A tale of Aeonia's greatest hero.
> A maiden of power, most lovely of form.
> Our hero, Evangelina Shadow-Storm."

THE ACTRESS PLAYING EVANGELINA SHADOW-STORM waltzed onto the stage. She wore a black dress so tight it might have been painted on. Alaric found the back of Stefan's head in the audience and glared at it. If they were going to produce his play, the least they could do was stick to his designs. The costume he had sketched for Evangelina had been loose and flowing with a long cape. She was supposed to be covered in shadows, not painted in ink.

"A heroine beautiful without a flaw
Joined by her faithful companion Luca.
A donkey most loyal, by her side he'll walk.
But this donkey is different than most. He can talk."

ALARIC GRINNED IN SPITE OF HIMSELF. THEY MADE THE Luca costume just right. He had always been secretly proud of that design. It wasn't easy to make a human actor look like a donkey, but he had managed it with an intricate system of straps and levers. The result was a wearable marionette that gave the actor full control over the donkey ears. A perfect tool to enhance the acting.

Alaric glanced at Carina. She did not look impressed by his feat of engineering. Well, fine. He found Lina's face in the crowd. She was clever. Surely she would appreciate-

No. Blast. She was crying.

❧ 26 ❧

Tears streamed down Lina's face. She couldn't help it. This was how Luca was remembered? They thought he was an actual donkey? She hadn't been serious when she made his password "I have donkey breath." Luca was a hero as much as she was.

The costume was an abomination. The actor wore ears attached to strings, so he could move them at will. He kept moving them. Twitching them for comedic effect. The crowd laughed. Lina seethed.

How had this happened? How could they be so wrong about everything?

The dancing goblins came back and mimed smashing up a town. The set included miniature buildings made of paper. One of the goblins pretended to stub his toe kicking a house. He limped around the stage. The audience laughed.

These people had never seen a goblin. They had no idea what they could do. Lina rubbed the bruises under her glove. If this was how they thought creatures of darkness acted, they would be helpless in a raid.

She could only hope the seal held.

Onstage, Evangelina and Luca explored the damage left by the goblins. Lina glared at her stage counterpart. What was with that dress? There was no way anyone could fight in that. It was far too tight.

She turned around to glare at Alaric. He was the one responsible for this atrocity. To think she had almost told him her secret! How he would have laughed.

To her surprise, Alaric was watching her. Their eyes met. Lina wiped tears away and glared at him. He had disrespected Luca's memory. He had-

"I must travel to the realm of shadows!"

Lina turned her attention back to the play.

"No, Evangelina," the donkey-Luca said. "You don't have time! It is too dangerous!"

"I don't have time to waste! Watch my back, Luca!"

The actress swooned onto the floor. Stage hands pulled curtains in front of her. The donkey Luca paced the stage and addressed the audience.

"She will travel to the realm of shadows. She wields the powers of darkness, but do not think she is evil! We will work together. I am a master of the light!"

He held his hoof up and raised his ears. A spotlight shone down on him.

"You think it is strange for a donkey to be a master of light magic? Perhaps it is. But the light will be wielded by those who protect it! When light and shadows come together, we can defeat any foe!"

The stage hands removed the curtain surrounding Evangelina. She moved to the other side of the stage. Dark curtains fell and blocked the scenery. Clearly they were meant to represent the realm of shadows.

Evangelina had changed costumes while Luca delivered his speech. Her new dress was even tighter and only covered her to her knees.

Lina stared. What was wrong with her legs? They were—hairy? The actress clopped across the stage. Lina gasped when she stepped into the spotlight.

Goat legs. The actress had goat legs now.

And horns, now that Lina looked. And furry sleeves over her arms. The trip to the realm of shadows had turned the girl into a goat.

The actress scampered in a circle.

"Goblins, I know you're there! Show yourself!"

The goblin actors crept across the dark stage. They jumped at Evangelina. She kicked them with her goat legs. She rammed them with her goat horns.

The audience cheered. Lina glanced around. They were actually enjoying this? This was an atrocity. It made her nauseous.

The goat Evangelina jumped and spin kicked a goblin in the head. He toppled backwards into the set, knocking down a column. A stage hand steadied it and pushed the goblin back into the fight.

More goblins rushed the stage. They surrounded Evangelina.

Lina leaned forward in her chair in spite of herself. She remembered this all too well.

"Luca!" the actress called. "Luca, can you hear me?"

"Hee haw!"

"Luca, I know how to stop them! Cast the sleeping curse!"

"No, Evangelinaaa!"

"It's the only way! Do it, Luca!"

The donkey actor ran across the stage. He tossed glitter over everything. Some of it caught a breeze and blew into the audience.

Lina leaned back into her seat. She should have known they would get this wrong too. It hadn't been a quick decision to use her magic to seal the goblins away. It had taken months of preparation. Months of secrecy. Even her parents hadn't known their plan until a few days before.

Onstage, Evangelina and the goblins collapsed to the ground in a cloud of glitter. Evangelina reached for Luca.

"I will sleep for centuries," she gasped.

Lina wasn't sure she was acting. She seemed to be choking on glitter. The actress coughed before continuing.

"Bury me on the mountain," she said. "Bury me where no one will ever find me. I will fight the goblins for eternity."

"Evangelinaaaa!"

"Do it, Luca! Please!"

Lina bit back a sob. Inaccurate as it was, this play stirred up too many painful memories.

She wasn't the only one crying. Most of the audience seemed moved. She caught Eirwyn wiping tears from her eyes.

The actress collapsed onto the stage. Stage hands pushed a set over her. A marble temple with a wolf statue. Its eyes glowed green.

The actor playing Luca stared sadly at the tomb. He sat in front of it and drooped his ears. The curtain closed.

The audience clapped enthusiastically. A few people jumped to their feet. The crowd had enjoyed the production.

The musicians returned to the stage and played the song again.

"Evangelina. Evangelina.

Won't you be my queen-ah? Be my queen-ah?"

The goblins danced and gestured to each actor in turn. The audience clapped in rhythm with the music.

Lina felt buried. Felt the walls closing in around her. It

was too much, watching the donkey Luca dance with the Evangelina Shadow-Storm actress.

She stood and elbowed her way out of the crowd. She ran down the hallway searching for a window. She needed to get out. Needed fresh air. Lina pulled her left glove off and blew her nose into it. She dropped it and pulled the right one off to wipe her eyes. She could hardly see well enough to walk.

Lina found an open window and crawled onto the ledge. It was wide enough to sit on. Practically a balcony. She wrapped her arms around her legs and buried her sobs in her knees.

A laric stood and bowed politely. Most of the crowd focused on the actors, but it was only a matter of time before they turned their attention to him.

He nodded an apology to Carina and slipped out of the theater before Stefan could call him to join the actors onstage. That would be unbearable.

Alaric breathed deeply as he walked down the hallway. Finally, he could relax. The play had not been as terrible as he feared. The audience seemed to like it. The costume designs were actually quite clever.

It could have been much worse.

A faint sound echoed through the hallway. Alaric followed it. Was someone crying? The cries seemed to come from an open window. He stuck his head out.

Someone was curled up on the windowsill sobbing. One of the princesses, judging by the purple dress she wore.

"Are you alright, miss?"

She jumped. Alaric reached for her in case she fell, but she caught herself.

It was Lina. Her eyes were swollen, and her face was red.

She looked absolutely miserable. Grief contorted her features. Alaric stared for a moment. He had never seen such raw sorrow.

"Was it that terrible?" he whispered.

Lina turned her head away. Her shoulders shook with silent sobs. Alaric climbed out onto the ledge. He pulled the window shut behind them, careful not to let the latch click.

"There," he said. "You can cry as loud as you want."

"Go away."

Her voice was hoarse. He could barely make out the words.

"Lina–"

"Leave me alone!"

Alaric leaned against the window. Whatever this was, it had to be about more than the play. He sat and waited. He didn't know what else to do. Her cries broke his heart. He leaned his head back and stared up at the stars. It was a nice night. Maybe he could stay here forever. Maybe he could forget about the Princess Test.

Lina's shoulders stopped shaking. She sniffed and wiped her face with a glove. Her bare arms gleamed in the moonlight. Alaric studied her.

"I don't want to talk about it," she said.

Something haunted her eyes.

"Do you want to tell me what you were going to say earlier?"

"No."

Something had changed between them. Alaric couldn't imagine what. Some of her emotion seemed directed at him.

He sighed.

"You're angry with me."

She turned her head away and didn't deny it.

"Why?"

She wouldn't look at him.

"Is this still about the genealogy?"

She shook her head. Alaric didn't believe her. What else could she be angry about?

"I don't like it either," he said. "Legend says they disappeared. My father thinks they were assassinated in secret."

She turned to him.

"What do you think?"

"I'm not a historian, although I have researched the matter as thoroughly as I can. There's no evidence of assassins. They just seem to have vanished. I don't know what the Council expects me to do. I can't call them back from the grave."

She smirked. Alaric stared at her.

"Nothing about this is funny, Lina! They're gone, but we're still here. Aeonia is finally at peace. We're prospering! I want that to continue. I think I'd be a good king!"

She laid her left hand on his arm.

"I'm sure you will be. That's why you want to marry Carina? To secure your position?"

He nodded.

"I tried to find another way. The Council doesn't accept me as royal. The only way to earn their respect is to marry a true princess."

Lina pulled her hand away and stared into the night sky.

"I understand."

"Really?"

She nodded.

"Sometimes you have to make sacrifices to protect what you love."

She stared at the stars with an intensity Alaric didn't understand. She was still a mystery. At least she didn't seem angry at him anymore.

"My father gave me the idea," he said. "Not directly. He was against the Princess Test at first. Aeonia was split after my family took the throne. He ended the civil war by marrying my mother. He united Aeonia."

"Was she an enchantress?"

Alaric nearly fell off the windowsill. He grabbed the ledge to restore his balance.

"What?"

"Some of the other princesses said you'd had a queen that was magic. Was it your mother?"

"No."

"And not Marta?"

Alaric tried to swallow. His throat had gone dry. Memories of Cassandra had that effect on him.

"Father had another wife. They married shortly after my mother died. She was dark. Evil. She tried to kill him. To destroy the country."

"Oh. With magic?"

Alaric nodded. Just thinking about Cassandra's magic made his skin crawl.

"I used to climb the mountain to hide from her. I searched for Evangelina's Temple as often as I could. I thought if I found Evangelina Shadow-Storm, she'd help me defeat my stepmother."

Lina smiled.

"Did you find her?"

"No. But I found Marta. She grazed her goats there sometimes. When I told her what was happening, she gathered the Society of Evangelina to help me. To overthrow Cassandra. That's how she met my father."

"That's a nice story."

Alaric's eyes widened.

"Nice? The kingdom was almost destroyed by an evil sorceress! What's nice about it?"

"You defeated her. The citizens of Aeonia gathered around you and helped you when you needed it. The other kingdoms may not see you as a prince, but the people of Aeonia do. Those ladies at the archive-"

She chuckled. Alaric grimaced.

"That was a dirty trick, and you know it!"

"Yes, it was. Do you know what they were doing there?"

"Looking for royal gossip?"

"Checking their lineages just in case they missed the fact that they were a princess. They wanted to enter the Princess Test and have a chance to marry you."

Alaric's face turned bright red.

"They what?"

"You have quite a following. They think you're handsome. And very helpful with trade agreements. And a good military commander. In their eyes, you are a prince."

"They said that?"

Lina nodded. She shivered. The night had grown cold. Alaric slipped off his cloak and handed it to her. She grabbed it with her left hand and tried to wrap it around her shoulders.

She couldn't do it one handed. Lina raised her right arm and winced.

Her arm. She had been hiding it all day. Alaric leaned forward to get a better look and nearly fell off the windowsill again.

Ugly bruises circled Lina's wrist. It looked like someone had grabbed her arm and squeezed and squeezed. Someone with enormous hands. The swollen bruises were so dark purple they were almost black.

"You're hurt!"

Lina glanced at her arm. Panic flashed through her eyes. She pulled the damp glove back on, wincing as she did it.

"Who did that to you?"

Alaric felt sick. He had worried about Lina hurting someone, but she was the one being mistreated.

"When did that happen?"

Lina shook her head.

"Lina, you can trust me."

She buried her injured arm in the folds of her skirt and turned to him. The pain in her eyes went far deeper than bruises on her arm. She looked like her very soul had shattered.

"Tell me about the play," she said.

"What?"

"The play. How much artistic license did you take? Is that how the story really goes?"

"Lina, don't try to change the subject."

"Just tell me!"

Alaric stared into her green eyes.

"Yes, that's how the story goes. I added the dancing goblins and the song, but that's all. It seemed like a good idea at the time."

He laughed. Lina's face stayed bleak.

"So you think Luca is a donkey? You think Evangelina is a goat shape shifter?"

Alaric nodded. He didn't understand. Was she trying to distract him by changing the subject? Or had his writing been the problem all along? He knew the play hadn't been great, but had it been bad enough to cause this much heartache?

Lina leaned against the window and took a shuddering breath.

"Someone hurt you," he tried again. "I won't allow it. Tell me who it is, and I'll stop them."

Lina fixed her sad eyes on him.

"You can't."

Alaric's heart twisted at the pain in her voice.

"Yes, I can. Lina, I don't care if it's the King of Gaveron! I'll see whoever is responsible for this put in prison."

Lina laughed. A little half chuckle that twisted the corner of her mouth into a smile.

"It isn't the King of Gaveron."

The corner of her mouth stayed twisted up for a moment as she studied his face.

"Thank you, Alaric."

"Don't thank me yet. Thank me after I catch the wretched fiend who hurt you."

She reached a shaking hand up and stroked a strand of hair out of his face.

"You've been kind," she said. "Mostly."

"Lina-"

She shook her head.

"Alaric, I've failed. The Council won't listen to me. There's nothing more I can do here."

"What were you trying to tell them? Lina, please let me help you."

Alaric couldn't explain it, but he needed this. Needed her beside him. Needed to know she was safe. That she was protected from whoever had grabbed her arm.

"I'll protect you. Whatever you're running from, I'll protect you."

The corner of her mouth twisted up a little further.

"I know you'd try. But my story is difficult."

"Tell me."

"Maybe someday."

"Tell me tonight."

She leaned closer to him. Alaric reached over and pulled the cloak further around her shoulders. He left his arm there. Lina looked into his eyes.

"I'm sorry. I can't. But I can tell you that you're in danger."

She nodded to her arm.

"This won't be the end of it. You're under attack."

"You know this because of the magic ring?"

"And because of the bruises."

"Lina, just tell me who's threatening you! I'll have the guards take care of it. I'll take care of it myself, if it needs to remain a secret."

"The threat isn't that straightforward."

She glanced at her ring again. Alaric swallowed.

"Magic?"

She nodded.

"Be careful, Alaric. I'm doing what I can, but I'm only one person. And I'm wasting a lot of time with the Princess Tests."

"We defeated dark magic before. We can do it again."

"Maybe. I need to get to bed."

She slipped out from under his arm and tried to raise the window. She couldn't manage it with only one good hand. Alaric helped her lift it, and she climbed back into the castle.

She favored her right arm in a way that made Alaric suspect her injuries went further than the bruises. When she jumped off the window, her right leg buckled. Alaric scrambled to help her, but she stood upright by the time he reached her.

"You should go back to the theater," she said. "Show those kings that Aeonia has a strong prince. And an artistic one."

She smiled a little.

"You were crying during the play," he said. "Was it really that bad?"

"No. It reminded me of something else. But you know goblins don't dance, right?"

Alaric shrugged.

"They're a fairy tale creature. I'm not sure there are rules about them."

Lina slipped his cloak from her shoulders and handed it to him. Whatever defenses she had lowered on the windowsill were back in place. Alaric couldn't read her face, but he suspected he had angered her again.

"Lina, whatever I keep doing to offend you-"

"It's nothing. Go, be a prince. Win your princess. And be good to Carina. She's more special than you know."

Alaric's heart twisted in his chest as she walked away. He wanted to follow her. Wanted to tell her- what exactly?

He swallowed. He couldn't. Lina was right. Aeonia needed a strategic prince right now, not a lovesick one.

❧ 28 ❧

Lina stumbled down the hallway towards her room. She was weaker than she had let Alaric see. Her strength was spent. The day had been physically and emotionally exhausting.

She nodded to the guard in the hall and slammed the door to her room shut. She leaned against the doorknob for support.

Should she have told him? She pictured Alaric's face. He had been nicer than she expected. Kinder.

And willing to do whatever it took to protect Aeonia.

Lina told herself her heart only beat fast because she was tired. It fluttered annoyingly every time she thought of Alaric's smile.

She turned to go to bed.

Only, she didn't have a bed anymore. Lina's jaw dropped.

A tower of mattresses sat in the canopy bed's place. Lina counted them. Twenty-one mattresses in a pile. One for each princess.

She opened her door and waved to the guard.

"What happened to my bed?"

"I'm not supposed to talk about it."

"Are there supposed to be twenty-one mattresses in my room?"

"Yes."

"And I'm supposed to sleep on them?"

"Yes."

"Do all the princesses have this many mattresses?"

"Yes."

Lina slipped back into her bed and closed the door. There was no way she could climb the tower with her injured arm. She would sleep in the chair.

The chair was gone. They had removed every piece of furniture except the wardrobe of dresses and the towering bed.

Lina walked around the tower. She pushed it. The mattresses seemed sturdy enough. There was a ladder on the other side.

What kind of princess test was this?

Lina's heart leaped in her chest. The pea! Had they removed the pea?

She forced her hand between the bottom two mattresses. If they were the same ones, then it should still be there.

Yes, there it was. Lina wrapped her hand around the gem and pulled it out. She breathed a sigh of relief. Thank goodness!

Lina circled the tower of mattresses again. There wasn't an alternative. She would either have to sleep on the floor or the ridiculously tall bed.

She tied the pea into her sash and climbed. Her right shoulder ached, but she kept going. Shadows pulled at her. Not now! If she went into a trance while climbing the ladder, she would fall.

Lina gathered the last of her strength and pulled herself onto the top of the mattress tower. She crawled to the center and collapsed. She had no energy left. She realized she was still in her gown. They would probably send a maid to help her change.

Too bad. She wasn't about to climb back down to change clothes.

Lina rested her head on the pillow. Her eyes were dry. She had no more tears to cry. Not even for Luca. Her heart was utterly and completely broken.

Half of her wished she had told Alaric the truth. She could have at least tried. Maybe the bruise would be proof where the ring wasn't.

The other half knew she had done the right thing. To claim to be Evangelina Shadow-Storm after watching that ridiculous play? He would think she was delusional. He might ask her to turn into a goat as proof.

Lina closed her eyes. She tried to fight the trance sweeping over her body. She didn't want to shadow travel. Didn't want to deal with the memories.

The trance took her anyway. Lina materialized in the realm of shadows. Her black gown and cape swirled around her.

She pulled up her skirt and looked at her legs. No, they weren't goat legs. Still very human. And rather shapely if she said so herself.

Something near her moved. Lina dropped her skirt and smoothed the fabric.

"Hello?"

Her voice echoed in the darkness. Lina shivered. That wasn't right. There shouldn't be anything for the sound to echo against. She reached with her senses, searching for the source.

Everything felt as it should be. The three stars on the horizon twinkled. Lina walked forward. She would check on the seal. Just a quick glance to put her mind at ease. Then maybe she could sleep.

She jumped and flew through the air until she neared the seal. Her left arm tingled. She looked down. Her ring flashed with red light. Lina stopped. Why was the gem doing that? She hadn't asked it to check for danger. Something must be very wrong.

She smelled it before she saw it. Goblin. A dark shape hurtled towards her. Lina reached for the pea emerald in her headband, but she was too slow. A solid mass slammed against her body. It crushed Lina to the ground. The flexible earth absorbed most of the impact. Lina used the flexibility to push back. The thing on top of her laughed. A clawed hand wrapped around her injured shoulder.

"Nog," Lina gasped. "You're- How?"

Nog didn't answer. He squeezed her shoulder. Lina screamed, but no sound came out. The goblin's weight had crushed the air from her lungs. It took her a moment to remember she was in the shadow realm. She didn't have to breathe.

Lina ignored the pain shooting up her arm and gathered her shadow magic around her.

"Lightning!" she shouted.

Black sparks exploded between her and Nog. They pushed the goblin into the air. Lina slid across the ground. She grabbed the pea with her left hand and held it in her palm.

"Sword," she said.

The pea glowed with green light and stretched into a massive sword. Lina grinned at the goblin.

"You've broken the seal. You know what that means, right?"

"I will devour the light you protect."

"No. It means there's nothing to keep me from killing you."

Lina jumped at the goblin. Her injuries from the body slam slowed her movements, but she was still faster than the hulking brute. She slashed with her sword. Nog roared. Lina grinned with a grim satisfaction. One more stroke should do it. If she could weaken him, she could push him back into the seal.

Red light flew from Nog's hand. It crashed into her face. Lina gasped in pain. The green sword's light flickered and went out. She floated in the air, vaguely aware of the goblin below her. Through the fog, Lina saw him extend his claws. This was it. Nog reached for her throat.

Lina couldn't move. The blow had paralyzed her. She watched the claw come towards her.

A flash of light hit Nog in the eye. He pulled his claw back and batted at the light as if it were an annoying insect. Another light joined the first and buzzed around his head.

Lina smiled. The stars were stronger than she'd given them credit for if they were able to annoy a goblin.

The third star caught Lina by the hair and dragged her away from Nog. When they were a safe distance away, it perched on her nose. Lina went cross-eyed staring at the tiny ball of light.

"Thanks," Lina said. "Who are you?"

The star twinkled but didn't respond. It was very faint. Speech in the realm of shadows was probably too advanced for it.

"You're a light wielder, right? Do you know any healing magic?" Lina asked.

The star hovered over her shoulder. A cool sensation spread over Lina's skin, but it didn't reach any deeper than that. The star dimmed.

"That's alright. Thanks for trying. You'd better go help your friends. Nog is nasty."

The star circled over her head.

"Yes, I'll be alright. I can make it from here."

The star bounced up and down and disappeared. Lina clutched her ribs. At least one of them was cracked from Nog's ambush. She held her diamond ring to her lips.

"Heal."

White light washed over her. The cracked ribs mended back together. They would be bruised, but at least she could breathe now. That would matter when she woke up. The piercing pain in her shoulder lessened a little.

Lina closed her eyes and focused on breathing. In and out. Slowly, she faded from the realm of shadows.

❧ 29 ❧

Alaric gritted his teeth at crowd in front of him. His admirers. They loved the play. Blast Stefan, everyone loved it. Nobles from every country congratulated him on a smashing success and wanted to know when his next work would be performed.

Alaric did his best to smile and nod. Carina stood by his side doing nothing. It was impressive how unimpressive she was. She seemed to fold in on herself, completely blending in to her surroundings. The rest of the princesses stood around her.

More than once, Alaric reached for the ring in his pocket. The play had been a triumph. She had said she would accept him. He should make the engagement official. He ducked backstage and pulled the ring out of his jacket. The green stone glinted. Even cut as a sphere, it had more sparkle than Princess Carina.

Lina had called her special. Alaric couldn't see it.

Lina. Now there was someone special. Half of Alaric thought she was crazy. Ranting about danger. Trying to enlist the King of Gaveron to help her.

Crazy or not, she was sincere. And she had some proof. The magic ring, which Alaric had mixed feelings about. And the bruises on her arm.

His feelings about that weren't mixed at all. He would find whoever hurt Lina and make him pay.

He tucked the ring back into his jacket. According to the rules of the Princess Test, he wasn't expected to propose until the last test had been completed. He had promised to do it the third night. Tomorrow night.

To propose early might raise some eyebrows.

He returned to Carina's side. She gave no indication that she had noticed his absence. The crowd was thin now. Only a few Aeonian nobles and the crowd of princesses. They stood behind him. Fiora jostled through the group until she stood next to him.

Alaric wished they would go. Maybe he would like Carina better if he spent time with her without the pressure of the Princess Test. But if the princesses left, he would be alone with her. That was against the rules.

Thank goodness no one saw him talking to Lina. The prince talking to a princess alone on a windowsill might cause enough outrage to end the Princess Test altogether.

He needed to be more careful.

The last of his admirers finally left the theater. Queen Marta joined Alaric and the princesses on the stage.

"Princesses, thank you for a lovely evening. I am sure you are all tired. The guards and I will escort you to your chambers."

The princesses curtsied and left the theater. Alaric hesitated just a moment before following them. He wanted to speak with the guards on duty. Maybe they had seen Lina's attacker.

He watched around the corner as each princess went into their room. Most of them came back out immediately.

"What is the meaning of this?" Fiora demanded. "What have you done with my bed?"

Queen Marta clasped her arms behind her back.

"Everyone has received the same treatment. Ask the other princesses."

"She's right," said the princess who was either Brigitta or Colette.

Fiora glared at the queen. She clearly wanted to yell at her.

And she clearly couldn't. She huffed into her room and slammed the door. The other princesses followed her lead.

Alaric met his stepmother in the hallway.

"What did you do to their beds?"

"Alaric! Don't sneak up on me like that!"

"Sorry. Why are the princesses angry?"

"It's nothing. Just another test."

"Sleeping without a bed is a princess test?"

"Oh, they've got a bed."

Queen Marta chuckled to herself in a way that made Alaric nervous.

"I need to speak to the guards," he said. "That won't get me disqualified, will it?"

Marta shook her head.

"I'll wait for you here. No need to risk the appearance of impropriety."

Said the woman who had obviously done something devious to anger Fiora.

Alaric crept back down the corridor and checked the Princess's hallway.

"They've all gone to bed?" he asked.

The guard nodded.

"Has anyone unusual visited them? Has anything strange happened?"

"Like what, Your Highness?"

"I have reason to believe someone has threatened one of the princesses. Has physically harmed her."

The guard's brows pushed together.

"I haven't seen anything, Sire. I will check with my men."

"Excellent. Make sure none of them leave the girls' rooms unattended. It would be a disaster if something happened to one of them."

The guard nodded. Satisfied that he had done all he could until morning, Alaric walked Marta back to her room before going to his chambers.

Stefan lay stretched across Alaric's bed. He propped his feet up on Alaric's pillows and grinned.

"Ah, the master of theater returns triumphant."

"Shut up, Stefan."

"Come on! Can't you admit I was right? Everyone loved the play!"

"Lina didn't. It made her cry."

"She wasn't the only one. Your noble story of Evangelina Shadow-Storm's sacrifice left hardly a dry eye in the house."

"No, she was really upset. I found her sitting on a window ledge sobbing. Her arm is bruised. Someone hurt her."

Stefan shrugged.

"She also tore her sleeve by running into a door. I think she's just clumsy."

Alaric glared at him. Stefan sat up.

"Oh, you're serious. It's hard to tell. You're always serious."

"She has bruises around her wrist. Like someone grabbed her. She wouldn't tell me who."

Alaric grabbed his own wrist, mimicking the gesture that might have led to Lina's injuries.

"I haven't seen anything," Stefan said. "The guards have been instructed to keep the princesses in and intruders out."

"You don't think one of them hurt her?"

"Alaric! You honestly think one of our soldiers would assault a princess? You've trained many of them. Besides, there's always multiple guards on duty. They would report anything that happened."

Alaric slumped into his chair.

"Why won't she tell me? That's what I don't understand. Who is she protecting?"

Stefan grinned.

"Stop making that face," Alaric said.

"You like her. I knew it!"

Alaric shrugged. It was admission enough to make Stefan to jump around the room.

"I knew it! I told you so! You like Lina! So why on earth did you pick the seagull princess? She brings the interest level of a room down just by standing in it."

"I know."

"While Lina adds interest."

"I know."

"So why didn't you choose her?"

"You know why. I need a true princess from one of the old families, and we don't know Lina's rank. She practically told me she wasn't a princess tonight. I can't choose her."

"Isn't that the point of being king? Being able to do whatever you want?"

Alaric rolled his eyes.

"Thank goodness you're the second son. Aeonia would collapse in fire and ruins under your reign."

Stefan shrugged.

"So, what are you going to do about Lina?"

"Find who's hurting her and stop them. Beyond that, what can I do? She's convinced we're all in danger. But whatever she expected from the kings she talked to, she didn't get. The King of Gaveron was furious about whatever she told him."

"Did she tell you where she's from?"

Alaric shook his head. Stefan smiled.

"Lucky for you, I'm here. I researched all records of countries and provinces who have ever sent princesses to the Princess Test. Some of these nations haven't participated in a while, but maybe they decided to join again at the last minute."

"You did research?"

"Only for you, brother. Only for you."

He handed Alaric a parchment with a list of countries. A long list.

"If she isn't from one of these kingdoms, she isn't noble."

"Stefan, this is- Thank you."

Stefan smiled.

"I told you I'd help you find love. If this is what it takes, I'll do it."

Alaric skimmed the list. They were mostly small countries. Remote islands. Some weren't countries any more. They had been annexed by larger neighbors.

But it was a start. As Stefan said, if Lina wasn't from one of these countries, she wasn't noble.

He patted the ring in his pocket and smiled.

❧ 30 ❧

Something pulled Lina back to consciousness. A voice. A vague echo. She followed it reluctantly. Every part of her body ached. Even opening her eyes hurt.

Hilda stared down at her.

"Princess," she whispered. "You must wake up."

Lina blinked at her. She tried to speak, but all that came out was a groan. Hilda blinked back. She didn't seem alarmed.

"She's awake, Your Highness."

"Oh, thank goodness!"

Lina heard a scuffling sound. Queen Marta's head popped over the edge of the mattress. Her face was flushed.

"Perhaps the mattress towers weren't the best idea," she said. "I wasn't expecting to climb one myself. But did you see Fiora's face?"

"I wasn't present at the moment, Your Majesty."

"Oh. Yes. Well, it was worth it."

Lina did her best to follow the conversation, but it didn't make much sense. She turned her head. Pain pierced her skull as she focused her eyes on Queen Marta's face. The queen's brow wrinkled.

"Lina, are you alright?"

Lina groaned again. She tried to nod.

"Get the charm, Hilda."

Hilda's head disappeared as she climbed down her ladder. Marta stroked a piece of hair away from Lina's face. Lina took a rasping breath.

"Goblin. Please."

Marta nodded.

"Of course. Stay still now."

Lina tried to sit up, but Nog's body slam had bruised every inch of her skin. Her newly healed bones ached. On top of all that, she was tired. She felt like she hadn't slept a wink all night.

Hilda returned with a small silver box. Queen Marta opened it and poured the contents on Lina's forehead. A cool tingle spread over her skin. Her breathing became easier.

"You're in danger," she rasped. "Please, Queen Marta."

"Don't speak," Queen Marta said. "This potion will ease your pain, but the actual healing takes time."

"Please," Lina said. "You're not on the Council, but you have to believe me. My name is-"

"Evangelina Shadow-Storm. I know, dear. I have donkey breath."

Lina sat up and stared at the queen. Her muscles screamed a protest, but she ignored it.

"That's Luca's password! How?"

Queen Marta pushed Lina back down on her pillow.

"I'll tell you, but you must stay relaxed so the potion can heal you. Do you understand?"

Lina nodded. Sitting up had taken the last of her strength. She couldn't move again if she wanted to. Queen Marta climbed onto the mattress tower and took her hand.

"We know who you are because we've been waiting for you. I'm part of a group called the Society of Evangelina.

Most of Aeonia thinks we're a philanthropic society. And of course we do help people. We know you and Luca would want that."

Lina's gripped Marta's hand.

"Luca isn't a donkey."

Queen Marta chuckled.

"Is that what upset you so much last night? No, we know he isn't a donkey. Luca is the one who founded the Society of Evangelina. He wanted to make sure you'd have someone to look out for you after he died."

Tears ran down Lina's cheek. Queen Marta patted her hand.

"Yes, I'm afraid he is gone. You slept for over a century. We weren't sure you would ever wake up. Luca had a good life. He protected Aeonia in difficult times. He married and had children. I'm a distant relative of yours, actually."

Lina smiled. It hurt her face, but she didn't care. Luca had lived. He hadn't died in the goblin wars. He hadn't died in the invasion.

He made sure she would be protected.

"Luca rose to prominence in Aeonia after you fell asleep," Marta said. "As half of the team that sealed away the goblins, he was regarded as the most powerful enchanter in Aeonia. He was a close adviser to King Dacian and King Thaddeus."

Lina chuckled. She couldn't imagine Luca talking to a king, much less advising one. Had he played pranks on them like he had on the generals who oversaw their missions?

"The invaders," Lina said. "The royal family's disappearance. What happened?"

Marta frowned.

"They weren't invaders. They were troops that broke away from Aeonia's army. Our own people. There were faults on both sides. King Thaddeus pushed the citizens of Aeonia to the breaking point. There was a drought and famine, but he refused to help those in need. Soldiers from the affected regions banded together and sent messengers to plead with the king. Negotiations might have solved the problem peacefully, but King Thaddeus refused to speak with them. He wanted to crush the delegations with magic to set an example."

"Luca wouldn't have liked that."

Marta smiled.

"You know your brother well. He refused to aid Thaddeus. He disapproved of fighting our own people and was afraid to pull magical resources away from the seal. The king banished him from court and found a few enchanters who weren't loyal to Luca. They fought the army, but by then it was too late. The people of Aeonia had rallied behind them. The enchanters weren't strong enough to defeat the entire country."

"The parchments said they killed everyone," Lina said. "The whole royal family. The genealogy just ended."

"Many people died in the war. Every nobleman who fought was killed, but Luca stayed hidden. He sheltered those nobles who didn't want to fight. They became goat herders. No one thought to look for members of the royal family amongst all those smelly goats. He also hid you. He blotted your name in the royal genealogy. He buried the wolf statue and transformed your story into a myth."

Lina laughed.

"He made himself into a donkey?"

"To keep you safe, yes."

Lina closed her eyes. It was a lot to take in.

"You fought a goblin last night," Queen Marta said. "D you defeat him?"

"No. Nog escaped the seal and ambushed me. He away. He might have killed me except I received help three stars. Were those members of the Society?"

"The stars that aided you were my sons: Cael, Henry, and Benjamin. They aren't very powerful light wielders. We haven't had anyone to train us, and King Thaddeus burned most of the scrolls about magic before his death. But we do have some powers."

"Does your husband know about this?"

Did Alaric know?

Queen Marta frowned.

"No, I haven't told my husband or stepsons. The Society of Evangelina has kept you secret for over a century. It wasn't my secret to tell."

She fixed her eyes on Lina. Lina swallowed.

"Oh. You mean, if I wanted to tell them, you wouldn't mind?"

"Our goal has always been to protect you. Now that you're awake, we will follow your lead."

Lina swallowed. It hurt her throat.

"I'm not a leader. I wasn't even a senior member of the special forces in my century."

"You are a trained shadow warrior. You have experience fighting goblins. You're the best leader we have."

Lina took a deep breath. Queen Marta was right. Like it not, she was the best chance Aeonia had.

"I don't think they'll believe me," she said. "I tried to tell 'ng of Gaveron. He laughed in my face and called me a

King of Gaveron is not the brightest. Besides, we ts that might help. I'll send word for Cael to fetch want to tell the whole council?"

shake her head. Too much effort.

ust the King of Aeonia and Alaric at first? ey react. And they can give us the help we

they will believe us. Noam is very fair

minded and will listen to reason. And Alaric has been trying to prove the existence of Evangelina Shadow-Storm since he was a child."

Lina nodded.

"I've tried to tell him a few times, but I couldn't. Not after the way everyone else reacted."

Queen Marta laughed.

"I can imagine! I don't think he'll be hard to convince. He likes the story a lot. I think Evangelina is his ideal woman."

She winked at Lina. Lina laughed. It hurt less. The healing potion was working.

"I'm not sure that version of Evangelina exists," she said. "The story has been embellished over the years. And I don't turn into a goat."

Marta laughed.

"Another of Luca's additions. And that's not what Alaric likes about the story. But maybe I should stop speaking for him. We'll find an opportunity to tell him soon enough. Will you stay in the Princess Test, Lina? It will be easier for us to work together if you're in the castle."

"Work together?"

"To defeat Nog, of course. He can't be allowed to run free. Our magic is weak, but we will help you as much as we can. And I'll have Cael get enchanted gems from the secret vault."

"Vault?"

"Yes. Luca spent the last few years of his life gathering everything you'd need when you woke up. We have enchanted gems, potions, magic mirrors, and things we can't identify. We're not sure what half of it does, to be honest. Luca collected enough to fill our vault, but he didn't organize it very well. It's all yours."

"That will help a lot."

"And there are letters. Luca wrote you a letter every... Our vault is full of them."

Lina's throat swelled. Letters from Luca. To know exactly what happened while she slept. How he felt about it. That was too much.

"Those can wait," she said. "Fetch the gems first. One of each kind that you have. I'll look through the vault once we've defeated Nog."

"Yes, of course. The vault can only be opened at night, so we won't be able to access the gems until the sun goes down. Now, do you think you're healed enough to come to breakfast? Princess Fiora is bound to demand your disqualification if you don't attend."

"She'll demand it before that if she knows you were here."

Queen Marta grinned.

"You think I'd put Evangelina Shadow-Storm in a room without a secret passage? Fiora will never know we were here."

I
it

day.

❧ 31 ❧

Alaric walked into the dining room. The princesses stood in a line as usual. Today they wore pale yellow dresses covered in lace.

Alaric searched the line. The princesses looked tired. A few yawned at him. Some had dark circles under their eyes.

Whatever Marta had done to their beds had affected their sleep. Alaric found Lina in the group. His heart missed a beat. He gritted his teeth.

Her whole face was bruised. Her right eye was nearly swollen shut. Patches of blue and purple on her arms peeked through the lacy sleeves of her gown. She leaned on Carina for support.

Alaric wasn't the only one to notice Lina's bruises. Princess Fiora watched her from down the line. Probably trying to figure out how to disqualify Lina for her injuries.

Queen Marta stepped forward and smiled at everyone.

"Good morning, princesses. Please, have a seat."

Alaric sat at the head of the table. Princess Fiora rushed to the chair by his side. Lina hobbled to a chair near Queen Marta. Carina helped her across the room.

"I trust you slept well last night, Your Highness?" Princess Fiora said.

Alaric nodded. He kept his eyes on Lina.

"It looks like not everyone did. Honestly, some girls will do anything to stand out."

Fiora was one to talk. She stood out in every way that was unpleasant.

Queen Marta tapped her fork against her glass and beamed at everyone.

"My dear princesses, congratulations on completing another Princess Test last night."

The princesses looked at each other. A flurry of whispers filled the room. Queen Marta smiled.

"Allow me to explain. I am determined to find a true princess for Prince Alaric. There are many qualities that define a true princess, but one of the most important is delicacy. A true princess must be delicate."

She glanced around the room. Alaric frowned. What had she done now?

"Last night, I took the liberty of placing a single pea under each of your mattresses. I added a few more mattresses to make the test more challenging. A true princess would feel a pea under her mattress. She would not be able to sleep a wink."

Several princesses yawned. Princess Fiora stretched her arms to show how tired she was.

"One of you is even more delicate than I imagined possible," Queen Marta said. "Indeed, I must apologize for the discomfort this test has caused her. The clear winner of this princess test not only could not sleep, but the pea under her mattress has left her bruised and battered. She alone is truly delicate enough to be a princess."

Marta gestured to Lina. Lina nodded her head slightly. It seemed to be all she had energy for. Alaric tapped his foot under the table. There was no way a pea under a mattress could bruise someone that badly. They were covering something. Protecting someone.

Princess Fiora glared at Lina.

"She probably fell off the tower of mattresses," she muttered under her breath.

Tower of mattresses? What had Marta done?

"That, of course, means that these two lovely princesses are tied. One was chosen as winner of the music competition. One won the delicacy test."

Queen Marta waved her arm at Carina and Lina. Carina smiled. She looked a little too happy to be tied instead of the clear winner. Lina looked ready to pass out.

Of course. Alaric should have known Marta wouldn't leave well enough alone. She was matchmaking, blast her! She was making sure he had options. That he could choose Lina if he wanted to.

Lina. Alaric watched her while he ate his breakfast. What had happened? He couldn't imagine the force necessary to cause such bruises. She was black and blue all over.

Marta's ruse only made it worse. There was an explanation for the bruises now, however implausible. He wouldn't be able to insist that Lina tell him what was really going on.

He wouldn't be able to protect her.

"We have only a few tests left in the final day of the Princess Test," Marta said. "After breakfast, you will prove your skill with a needle in an embroidery test. Then we will have a period of rest for you to prepare for your final chance to interact with Prince Alaric before he selects a winner. We are having a picnic lunch on Mount Evangelina."

Alaric winced. He had forgotten that he had asked Marta to include that. It seemed a mistake now. Had he really thought he could fall in love so quickly? That he could find someone he wanted to share his favorite place with?

He glanced at Lina. She would like the mountain. He was sure of it.

Well, maybe not. Lina looked horrified. She stared at Queen Marta with eyes as wide as her bruises allowed. She seemed to be trying to get the queen's attention. To signal her without drawing attention to herself.

Was she that averse to spending time outdoors? Surely someone who climbed castles wouldn't mind hiking up a mountain. Maybe she was worried she would be too weak from her injuries.

Or was there something else going on? Perhaps she was afraid of being out in the open. Afraid that whoever hurt her would find her outside the castle.

Alaric clenched his fists. He needed to speak with her. Needed to find out the truth, blast it all!

"I love needlework," Fiora said. "My tapestries decorate the entire castle of Kell."

Alaric nodded. He didn't take his eyes off Lina.

Princess Fiora took a final bite of eggs and stabbed her knife into the table. It sunk deep into the wood. Alaric swallowed.

"I'm sure your tapestries are lovely," he said.

Fiora beamed at him. She had a bit of egg caught in her teeth. Alaric decided not to mention it.

The princesses finished their breakfast and stood to leave. Alaric jumped to his feet and opened the door for them. If he could just get a few words with Lina, to ask her what had really happened, maybe he could make this right!

Lina didn't meet his gaze as she limped past. She stood between Carina and a princess with black hair. They helped her walk.

Alaric took a step towards her, but Fiora stood in his way.

"I look forward to the picnic," she said. "I have heard that Mount Evangelina is beautiful."

She still had egg in her teeth. Alaric nodded at her. Queen Marta patted his shoulder as she passed.

"Marta, I-"

"I'm sorry, Alaric, I don't have time to chat. We must begin the needlepoint test immediately so we have time to travel up the mountain by lunch."

"Cancel the picnic. I've changed my mind."

Marta shook her head.

"Oh, it's far too late for that now. I put it on the official schedule. Besides, you don't want to miss an opportunity to share your favorite place with the princesses."

Yes, he did. He definitely did.

Marta smiled at him again and bustled away to join the group of girls. Alaric ran down the hallway in the opposite direction. Towards the princess's bedrooms.

A guard blocked his path when he reached it.

"I'm sorry, Prince Alaric. We've been ordered not to let anyone into this wing of the castle."

"Yes, I know. Were you on duty last night?"

"No, Your Highness. Those guards are off duty now. Guards need rest too."

"Yes, of course. Thank you. Will you let me know if you see anything suspicious?"

"Of course. We are all watching and ready to report at the first sign of trouble."

"Thank you."

Alaric frowned and walked back to the dining room. Maybe the servants clearing away the meal had noticed something. They might know which maids had been assigned to which princesses. If he could question Lina's maid, he might learn something.

The servants hadn't cleared the table yet. Stefan sat at the end eating the remains of the breakfast. He waved a fork full of eggs when Alaric entered. Alaric sat beside him.

"Have you seen Lina?" Stefan whispered. "All the guards said she was bruised or something."

Alaric grabbed Stefan's arm. The eggs on his fork flew across the room.

"You've talked to the guards? Did they see anything suspicious?"

Stefan frowned at his now empty fork.

"No. They woke up the guards who worked last night to question them. Lina didn't leave her room last night. No one has visited her."

"That's impossible. There's no way those bruises are from a pea."

"Maybe she fell off the mattress tower."

Alaric crossed his arms.

"Mattress tower?"

"Marta made each princess sleep on twenty-one mattresses last night."

"What? That's ridiculous."

"I know. This delicacy test really went to her head. But a fall from that height would explain the bruising."

"And the mattress tower grabbed her arm?"

Stefan shrugged.

"Alaric, there isn't anything you can do. If you're caught talking to her alone, she'll be disqualified. Our guards are trustworthy."

Alaric pushed his chair away from the table.

"Maybe the servants saw something the guards didn't. I'm going to question them."

Stefan raised an eyebrow.

"Won't that look suspicious? You asking the servants about one of the girls in the Princess Test?"

Alaric slumped.

"I suppose. But our servants are discreet."

"Hmm. You'd better let me take care of this. I've got a few contacts I trust."

"What? Since when do you have spies?"

"Since I've been trying to learn the identities of the princesses for you. Not that it matters since you're obsessed with Lina. I don't suppose you even care that I've figured out which princesses are Marian and Merinda."

"Really?"

Stefan grinned.

"See? My informants are excellent. They suspect the other princess Lina befriended is Eirwyn of Gaveron, but they aren't sure."

Alaric considered this.

"Marian is a king's niece, not daughter. That would do me no good."

"Ah, but Merinda is from Eldria. One of your top two choices if I remember correctly. Or have you changed your mind?"

He grinned at Alaric. Alaric brushed his hair back.

"No. I've already decided on Carina. Tell your informants to stop trying to identify princesses and start searching for information about the person hurting Lina. I'll go to the archives to research the list of countries you gave me. If I can discover where she is from, I might be able to identify any enemies who would want to harm her."

"You think a political enemy of her country is sneaking past our guards and hitting her in her sleep while she's on a mattress tower?"

Alaric glowered at Stefan.

"It's possible. I need to do something! I feel useless, Stefan!"

Stefan picked up a bit of egg with his fingers and chewed on it.

"You're irritable today. I've heard men in love get that way, but I never expected it of you."

"Stefan, be serious!"

"I am serious. I'll help you on one condition. You promise to marry Lina if we figure out which kingdom she's from."

"Stefan, I'm marrying Carina."

"Maybe Lina is Carina's sister. Maybe she's from Santelle. Their names rhyme. They spend all their time together. That has to mean something."

"No, it doesn't. Besides, they didn't arrive together. Are you going to help or not?"

Stefan shoveled another bite of eggs into his mouth. He wiped his hands on his tunic.

"Fine. More research. I'll talk to the servants. You go to the archives and search for more information about the girl you feel absolutely nothing for."

🌺 32 🌺

Lina wielded her needle like a sword. She stabbed her fabric and imagined it was Nog's face.

His stupid, smirking, goblin face.

This was unbearable! She shouldn't be sewing! She should be on the mountain hunting for the goblin!

Carina cast a sideways glance at Lina. Her own embroidery project looked better, but it still wasn't great. They were supposed to be embroidering snowbells. Lina's were lopsided, and Carina's were too pointy.

"I don't embroider much," Carina whispered. "Do you think Prince Alaric will change his mind about me if my sewing is terrible?"

"Worth a try."

Carina smiled and tied a knot in the middle of her thread.

"I should be out there helping," Lina said. "This is a waste of time."

"You're so bruised you can barely stand. You need rest more than anything. Could you walk all the way up the mountain right now?"

Lina frowned. No, she couldn't. She stabbed the fabric a few more times with her needle.

"This picnic is a mistake," she said. "The mountain is dangerous right now."

Carina tied another knot in her thread. Her embroidery had become a tangled mess.

"Can't you use your ring to protect everyone?"

"No, the ring's magic is limited. It mostly helps me focus my power. And my powers are strongest at night. Just when the danger will be strongest."

"If the danger is strongest at night, we should be fine at the picnic. We'll be back to the castle long before nightfall."

Lina sighed. Carina had a point.

"I suppose."

"Then you can use the picnic as a way to get to the mountain. A free ride. Once we're there, I'll distract the prince so you can sneak away."

"Really? What about blending in? Your strategy?"

Carina frowned.

"That won't work anymore. If he's decided to choose me, he's going to choose me no matter what."

"Carina, I'm sorry."

Carina pulled her thread tight and shook her head.

"There's nothing to be done about it."

Across the room, Fiora glared at them.

"Are you sharing patterns? If you are, I'll-"

"Have us disqualified," Lina and Carina said in unison.

Fiora huffed and returned to her embroidery. Eirwyn caught Lina's eye and smiled. She sat in a small group of princesses who hadn't said a word the whole embroidery test. They were focused on their sewing. They looked like they actually knew what they were doing.

"Who are they?" Lina whispered. "Is it bad that it bothers me not to know their names?"

"No, I found it strange my first test. It took me a few times to figure out who everyone is. The one in the corner is Marian. She's from Fletcher. The other two are Brigitta of Ostenreich and Colette of Montaigne."

"I guess you get to know each other pretty well coming to these tests."

Carina shrugged.

"In a way. Some of the girls are very competitive. If you're a princess, you're the enemy. Most of them are nice though. Colette's castle is close to mine. We visit each other a few times a year."

Queen Marta stood and rang a tiny silver bell.

"Princesses, the embroidery test is over. Please put your needles away and bring your fabric to Bastien for inspection. He will determine who has embroidered the most acceptable snowbells."

The princesses formed a line and handed their cloths to the tailor. Bastien studied them with a careful eye and wrote numbers on a parchment. Fiora went first. She had sewed ten perfect snowbells during their time.

Bastien frowned when Lina handed him the fabric.

"You were informed that you were to embroider snow-bells, Princess?" he whispered.

"Yes."

"Have you ever seen a snowbell?"

"Yes."

He looked from Lina to the cloth and back to Lina.

"Do your eyes work properly?" Bastien whispered. "Perhaps your injuries impeded your skill?"

"Just give me zero snowbells."

Lina snatched the fabric back and limped away. The tailor watched her go. He wrote something by Lina's name. Lina didn't want to know what it said.

Carina went next. Bastien stared in horror at Carina's

tangled mess of thread. Carina beamed at him as if she were presenting a masterpiece. He sputtered and searched for something to say. Lina giggled. Carina joined her.

"He thinks I was sabotaged. He asked if anyone touched my thread beforehand."

"I wouldn't put it past Fiora to tie knots in your thread if given the chance."

When all the princesses had presented their embroidery, Bastien presented his parchment to Queen Marta. He circled a name with a flourish of his quill. Lina followed his gaze.

Uh oh.

Queen Marta held up the parchment.

"The winner of the embroidery test, with ten perfectly embroidered snowbells, is Princess Fiora."

Princess Fiora smiled at Lina and Carina. She looked absolutely fierce. Lina glanced at Carina. They both raised an eyebrow.

The other princesses lowered their heads. Some looked disappointed. Some looked relieved.

"We have three winners now," Queen Marta said. "The winner of the singing contest, the delicacy contest, and the embroidery contest."

She nodded to Carina, Lina, and Fiora in turn. They curtsied.

"And now you may retire to your rooms. Your maids will help you prepare for the picnic."

The princesses filed out of the sewing room. Lina tried to catch Queen Marta's attention, but Fiora blocked her path.

"We're even now," she said. "Prince Alaric could choose any one of us."

She walked beside them. Carina took Lina's arm and supported her weight.

"Good stitching," Carina said.

Fiora beamed.

"I practiced all the traditional skills to prepare for the Princess Test. My father hired tutors for me. I'm glad it finally paid off."

"Yes, I'm sure sewing is the way to the prince's heart," Lina said.

"It shows an eye to detail. Perseverance and focus. Much more important qualities than delicacy."

Lina gritted her teeth and stepped towards Fiora. Carina pulled her back.

"We need to get ready for the picnic," she said.

Lina took a deep breath. As much as she hated to admit it, playing along with the Princess Test was the best way to make it to Mount Evangelina. The carriages would get her there much faster than walking.

She took Carina's arm and walked with her back to their rooms. They reached their corridor. Carina didn't let go of Lina's arm. She glared at the guards, daring them to stop her from going into Lina's room.

They didn't.

"I'm fine," Lina said. "I can walk now."

"You're clearly not. What happened to you last night? You can tell me now that we're alone."

"You heard the queen. She put a pea under my mattress."

"Lina, do you honestly expect me to believe that? This has to do with the danger, doesn't it?"

Lina sighed.

"Carina, you wouldn't believe me even if I told you."

"Try me."

Carina stood by Lina, arms crossed.

"Carina, go back to your room. You'll get yourself disqualified."

"Good. Now tell me what is happening."

She sat on Lina's bed. The tower of mattresses had been removed. Lina sat beside her.

What could she say? Carina watched her with bright blue eyes, daring her to lie.

Lina sighed.

"I-"

A grating sound interrupted her. The wall beside the fireplace slid open. Carina jumped up and moved in front of Lina.

"I knew someone was attacking you! Don't worry, Lina. I'll take care of them."

Lina pulled herself to her feet.

"Carina, don't be silly."

"You think you're the only one who can fight? You're clearly not great at it, judging by how bruised you are. I'm from Santelle. I can handle myself."

Carina kicked off her shoes and took a fighting stance. Lina bit back a laugh. Carina's face was serious, but the overall effect was comical. Her fierce pose didn't match her lacy yellow gown and glossy blond curls.

Hilda stepped out of the hole in the wall. She took one look at Carina and stepped back in.

"We've got the wrong room, Your Majesty."

"What are you talking about, Hilda?"

Queen Marta slipped around Hilda. She frowned when she saw Carina.

"Lina, I don't think getting help from another princess is a good idea."

Lina limped over to the fireplace. Carina followed just behind her, still ready to pounce.

"She's been helping me. I told her about the danger."

"Is the queen the one who attacked you?" Carina asked.

Marta bristled.

"Of course not. It would be better if you left, Princess. This is a serious matter."

"And I'm too delicate to handle it?"

Marta studied Carina. She laughed.

"Well, you certainly have more mettle than I thought."

"She's just been trying to blend in," Lina said. "She's actually very clever. I'd like her to help us."

Marta shrugged.

"If you insist."

Carina turned to Lina.

"So they aren't the ones who hurt you?"

"No," Lina said. "In fact, they've been healing me. Please don't attack them."

Carina dropped her arms and resumed her normal bland expression. She curtsied to Queen Marta.

"Please, everyone have a seat," Queen Marta said. "And keep your voices down. It would be a disaster if anyone found us here. Lina, drink this potion. It will help your stiffness."

Lina took the tiny vial and drank it in a single gulp. It tasted bitter and made her tongue tingle. Carina darted across the room and blocked the door with a chair. Then she sat beside Lina looking as unremarkable as ever.

"The king and Alaric couldn't join us?" Lina asked.

Marta shook her head.

"I couldn't pull my husband away from the Council meetings without creating suspicion. Alaric and Stefan have left the castle. I'm not sure where they've gone."

Lina nodded.

"What is this about?" Carina asked. "What is this danger?"

"A goblin."

Carina raised an eyebrow.

"Like in the play? Does he dance?"

"No. Goblins don't dance. They're hulking brutes. They'll smash anything. Eat anything."

Carina swallowed.

"But goblins aren't real. They're legends. Fairy tales."

Queen Marta cleared her throat. Lina took a deep breath.

"They are real. They haven't been seen for over a century because they were sealed away. I sealed them away. Carina, I know this is hard to believe, but I'm-"

"Evangelina Shadow-Storm," Carina said with a nod.

"What?"

Lina jumped out of her chair. The potion seemed to be working. She wouldn't have been able to move that quickly before.

"How could you possibly know that?"

Carina shrugged.

"I only know of one goblin sealing warrior. If goblins are real, and you're fighting them, it makes sense. You're certainly not a princess from anywhere near here. You know magic but not The Snowbell Song? You sneak away from the test to search the castle? That isn't typical princess behavior."

Lina sank back into her chair. Her muscles protested from the sudden movement of jumping.

"Besides, you didn't get those bruises from a pea," Carina said. "Did you sneak away and confront the goblin last night?"

"Something like that. He ambushed me in the realm of shadows."

Queen Marta tapped her chair.

"Now that the princess has proved her cunning, we need to make a plan. From what I understand, goblins are weak during daylight hours. Is that true?"

Lina nodded.

"A very strong dark creature might be capable of attacking in daylight, but they prefer to wait for night. They gain physical strength and magical abilities when the sun goes down."

"So we attack it now," Carina said. "We rally the army and destroy it before sunset."

Lina laughed.

"And you accuse me of not being a typical princess? I wouldn't think fighting goblins was your idea of a good time."

Carina shrugged.

"I know my way around a battle. Military training is standard for everyone in Santelle."

She looked at Queen Marta and flushed.

"Oh. I mean- Blast, it isn't like it was a secret anyway. Alaric would never have chosen me if he didn't know I was from Santelle."

Marta winked.

"I won't tell anyone. We can't have Fiora demanding your disqualification."

"Talk about militant," Lina said. "Anyway, I don't think we'll be able to find Nog in the daylight. His magic will be weak. He probably won't be able to manifest a physical form until evening."

"So we wait?" Marta asked.

Lina shook her head.

"No, I still want to go back to the cave and investigate. That's where Nog would have appeared if he was strong enough last night. I want to check the seal in the realm of light. I may find something that will help us."

"The Society of Evangelina can investigate," Marta said.

"No. I want to go myself."

"We're in the middle of a Princess Test," Queen Marta said. "But perhaps you could miss the carriage after the picnic and stay on the mountain to search. I can have one of my sons help you."

"I'll just get Fiora to disqualify me. Defeating Nog is more important than a Princess Test."

"There's no need to do anything drastic," Queen Marta said.

"You haven't seen a goblin! You don't know what they're capable of! I need to get to the mountain and investigate!"

"And so you will. But wait a few hours. Wait for the picnic. We'll all take carriages up there together."

"Queen Marta, please reconsider the picnic. What if Nog attacks? I can't guarantee everyone's safety."

"We'll be away long before sunset. Now, I'd better make sure everything is ready."

Queen Marta and Hilda slipped through the secret tunnel before Lina could protest. Carina gave her a sympathetic look.

"I'm sure they'll bring guards. It will be alright."

"Guards won't be much good against a goblin."

They had no idea what they were dealing with. They were bigger donkeys than Luca! Lina pulled the pea from its hiding place under the mattress and tucked it into her sash. She had a feeling she would need it.

❦ 33 ❦

The carriage jolted as it turned onto a narrow mountain road. Alaric turned to Marta.

"Is it wise to take the princesses so far from the castle? It isn't too late to cancel."

"Alaric, relax. This was your idea, and it's a good one. A picnic will give you a chance to interact with the princesses in a less formal setting."

Alaric narrowed his eyes.

"Marta, I've already made my choice."

"Of course you have, dear."

Alaric stared out the window. Blast. This was all his fault. He had been the one to suggest a picnic on the mountain.

"Where exactly are we going? What part of the mountain?"

"I told the drivers to stop at the hill just below Evangelina's Temple. That way you can have a romantic stroll to the top with the lady of your choice."

The proposal. Alaric grimaced. This was it. His final chance to propose in private before he faced the Council of Kings to announce his choice.

It had to be done.

"Will that be alright, Alaric?"

Alaric shrugged. He just wanted to finish this whole ordeal.

Stefan poked his head in the carriage window. He rode a horse alongside it, leading the guard that surrounded the caravan of carriages.

"He's just mad that he couldn't find anything about Lina at the archive."

"Stefan, don't stick your head into a moving carriage," Marta said. "That's dangerous."

Stefan smirked at Alaric and removed his head. Alaric leaned back against the seat, trying to relax. Marta studied him like she had so many times when he was a young child. He knew that look. She was assessing the situation. Deciding what was wrong and what was the best way to solve the problem.

"Don't," he said.

"You've been researching Lina?"

"You have to admit the circumstances around her arrival are suspicious."

"Unusual, perhaps."

"No. Suspicious. I've seen her several times in the archive looking for something. She's sneaked out of the castle. She's bruised overnight and won't tell anyone how it happened."

Marta opened her mouth.

"Don't tell me the pea story again. No one with sense believes that. Besides, she was bruised before the pea test."

Marta smiled.

"You're more taken with her than I thought."

Alaric sat straighter.

"Of course not. If there's a security threat to Aeonia, I need to investigate."

"Alaric, she is a princess. I was expecting her. I had a room ready for her. Gowns for her to wear."

"Yes, I've been wondering about that. Only twenty princesses responded to the invitation. How were you expecting twenty-one?"

"I told you. She's a princess."

"Marta, please. Tell me the whole story."

Marta shook her head.

"The story is Lina's to tell. I'd rather you hear it from her."

"Marta, we're in the middle of a princess test! She'll be disqualified if she tells me who she is! Anyway, she won't. I've already asked."

"She might. Try asking again."

"When? This is the last day of the Princess Test. I told the Council I'd announce my choice tonight."

Marta started.

"Tonight? Alaric, you have the rest of the week to consider your choice. That is traditional. No one would question it."

Alaric shook his head. If he delayed once, he might not work up the courage again.

"I've already told them it will be tonight. I've made up my mind. Carina may be bland and boring, but an alliance with Santelle will secure Aeonia's future."

Marta laughed.

"What's so funny?" Alaric asked.

"I'm not sure Carina is as bland as you think."

"Marta, don't try to twist this around. I don't want a boring wife. I'm just stating a fact."

The queen glanced out the window, still smiling.

"Marta, whatever you're planning, stop it right now."

"I'm not planning anything, Alaric."

"Yes, you are. You've been trying to convince me to choose Lina since she got here. Why?"

"Alaric, I'm a simple goat herder, not a matchmaking courtier."

"Is that so?"

Marta smiled innocently at him.

"Of course. But since you brought it up, Lina is a charming girl, isn't she?"

"I can't afford to fall in love, Marta. You know that. You know I have to make a strategic match."

"I just want you to be honest with yourself, Alaric. If you weren't crown prince, who would you choose?"

"It has only been three days. I don't know any of them well enough to marry if I didn't have to."

Alaric turned to the window. He watched the familiar scenes roll by. Fields of snowbells. Herds of goats.

If he was honest with himself, he knew exactly who he would choose. But it bothered him that he didn't know exactly why. He barely knew Lina. They had shared only a few conversations. He didn't really think she was a spy anymore, but she was certainly more than she seemed.

Was that what intrigued him?

Alaric frowned and took a deep breath. He couldn't afford to think like this. He didn't have a choice in this matter, so why pretend that he did? It would only break his heart even more.

❦ 34 ❦

Lina watched the scenery pass as the carriage rumbled up the mountain path. Much had changed while she had slept, but the mountain felt the same. The same sweet scent of snowbells.

Mixed with the not so sweet odor from the goat herds.

Smelly, but it felt like home.

She leaned against the seat, closed her eyes, and took a deep breath. All was just as it should be. She was on a mission with her team. Playing tag with Luca. Picking flowers for her mother.

"Do you think they'll have another official test at the picnic?" Fiora asked.

Lina closed her eyes tighter. She tried to hold the daydream, but Fiora's voice destroyed it.

"I doubt it," Eirwyn said. "It is traditional to have one competitive test per day. We have had three."

"But one of them was at night. I'm not sure that counts."

Lina opened her eyes just wide enough to glare at Fiora. The healing potion had helped, but she still had enough bruises to prove her victory if Fiora questioned the results of the pea test. It was a ridiculous story, but if it helped her stay close to Marta and the Society of Evangelina, she was willing to defend it.

"Of course it counts," Carina said. "You heard Queen Marta. Delicacy is the mark of a true princess."

Everyone laughed.

"As if a former goat herder believes that," Fiora said. "What really bruised you, Princess?"

Lina closed her eyes again.

"A pea under the mattress. Couldn't you feel it? The bed was so uncomfortable that I tossed and turned all night."

"I didn't sleep well, but it had nothing to do with the pea," Eirwyn said. "I was too afraid I'd fall off the bed."

The carriage halted without warning. Eirwyn screeched as she flew out of her seat.

"Get off me!" Fiora said.

She pushed Eirwyn off her lap.

Lina stuck her head out of the carriage window. Queen Marta had set up a pavilion with tables in the middle of a field of snowbells. She smiled in spite of herself. The waving flowers smelled even better from outside the carriage.

The door opened. Someone took her hand and helped her down. Alaric.

Lina nodded at him. She was still stiff from her bruises. She accepted his hand and stepped down. He leaned close as if to whisper in her ear. She pushed his hand away and hurried out of reach.

Alaric frowned at her and turned to help Eirwyn from the carriage.

Lina examined the terrain. It wouldn't be easy to sneak away. She would have to climb over a rolling hill of snowbells before she was out of sight.

"Eat lunch first," Queen Marta whispered as she walked past Lina.

"No, I want to investigate immediately."

Marta slipped something into her hand.

"I thought you might say that."

Lina glanced down. Marta had packed her a separate picnic basket. She held it against her side and wrapped her skirt around it.

At the carriages, Alaric reached to help her Carina to the ground. Lina caught her eye and gestured for the hill. Carina nodded. She jumped into Alaric's arms.

"Oof!"

He stumbled under her weight.

"Oh, forgive me, Your Highness! My foot slipped."

Carina clung to Alaric's neck like a barnacle on a ship. He tried to extract her from his arms while maintaining some sense of decorum. Carina made an equal effort not to be extracted.

Everyone in the camp rushed over to help. Lina tore her eyes away from the spectacle and ran up the hill. She made it to the top and collapsed on the other side to catch her breath. She was safe now. Out of sight. She pulled an apple from the basket and ate it while she walked to the cave.

﷼ 35 ﷽

A laric struggled with the mass of princess and gown clinging to him. Blast Carina! It was like she was trying to get tangled in his arms.

Stefan tried to help. He grabbed Carina's waist and pulled. Alaric pushed on her shoulders. She didn't budge. Had she wrapped her legs around him? Surely not, but it felt like it under her voluminous skirt.

"Princess, please let the prince help you down," Queen Marta said.

"Is it safe?" Carina squealed. "I don't want to fall!"

"Yes, quite safe."

Carina relaxed. She fell backwards into Stefan and nearly knocked him over. He recovered enough to catch her and set her on her feet. Carina curtsied and walked to the pavilion.

Alaric and Stefan shared a glance. Stefan shrugged.

Alaric helped Fiora out of the carriage next. She studied him, doubtless trying to decide if she could disqualify Carina for slipping. Alaric helped each princess step down before joining them at the picnic table. He took their hands carefully and did his best to make sure no one else fell onto him.

Stefan rolled the dice for seating. Alaric had little faith in Stefan's dice at this point, but at least the rigged seating would let him talk to Lina.

It was not a surprise when Carina sat at his right. It was a surprise when Fiora ended up on his left. She smiled too triumphantly for Alaric's liking.

He raised an eyebrow at Stefan. Was he angry? Was this some kind of revenge? Why wasn't Lina beside him?

Alaric pushed the thought away and kept his eyes down. It was better this way. He wouldn't allow himself to look for Lina. Wouldn't allow himself to catch her eye.

He smiled at Carina. She smiled back a little too brightly.

"Do seagulls fly this far away from the ocean?"

Alaric groaned. Not this again. Fiora answered before he could.

"They certainly could, but why would they? What would a seagull do on a mountain?"

Carina frowned at Fiora and looked back to Alaric.

"What indeed? What do you think a seagull would do on a mountain, Your Highness?"

"They would do nothing," Fiora said. "What a foolish question. Tell me about the cashmere goats of Aeonia, Prince Alaric. I understand they live on this mountain."

Carina's face brightened.

"Those wonderful goats live on this mountain? Oh, they must be so soft! I adore cashmere wool."

Fiora glared at her.

"Yes, their wool is very soft. Kell imports an enormous amount of cashmere wool each year. We are a valuable trading partner for Aeonia."

Alaric focused on his bread. The girls didn't notice they had lost his attention. They bickered about goats for the remaining three courses of the picnic. Alaric didn't eat much.

Queen Marta stood after everyone finished eating.

"I thought we might play picnic games now. A diversion since everyone has been working so hard."

Fiora's eyes gleamed.

"Is this an official test?"

"No. This would be simply for fun."

"Oh, I see. Queen Marta, I think rest might be more appreciated. And perhaps some conversation?"

She batted her eyelashes at Prince Alaric. He gulped. Fiora stared at him with her fierce eyes. Carina watched him with no expression at all.

This was it. His chance to propose.

Alaric smiled at Carina.

"Princess, would you join me on a stroll up the mountain?"

She blinked at him.

"Are the hills higher up the mountain better than these?"

"There is a place I would like you to see."

"If you stroll with her, you must stroll with all of us," Fiora said. "She cannot spend extra time alone with you."

Alaric sighed. He hoped he wouldn't have to stroll with every girl once he had proposed to Carina. Surely a proposal marked the end of the Princess Test rules. He nodded to Fiora. That was far from a promise to stroll, but she seemed satisfied. Alaric turned back to Carina.

"Princess, will you join me?"

He held his hand out. She took it without enthusiasm and followed him away from the picnic.

She didn't say a word as they walked over the hills. Alaric considered starting a conversation and decided against it. Given Carina's awkwardness, he preferred silence.

Of course, he would have to speak to propose.

Would she be able to turn that conversation to seagulls?

At this point, she seemed capable of anything.

Alaric had intended to lead her all the way to the rumored

site of Evangelina's Temple. The place he discovered the emerald. It had a magnificent view of the city and the ocean.

The ocean.

Seagulls.

Alaric stopped. Maybe it was better to do it here. He glanced around. This spot wasn't bad. They were around the corner from the picnic, so at least they had privacy. They stood in a field of snowbells.

Yes, this was a fine place for a proposal. He turned to face Carina and took her hand.

Lina's heart sank when she climbed the final hill. The grass around her cave had been trampled into a muddy mess. The rock door had a deep gash in it. Nog had tried to break it down. He had unearthed the wolf statue and smashed it to pieces. Lina sifted through the marble shards but didn't see the other emerald.

Of course Nog wouldn't have left that.

Lina took a deep breath and slid her ring into the keyhole.

"Is that where the entrance is?"

Lina pulled her hand from the rock and spun around.

"Eva! What are you doing here?"

The goat herder smiled and curtsied.

"I'm here to help, Lady Evangelina!"

"Oh. Um, how do you know about me?"

"I'm Marta's niece of course! I'm sorry I didn't recognize you when you first arrived! I had a hunch, but I didn't want to give away the secret if I was wrong. I sent a message for the princes, but you left before they arrived!"

Lina took Eva's hand and pulled her to her feet.

"You have nothing to apologize for. Your kindness was incredibly helpful. Thank you."

Eva blushed.

"You're really Evangelina Shadow-Storm? I can't believe I get to meet you. I'm named after you. I want to be a shadow warrior when I grow up."

Lina studied the girl's face.

"Haven't you learned light magic like the others?"

"I tried. Honestly, I did. I practiced every day. But I haven't been able to work a single enchantment."

"Shadow magic abilities are rare, but I will test you if you like."

A huge grin split Eva's face.

"Really? Can we start now? I'll help you fight the goblin!"

"No, there isn't time now. It takes years to perfect shadow magic."

"Oh. Later, then. Can I go in the cave with you?"

Lina studied the rock. Deep scratches covered the stone, but it didn't seem that Nog had been able to force it open. It should be safe to bring Eva in there.

"Yes, but you must do exactly as I say."

A man's voice echoed over the hills.

"Eva! Wait!"

Eva bobbed up and down.

"Oh, right. I forgot. Cael and Henry are behind me. They're coming to help you."

"Marta's sons?"

"Yes. They're light wielders, but they can't run as fast as I can."

Eva grinned as the two princes climbed over the hill. Lina studied them. They wore the loose clothing typical of goat herders. Their faces were smudged with dirt. Their features were sharp, but Lina saw a resemblance to Marta. Mostly around the mouth. They had the same mischievous smirks. Wool caps covered their hair.

No wonder the royal family hid successfully for a century. They had perfected the goat herder disguise. Lina wouldn't give the princes a second glance if she saw them with a herd of goats.

The taller of the two reached them first. He bowed.

"Lady Evangelina, it is an honor. My name is Cael. I'm at your service."

Lina curtsied.

"I'm pleased to meet you, but I think we've met before. You were the stars that helped me, weren't you?"

The second brother reached them. He bowed as well.

"Henry at your service, Lady Evangelina. Yes, we were the stars that aided your fight. The third was our brother Benjamin. He's away at school at the moment but will do his best to help us from there."

"Please, call me Lina. Thank you for your help."

The brothers shared a glance.

"Lina?" Henry said. "I'm not sure we should. That seems so informal."

"I don't mind. Evangelina is a bit of a mouthful. Most people call me Lina."

"I want to be called Lina," Eva said. "That's a nicer nickname than Eva!"

Cael ruffled her hair.

"Eva, that would get confusing. You be Eva. Lina can be Lina if she wants. Although I agree with Henry. It feels too familiar to call a hero by a nickname."

Lina grinned.

"Strange to meet me in person?"

Cael laughed.

"You have no idea. I've heard stories about you since I was

a child. To be honest, I thought it was all made up. A fairy tale to keep us content herding goats."

"Nothing would keep you content herding goats," Henry said.

Cael shrugged.

"They're not terribly exciting. And they smell."

"They're nicer than most people. With a goat, at least you know where you stand."

"Henry likes herding goats," Eva whispered to Lina. "He'd rather do that than be a prince at the castle. He's crazy."

"Eva, what are you telling her?" Henry said.

Lina squeezed Eva's shoulder to quiet her.

"Nothing. Now, are we ready to investigate the cave?"

All three nodded.

"I can't believe it was here all along," Cael said. "We bring our goats to graze here all the time. We were so close to you."

Lina unlocked the door with her ring. Henry and Cael helped her pull the rock open. Eva darted inside.

"Eva! Come back!"

"It's dark in here! I'm in Evangelina's Temple!"

Eva's voice echoed through the cave. She laughed.

"Light. Illuminate," Lina said.

Her diamond lit the cavern with a soft glow. She located Eva and pulled her back.

"Don't run off like that! What if Nog had been in here?"

"Oh. I didn't think of that. Is he?"

Lina sniffed.

"No. We'd smell him."

Cael nodded.

"That thing smells worse than the goats. Normally my senses are dull when I'm wielding light, but the stench was overwhelming."

"Your senses should be stronger when you're wielding

light," Lina said. "You should be able to sense more in both realms."

Henry adjusted his hat.

"I'm afraid we're not very accomplished light wielders. We don't have a teacher. You can only learn so much from scrolls, and not many of those survived the war."

"Oh. Maybe I can teach you a few things. Luca was always bragging to me about his technique."

"You know Luca's techniques?" Cael asked.

"Of course she does," Henry said. "Luca's her brother. They trained together."

Cael cleared his throat.

"Yes. Forgive me. It's just, the possibility of learning something like that is overwhelming. Luca was one of the strongest light wielders in history!"

Lina snickered.

"Really? Does it say that in his scrolls?"

"Um, yes. Wasn't he?"

"He was strong, but he was also a bragger. I wouldn't take his assessment of his own abilities too seriously. Still, I'm happy to show you what I know."

Cael's face fell. He scuffed his feet along the cavern floor. It kicked up a small cloud of dust.

"Luca is his personal hero," Henry said. "He's always wanted to be an adventurer just like him. Be careful what you say. He'll take it personally."

Lina considered this. Luca as someone's personal hero? Especially someone as serious as Cael seemed to be? Luca had been too busy playing pranks to practice magic. She stifled her laugh when she glimpsed the expression on Cael's face. She put her hand on his shoulder instead.

"I'm glad Luca has admirers. He was a good brother and a good warrior. My best friend. He deserves better than to be remembered as a talking donkey."

Cael smiled at her.

"You'll have to tell me about him sometime, Lina."

"I'd like that."

Ahead of them, Eva peeked her head out of the door to the sleeping chamber.

"Is this where you slept? No wonder you were so dirty!"

"Yes, that's the place. If I'd known I would sleep for a century, I would have set some cleaning charms."

Lina examined the floor. Eva's footprints crisscrossed with hers, but nothing else disturbed the thick layer of dust.

"Nog hasn't been here," she said. "There would be footprints. He would have smashed everything."

Cael and Henry paused in the doorway. They stared at the cavern with wide eyes until Lina felt awkward.

"Welcome to Evangelina's Temple," she said.

She was trying to lighten the mood, but the brothers kept staring.

"We should take off our hats, right?" Henry said. "That's a respectful gesture, right?"

He slid his hat from his head, revealing a tangled mess of brown curls. Cael left his on. He stood frozen, not even blinking, as he examined every corner of the room.

"Ben will be sorry he missed this," Henry said. "He's more scholarly than the rest of us."

"Except for Prince Marcus!" Eva said. "He comes up the mountain all the time and asks me questions about Evangelina and goats."

"Marcus?" Lina asked.

"The king's youngest son. He and Benjamin are studying at the same school. He is something of a scholar. Even more so than Alaric."

"He said he'd tell me if he found any scrolls about shadow magic," Eva said. "He's been researching it."

"Oh. That is interesting," Lina said. "He doesn't know the truth about you?"

Henry shook his head. Cael finally snapped out of his daze and answered.

"No. No one does. It wasn't our secret to tell."

Lina pushed a strand of hair away from her face.

"We'd better start searching for Nog. If he tried that hard to break into the cave, I don't think he'll be far away. He'll be in the realm of shadows until nightfall, but we may still be able to track him."

Cael's attention was on the mirror.

"Did Luca enchant this?"

Lina nodded. Cael placed his palm on it. A spark of light crackled from his hand across the surface of the glass. Cael pulled his hand away, and the mirror shattered. He jumped back.

"Lady Evangelina, I am so sorry! I thought I could restore the enchantment! I didn't mean to destroy it! I should have asked your permission before touching it."

Lina pulled Eva away from the broken glass.

"Cael, it's fine. You didn't mean to break it. The enchantment was gone, anyway."

Cael stared at the broken glass like he might cry.

"It was a relic," he said. "An antique. Priceless. I'm so sorry."

Henry pulled his brother away.

"Calm down, Cael. It's just a mirror. We need to find Nog."

Lina nodded.

"Now that we have proof Nog was here, do you think you could convince Marta to take the princesses back to the castle? I don't want to risk their safety."

Henry's jaw dropped.

"Mother brought the princesses here? Why didn't you tell her there was a goblin loose?"

Lina bristled.

"I did. She wouldn't listen to me."

Cael made a face.

"Of course she wouldn't. She's stubborn. And she's always had too much confidence in our abilities. I'll try to talk some sense into her. You and Henry can search for signs of the goblin."

Lina smiled at him.

"Take Eva with you. I don't want to put her in any danger."

Eva looked up from where she had been drawing hearts in the thick dust on the floor.

"I don't mind. I can help."

Cael put his hand on her shoulder and edged her towards the door.

"You can help me convince mother to return to the castle."

Eva brightened.

"Will the princesses be there?"

"Yes. All of them."

"Let's go!"

Eva grabbed Cael's hand and pulled him down the hallway. Lina and Henry jogged behind them. They stopped when they reached the cavern door.

Dark clouds had gathered in the sky while they were in the cave. The edge of a storm crawled over the mountains, blocking the sun.

"Run, Cael," Lina said. "Those clouds could be trouble. Get the princesses out of here."

❧ 37 ☙

Alaric studied Carina's face. He couldn't guess her thoughts. Her face was smooth as a statue. Empty. Alaric gulped. This was it.

"Princess, I am sure you have guessed my intentions. You are a woman of rare intelligence and charm."

Carina blinked at him. She looked anything but charming. She yawned, making her look even less intelligent than usual.

Now or never. For Aeonia. Alaric pulled the ring out of his pocket. Carina flinched. The green stone shimmered in the sunlight. Alaric dropped to his knee in a patch of snowbells.

"Princess, will you do me the honor-"

Carina made a face.

"What's that smell?"

Alaric blinked.

"I beg your pardon, Princess?"

"That smell. What is it?"

"Snowbells. We're surrounded by them. I thought it would make the moment romantic."

"I'm not talking about the flowers. Idiot."

Alaric stood and gritted his teeth. Now or never. For Aeonia.

"Princess, please do me the honor of becoming–"

The smell hit him like a slap in the face. His eyes watered.

"What is that?" he said.

Carina stretched her sleeve over her nose.

"I don't know. I've never smelled anything so bad in my life."

"Neither have I, and my stepbrothers herd goats."

Alaric slipped the ring back into his pocket. He couldn't do it. Not when this wretched scent made him gag every time he breathed. Part of him felt relieved. Part of him wanted to throw up.

"Oh," Carina's eyes widened. "I think I know what's causing this."

Alaric waited. Speaking meant breathing more. He pulled his cloak around his shoulder and covered the bottom half of his face with it.

"Goblin," Carina said.

"What?"

"A goblin. I imagine a creature of darkness would have a certain aroma."

Alaric blinked at her.

"I'm sure they don't smell good. But why is your first thought that there's a goblin? They're not real."

Carina shook her head at him and ran up the mountain. Towards the smell as far as Alaric could tell. He ran after her.

"Princess, come back!"

"Lina's up here! She might be in trouble."

Alaric caught up to her.

"What do you mean?"

"She was hunting the goblin. She must have found it."

Alaric grabbed her shoulder and pulled her to a stop. Carina glared at him.

"Unhand me!"

"You're talking nonsense, Princess. Are you well?"

"Lina needs our help! She's in danger."

Danger. Lina had been talking about danger since her arrival. Was this where she had gotten all her bruises? Had she managed to sneak out of the castle to battle-

To battle what, exactly?

Not a goblin, but certainly nothing pleasant.

"You're not making sense, Princess. We should to get back to the picnic."

"We need to get to Lina!"

Alaric sighed. He gagged on the stench.

"I'll go get Lina."

"I'm coming with you!"

"I am not letting a Princess of Santelle run up a mountain to face an unknown danger!"

"That is exactly the sort of situation when you need a Princess of Santelle!"

Carina looked far from bland now. She looked absolutely fierce. She pushed Alaric's hand off her shoulder.

"I'm not leaving Lina alone up there. We've wasted too much time already."

"Carina, please. Go tell the others to get in the carriages. Smell or not, I don't like the look of those clouds. We don't want to be trapped up here in a storm. I'll find Lina and bring her back."

Carina crossed her arms.

"So we're on a first name basis now, Prince Alaric?"

"Blast. I'm sorry. Will you go? Make sure the others get home safely? They can leave horses for me and Lina. My step-mother can be stubborn. She might refuse to leave without you."

Carina studied his face.

"It isn't a bad plan," she said at last. "But if you let

anything happen to Lina, I will push you off a tower. And it won't be made of mattresses."

So Marta had been right after all. Carina wasn't bland. Alaric lowered his arm so she could see his face.

"I'll bring Lina back safely. I promise."

Carina narrowed her eyes. Then she nodded and ran down the hill. Alaric ran up.

The stench got worse as he climbed. Yes, it was coming from somewhere up the mountain. Storm clouds billowed over the peaks. They needed to find shelter immediately.

A goblin, Carina had said. That was nonsense. Goblins weren't real.

"Lina!"

Alaric realized he had no idea where to find her. Instinct led him back to Evangelina's Temple. That had always been his place. He couldn't explain it, but that was where he needed to look.

Mist swirled around him. Alaric ran faster. Something was very wrong. This sort of mist was common higher up the mountain, but it shouldn't be at the base. It was like all of nature wanted to block the sun. To make him lose his way.

Alaric could find the Temple in the dark. He had done it before. He saw the two figures before he saw the wreckage of what had once been his favorite place in Aeonia. Someone, or perhaps something, had dug up the earth around the rock. Shards of white littered the ground. Bone? He ignored it and ran towards the figures.

Lina and Henry stood in front of a hole in the mountain. That hadn't been there before. It had been a mossy rock. They were arguing.

"I won't leave you alone," Henry said. "What if he attacks your body while you're in a trance?"

"I'll lock the cave. You need to get between him and the princesses. The clouds are blocking the sun, but it's still daylight. You'll be stronger than him. You can drive him up this way."

"So he can attack you? I'm not leaving."

They both dropped to fighting stances when Alaric appeared. And they both sagged with relief when they saw it was him.

"Alaric!" Henry said. "Thank goodness! Tell Lina there's no way she can stay up here alone!"

Lina bristled.

"Tell him there will be an international incident if something happens to the princesses while they're in Aeonia!"

Alaric looked from Lina to Henry.

"I- When did you two meet?"

Lina grabbed his arm.

"Alaric can stay with me. He'll protect me. Is that good enough for you, Henry?"

Henry narrowed his eyes.

"Will you stay with her?"

Alaric shook his head.

"We all need to get off the mountain now. There's a storm coming."

"There's worse than that," Lina said. "Alaric will stay with me. You get to the princesses before it's too late."

Henry glared at Alaric.

"You won't leave her alone?"

"Of course not. But-"

"Good enough for me."

Henry saluted Lina and jogged down the mountain. Alaric turned to her.

"What is going on? What are you doing up here?"

Lina let go of his arm and stared into the storm.

"I can't leave, but you don't have to stay. It's dangerous here. Especially for you since you don't have magic."

"I'm a trained soldier. I can handle this. Whatever this is."

Lina grinned at him.

"You think so? Wait until you see it."

Her expression made Alaric pause. He swallowed.

"What is it exactly? What's causing that smell?"

"A goblin. The smell is the most harmless thing about it."

"A goblin? That's what Carina said. Why does everyone think there's a goblin here? They don't exist!"

Lina turned to face him. She reached for his hand then thought better of it and pulled away.

"Alaric, I need to tell you something. I'll understand if you don't believe me, but please listen. Please try."

Alaric nodded. This was it. Whatever she said, he was prepared to hear it. He had considered everything. A spy. An assassin. A princess from a disgraced kingdom.

"My name is Evangelina Shadow-Storm. I awoke from my enchanted sleep a few days ago, and a goblin called Nog awoke with me. I'm real. I'm here to protect Aeonia, just like I did a hundred years ago. Luca erased all historical records of me to keep me safe while I slept. He was my brother. Not a donkey. Oh, and I don't turn into a goat."

Alaric's jaw dropped. So much for being prepared. He was vaguely aware that his mouth was hanging open. That he looked ridiculous.

"You what?" he said.

"I don't turn into a goat."

That hadn't really been the shocking part, but Lina had her arms crossed, ready to fight him if he contradicted her. He didn't plan on it. He met her gaze. Her green eyes stared straight into his.

He searched them. Searched her face. The story was unbelievable. Impossible.

So why did he think it was the truth?

"You said you were a princess. Or noble, at least."

"I am if you get technical with my genealogy. My grandmother was a distant relative of King Dacian."

"Why did you sneak into the princess test?"

"I thought some of the Council members would remember me, and I wanted their help to defeat Nog. Believe me, I didn't seek out the King of Gaveron because he's a charming man."

Alaric managed to close his mouth. He was getting a bad taste from the stench. The sky above them darkened as ominous clouds rolled over the mountain.

"And when you climbed the castle tower?"

"I was checking a secret room. We stored enchanted weapons there in my century. It was empty."

"The archives?"

"I was doing the same as you. Searching for proof of myself to see how long I'd been asleep. Alaric, think about it. Why else would I appear on your doorstep in the middle of the night? Why else would I refuse your offers of help when I clearly needed it? Why would I keep asking about Evangelina Shadow-Storm? Why would your play upset me so much?"

Why indeed? Alaric studied Lina's green eyes.

"Evangelina Shadow-Storm?" he said. "You're really Evangelina Shadow-Storm?"

Lina nodded. Alaric shook his head.

"That's impossible. She's not real. I've tried to prove her existence. I searched every record. Every scroll in the archive."

Lina raised an eyebrow.

"Every scroll? Talk about impossible."

"Alright, every scroll in the histories. Hundreds, anyway. There was nothing. Not a single mention of her. Of you."

"Because Luca made sure of it. Alaric, I went to sleep a few years before King Thaddeus was overthrown. Before the royal family was killed. They would have hunted me down. Luca erased me from the records to protect me."

Alaric's stomach churned. It had nothing to do with the smell.

"Those were my ancestors. They killed your family. Lina-Evangelina, I'm so sorry."

Lina blinked at him.

"You believe me?"

Alaric nodded. He did. He trusted her. Even when she told him the impossible. He swallowed.

"You must hate me. They would have killed your brother. Luca."

He turned away. Alaric had never been proud of his forefather's actions. Yes, some action had been necessary. King Thaddeus had wronged the people of Aeonia many times, but his ancestors should never have hunted down the innocent.

Lina rested her hand on his shoulder. He flinched.

"I swear I've been trying to make it right. I just want Aeonia to have peace. They hunted them down. Every member of your family. Lina, I know you must hate me."

"They didn't," Lina said. "And I don't."

She pulled his arm until he turned around to face her. He stood still and looked over her head. He couldn't meet her gaze.

Lina stepped closer. Alaric stood his ground. Whatever revenge she wanted to take, he was prepared for it. He would answer for his forefathers' crimes.

Had she brought a weapon? She was a shadow warrior. Surely she had. Was she going to kill him?

Alaric swallowed. He would let her. Maybe that was foolish, but he would. He wouldn't defend himself. He couldn't bear to hurt her. Alaric lowered his head and closed his eyes.

Lina stood on her tiptoes and kissed him.

❧ 38 ❧

He trusted her. The anguish on his face twisted Lina's heart. He took responsibility for his forefathers' actions even now. He was impossibly noble. The noblest man she'd ever met.

She stood on her tiptoes and kissed him.

Alaric didn't respond. He didn't move. Didn't breathe.

Lina stepped back. He believed her. She was impossible, and he believed her in a heartbeat. He trusted her.

Alaric looked shocked. The kiss seemed to have startled him more than her story. He stared at her, his eyes wide with disbelief. Thunder rumbled in the distance.

In retrospect, kissing him may not have been the best way to show she appreciated his trust. Lina's heart sank. What had she expected? That he would kiss her back? That he would love her?

She had ruined everything.

Why had she kissed him?

She thought he liked her. That only the Princess Test and her mysterious origins had kept him from pursuing her.

"I'm sorry," she said. "I shouldn't have done that."

Her voice was little more than a whisper.

Alaric's mouth moved, but no sound came out. Clearly he was in shock. Clearly she had been out of line.

Blast! What was she thinking? A goblin was materializing in the realm of light, and she was kissing a prince! She had never been this stupid in her own century.

She hadn't known anyone like Alaric in her century.

Lina wiped the tears away from her eyes. It was the stench. It had to be. The smell had affected her head. Clouded her judgment.

She had smelled goblins before. Worse than this. She hadn't kissed anyone then.

She glanced at Alaric. He gave up trying to speak and stood tall with his mouth closed, watching her every move.

A red lightning bolt pierced the sky. The flash showed a hulking silhouette in the mist. Horned head. Massive arms. Alaric's jaw dropped again.

"Is that?" he rasped.

Lina nodded.

"Nog the goblin. He escaped the seal and is taking a physical form in the realm of light. Normally we'd be safe until sunset, but these clouds are blocking the sun. He may be able to materialize sooner because of it."

"We need to warn everyone. The princesses-"

"Should be on their way home by now. Marta knows who I am. She knows about Nog. She'll take them to safety."

Alaric swallowed.

"Marta knows?"

"Yes. Your ancestors weren't as thorough as they thought. Some of the royal family escaped. They've been living as goat herders for the past hundred years."

"You mean Marta is noble? A descendant of the original royal family?"

Lina nodded. Alaric frowned.

"I always thought I was generous for welcoming my step-brothers into the castle. For treating them like princes in spite of their background. All this time, they were being nice to me. I was the newcomer."

Lina laughed.

"You're as much a prince as they are. From what I've read, your family has ruled well. You have nothing to be ashamed of. You'll be a great king."

"What? No, I can't now. It should be Cael. Or you. You're technically the oldest member of the royal family now."

Lina frowned. Was that why he didn't want to kiss her?

"You think I'm old?"

"What? Um, no. I mean- you were born first. Before them. Right?"

"Yes, but I didn't age while I slept. This could get confusing. You'd better just take the throne and leave it at that."

"But if you take the throne, the other countries will stop trying to annex us."

"They'll stop trying to what?"

"The King of Gaveron thinks I'm not fit to rule because I'm not noble enough. He has proposed that Gaveron should assume the rule of Aeonia so the people could benefit from a truly noble king."

Lina bristled.

"That's ridiculous! How dare he!"

"But you could solve the problem. He'd have to respect your right to rule. We could even cancel the Princess Test."

He flushed and looked away. Lina watched him. He had mentioned this on the windowsill. Said the Council didn't respect him. But would they truly use his lineage as an excuse to take over Aeonia? No wonder he pursued Carina. If the kings didn't recognize him as a noble by birth, he could become one by marriage. He could use an alliance with Santelle to prevent the takeover.

"Alaric, is that really why you chose Carina?"

He looked straight ahead, staring into the mist.

"Of course. But now-"

He looked at her. Lina's heart stirred. Maybe he did feel something for her. Maybe-

Laughter shook the mountain. It mixed with the rumbling thunder that was getting closer by the minute. Lina stumbled as the earth quaked. Alaric caught her arm and helped her stay upright.

"Show yourself!" Lina said. "We know you're there, Nog! We're ready for you!"

"Are you, goat girl? I doubt it. Let me into that cave and maybe I'll let you live."

His voice resonated in the air around them. Thundering footsteps rumbled through the hill. The first raindrops of the storm pattered around them. Alaric tightened his grip on Lina's arm. She placed her hand over his. His arm trembled. He was nervous.

That was the sane reaction. Especially if you hadn't seen a goblin before.

Lina wasn't scared. She was angry. She had endured over a century of sleep to seal away the creatures of darkness, and this goblin wanted to undo her work? Lina stepped back and pulled Alaric with her.

"I'll guard this cave with my life," she said. "I'll keep the seal safe."

A gust of wind blew the mist away, giving them a glimpse of the goblin. He wasn't quite solid yet.

But he would be soon.

"Get in the cave," she whispered.

"Lina, we need to run. He's slow. I told Carina to leave us a horse. We can make it back to Mias."

"You want to lead him to the city? Towards all those people? No, we need to keep him here."

Alaric glanced at the hole in the mountain.

"We'll be trapped."

"We'll be safe. Get in!"

Rain fell. The storm had finally arrived. Lina pushed Alaric into the cave. Nog roared and rushed towards them. Lina pulled the door shut and pushed her ring into the stone. She clicked the latch just as Nog crashed into the mountain.

❧ 39 ❧

Alaric blinked in the darkness. Nog's blows shook the whole cavern. Bits of rock fell onto his head.

"Where are we?"

"Light. Illuminate."

A soft glow filled the cavern. It came from Lina's ring. From the diamond.

Alaric stared at it. At Lina.

"Is this your temple?"

She smiled at him.

"More like my bedroom. So you really do believe me?"

"Given everything that's happened, yes. I believed you before, but I definitely do now."

"And you see why I couldn't tell you?"

Alaric nodded. Evangelina Shadow-Storm. She was here. She was real.

He wasn't sure what to feel. He had idolized this girl since he was a child, and now she was standing right in front of him.

Alaric realized he was staring at her and cleared his throat.

"Is that goblin what injured you?"

Nog's roar echoed through the cavern. The rocks shook as he pounded at the door.

"Yes. Let's go deeper into the cave. It will be quieter there."

Alaric followed her. The stone hallway was simple. A natural formation carved until the passage was wide enough for two people to walk side by side. Nog's roars faded as they walked through the cavern. Lina ducked into a door, and Alaric followed her.

"Be careful. There's broken glass."

Lina dodged the glass and sat on a large flat stone in the middle of the room. Alaric joined her. Dust coated every inch of the cave. Someone had traced hearts in the thick grime on the cavern floor. The cave was so silent he could hear her breathing.

He still couldn't believe it. He was in the Temple of Evangelina. With Evangelina Shadow-Storm.

And she had kissed him.

Alaric was still processing that. The more he thought about it, the more he wished he had wrapped his arms around her and kissed her back. He had been too surprised to do anything more than act like an idiot.

He had been expecting a slap at best. Part of him thought she would stab him to avenge her brother. Or blast him with shadow magic. Or throw him down the mountain.

But she had kissed him.

Alaric wanted to talk about it. Wanted to try kissing her again.

But a goblin was trying to break into their cave. And it wasn't the kind that danced.

He flinched at the memory of the play. The dancing goblins. They must have seemed ridiculous to her. She had battled hundreds of goblins. She had sealed them away with the rest of the creatures of darkness. He had written a play with them dancing to a song.

Evangelina. Be my queen-ah.

He wanted to kiss her. Blast it all, they were in mortal danger! He might not get another chance!

Alaric turned, but Lina had moved. She walked around the stone bed, tracing a silver vein in the rock with her fingers. Alaric looked at it. That stone wasn't natural. The silver moved and swirled around itself like oil in water.

Alaric jumped up. He looked at Lina. She nodded.

"Yes, that's the seal. What we can see of it in the realm of light, anyway."

"I was sitting on the goblin seal? Why did you let me sit on it?"

She laughed.

"You can't hurt it. The seal exists in the realms of light and shadow. You'd have to sit on it in both realms to make a dent."

"Then why is there a goblin on our doorstep?"

She frowned.

"I don't know. The seal may have weakened when I awoke. Or Nog may have learned new magic while I slept. His power is different than what I've seen before. He seems to be using light."

"But he's a creature of darkness."

"Exactly. It is strange."

Alaric crossed his arms. Until he convinced one of his stepbrothers or Lina to take the throne, he was Crown Prince of Aeonia. And he was a military commander.

It was time to act like one.

"How can we defeat him? Maybe I can get a message through to the army."

"No. Without magic, they wouldn't stand a chance. Nog is in both realms right now, just like the seal. We'll have to fight him in both to defeat him. Unless you have a troop of shadow warriors or light wielders, they'll be useless in a fight."

"He has a physical form here. Surely some well-placed arrows couldn't hurt."

"He wouldn't even feel them. Goblins have very thick hides."

Alaric ran his hand through his hair.

"He must have a weakness."

"Goblins aren't known to be smart, but Nog seems brighter than most. They are incredibly strong. They do everything by sheer brute force. That's how they're able to exist in both realms at once. Essentially, he's pulling the realm of light around him into the realm of shadow. They overlap wherever he goes."

"Is that possible?"

"Only for something as strong as a goblin. The rest of us who travel between the realms rely on technique. I trained for five years to learn how to materialize in the realm of shadows. It takes even longer to learn how to fight."

She glared at him.

"That process does not involve turning into a goat."

He threw his hands up in surrender.

"I'm sorry! That was what the legends said! I didn't know anything else about magic. I know I keep making you mad, but it isn't on purpose!"

She sighed.

"I know. As soon as the sun sets, I'll be able to travel to the realm of shadows and attack Nog there. Your step-brothers will aid me with their light magic. It should be enough to defeat him."

"You don't sound sure. What if it isn't?"

"Then you can call the army. Maybe you'll be able to defend the city. Marta mentioned a vault full of magical items, but it only opens at night. If there are enchanted weapons there, the army could use them and possibly stand a chance."

"What about me? What can I do?"

"You'll be my personal guard."

"Don't patronize me, Lina. I don't need a pity assignment. You're a shadow warrior. You're powerful."

Lina frowned.

"You really don't know anything about this, do you? When I travel to the realm of shadows, my body stays here. For all practical purposes, I'm sleeping. I'm helpless."

"Oh."

"I need someone to watch me in the realm of light while I'm defenseless. To protect me. It's an important job. Luca used to be my guardian."

Alaric ran his hands through his hair.

"Lina, I'll protect you with my life."

She smiled.

"A sword might be a better weapon. Did you bring one?"

"Of course I didn't. I came here to propose, not fight a goblin."

Lina's face fell. Alaric wished he could take back the words. They sounded too much like a complaint. An accusation. He wasn't upset that the proposal had been delayed. If anything, he should thank Nog for the diversion.

"We'll have to improvise then," Lina said. "A weapon enchanted with light magic would be best. You'll be a light wielder. Sort of."

Lina picked up a long, jagged piece of the broken mirror. It sparked in her hands. She traced the surface with her finger, and a black bolt of lightning flashed across the glass.

Alaric jumped.

"That's amazing!"

She grinned.

"It's nothing. Cael blasted this with light magic earlier. Let's see if he did any good."

She hit the mirror against the side of the cave. It didn't break. Lina tore the hem off her skirt and wrapped it around the thinnest edge of the glass to make a handle. She handed the weapon to Alaric.

"There. You are now a light wielder."

Alaric took the glass and weighed it in his hand. It looked like a jagged dagger. He touched the reflective surface. The glass sparked.

"Ouch! That burned."

"Why do you think I made a handle? You aren't trained in magic. You don't know how to handle it. Don't touch it again. You'll ruin the enchantment."

Alaric examined the mirror.

"There's something moving on it. Lights. Those aren't in the cavern, are they?"

Lina glanced at the mirror.

"No. The mirror's original purpose was to provide a portal to check on the seal. It lets you see between the realms. That's a reflection of stars in the realm of shadows. What light wielders look like there. They're your stepbrothers."

"Oh."

Alaric tried to think of something intelligent to say, but he knew nothing about magic. Not real magic, anyway. If magic had been the same as it was in the legends, he would have plenty to talk about.

Best not to mention that though. Apparently Lina was sensitive about the goat thing.

Alaric turned the glass over in his hands. He gasped.

"I see Nog!"

Lina nodded.

"You'll be able to see everything that happens in the realm of shadows. Including me once I'm there. You might hear me if you listen closely. Normally you'd need training for that, but Nog's presence has pulled the realms closer together."

Alaric looked into the mirror again. The stars buzzed around Nog's head.

"They're attacking him," he said.

Lina smirked.

"They're just bothering him. Like flies."

"Oh. So they're not powerful light wielders?"

"Not even close. They have potential, but they haven't had anyone to train them. I hope they've managed to pick up a few tricks though. I'll need a light wielder's help to defeat Nog."

"It won't be that dangerous, right? You've fought goblins before."

Lina grimaced.

"Yes, but I had help. And more weapons. All I have is one gem."

She pulled a round, green gem from her sleeve. Alaric gasped.

"That's an emerald, right?"

She nodded.

"Luca always called them peas. This was the eye of the protective wolf statue. I found it when I woke up. Nog destroyed the statue and other gem."

"No, he didn't."

Alaric pulled the ring from his pocket. Lina's eyes widened.

"The other pea! How did you get it?"

"I found it years ago when I was a boy. This is what made me believe in Evangelina Shadow-Storm."

"So you made it into a ring?"

"It means a lot to me. I wanted my bride to have it."

"Oh. Oh! You were going to propose to Carina with this!"

Alaric nodded. Thank goodness he hadn't. This ring

belonged to Lina, even if she wasn't his bride. He took her hand and slipped the ring onto her finger. It sparkled in the light of her diamond.

"A perfect fit," he said. "I hope this helps you defeat Nog."

Her eyes glistened.

"Alaric, you don't know what this means. To have the other pea. I-"

Nog's roar echoed through the mountain. Pebbles fell from the ceiling as the cavern shook. Lina's face turned grim.

"The sun just set. Nog's at his full power. I need to travel to the realm of shadows now."

❧ 40 ❧

The shadows pulled at Lina. They were stronger than usual. It made sense. The realm of shadows was closer thanks to Nog. She gathered them and wrapped them around her like a cloak. She couldn't delay her confrontation with Nog for a single moment.

Lina lay on the rock bed, on top of the seal, and smiled at Alaric. Part of her wanted to fight off the shadows. To stay and talk to him. She wanted to hear the story of how he found the pea.

She wanted to tease him about giving her an engagement ring. Wanted it to mean something.

But now wasn't the time. Now, she was just grateful that she had another weapon.

Lina grinned and winked at Alaric. Then she closed her eyes and sank into a trance. She appeared in the realm of shadows.

Ugh. The whole place smelled like goblin. Ghostly raindrops hovered around her. Nog hadn't pulled the realms close enough to make them solid, but she could see the results of the storm in the realm of light. Lightning flashes lit the darkness with an eerie glow.

She jumped to the seal and checked it. Her patch on the seal held. No more goblins would escape.

Now she just needed to take care of Nog.

Lina followed the stench. She considered using magic to block her sense of smell, but decided against it. The smell was the only way she could track him.

Three stars appeared over her head.

"Cael, Henry, and Benjamin, right?"

The stars flashed brighter. Lina smiled.

"I'm glad you're here. Nog is trying to break into the cave to get to the seal. Alaric and I locked him out, but I'm not sure how long the door will hold. Nog destroyed all the charms set up to protect it."

The stars flashed again. Lina wished they were strong enough light wielders to talk to her. That would make this a lot easier.

The stench grew worse. Lina stared up ahead. Nog stood in a pool of light. The mountain was visible around him. Lina could see faint outlines of the rock, the cavern door, and the field of snowbells.

She raised her left hand to her lips.

"Spear," she whispered.

The green light from the pea emerald in Alaric's ring mixed with the white light from her diamond. They stretched into a spear with a jagged point. Lina threw the spear as hard as she could. It flew through the air and landed in Nog's left shoulder.

Nog grunted and continued to hammer the rock with his fists. Water ran down his massive arms. Lina jumped towards him. She changed the other pea into a sword in midair. Nog was preoccupied with the rock. If she landed a few blows, she might be able to force him back to the realm of shadows.

Without looking away from the rock, Nog reached his hand up and backhanded Lina. The blow caught her chin. She staggered back. It didn't hurt as much as it should have. She caught her breath and studied Nog.

He was less solid than he should have been.

"You're trying to leave the realm of shadows!"

Nog turned and laughed at her.

"Wrong, goat girl. I'm pulling the realm of light completely into the realm of shadows. Your protective charms are holding this rock together, but that won't do any good when I pull it into my domain."

"That isn't possible!"

"Watch me."

Lina formed the second pea into another spear. She threw it at Nog's chest. It lodged where his heart should be, but he didn't stop digging.

"That was your mistake, goat girl. Thinking you could do this on your own."

"I'm not on my own. I have stars."

Nog laughed.

"Those pathetic pinpricks of light? They're not strong enough to hurt me."

Nog raised his hand and blasted the stars with a bolt of red lightning. They disappeared.

"No!"

Lina reached out with her senses, but the princes were gone. She and the goblin were alone in the realm of shadows. Nog laughed.

"Don't worry. They're not dead. Not worth killing. Who takes the time to swat every gnat that comes their way?"

"They'll be back."

"I doubt it. So what will you do now? It takes the power of shadow and light to defeat me. You're only shadows."

Lina dissolved her spears and formed the light from the

two pea emeralds and the diamond into an enormous sword. She couldn't defeat Nog without help from a light wielder. Not entirely. But maybe she could slow him down long enough for the stars to return.

🎐 41 🎐

Alaric watched Lina. She hadn't moved since winking at him and collapsing into a deep sleep. Her diamond ring still lit the cavern.

Not that there was much to see. Alaric picked his way around the shattered glass on the floor and walked the perimeter. He had always pictured the Temple of Evangelina as a grand structure. Something as intricate as the archives. Gleaming marble that crackled with magic.

Maybe this cavern had been magnificent once, but now it felt oppressive. He couldn't imagine staying here a few days, let alone a hundred years.

He finished his patrol, such as it was, and returned to Lina's side. She flinched in her sleep. A fresh bruise blossomed on her chin and spread up her cheek. He watched the purple mark crawl across her skin until it covered half her face.

Alaric gritted his teeth. Some protector he was. Some warrior. He felt useless, sitting here while she fought. Watching new injuries appear. Surely there was something he could do.

He held up the mirror fragment. At least Lina had his stepbrothers. She wasn't fighting alone. He blinked at his reflection. Lina's green eyes blinked back at him. He jumped and almost dropped the mirror.

He was looking at Evangelina Shadow-Storm in the realm of shadows! Alaric twisted the mirror to get a better view.

Lina stood in a field of faint snowbells. She wore a flowing black gown with a cape that billowed behind her like a cloud. She moved with impossible grace. Like she weighed nothing at all. She looked just like Alaric had always imagined she would.

Except she wasn't part goat. That was good. He liked her better as a human.

Lina held an enormous sword made of green light. She jumped around the goblin, attacking him in an impressive display of swordsmanship. Nog parried with his bare fists. He blasted red light at Lina, but she dodged.

Lina kept fighting, but she wasn't causing any damage. The goblin barely noticed her blows. Lina had said this would happen. She needed to work with a light wielder. With his brothers.

Alaric's stomach dropped. He studied the mirror from every angle. Apart from Lina and Nog, he saw only darkness.

Where were the light wielders? Where were the stars?

He turned back to Lina's sleeping form. Was it his imagination, or did her face look troubled? He checked the mirror. Lina definitely looked worried. Something had gone wrong.

Alaric knelt by Lina's side.

"Tell me what to do," he whispered both to her body and the mirror. "How can I help you?"

❧ 42 ❧

It wasn't working. Lina kept jumping around Nog. Kept hitting him with the sword. Nog batted away her strokes and kept working on the door. Scratching at it. Trying to dig through.

He had made a dent.

Blast it all! Lina stepped back. The sword wasn't doing any damage. Even with the extra gem, she was still shadow fighting darkness. She needed light!

A faint glimmer appeared by Lina's side. Not quite a star. Fainter than that. The presence felt familiar.

"Tell me what to do," the light said. "How can I help you?"

"Alaric?"

"Lina?"

The voice was faint, but it was definitely him.

Lina jumped high in the air and hovered above Nog. The glimmer of light followed her.

"How are you doing this?" Lina asked.

"I don't know. I'm just talking into the mirror. Lina, are you alright?"

"No. My attacks aren't working, and Nog pushed your

brothers away. He's in both realms. I can't defeat him without a light wielder's help."

"So let me help you."

"Alaric-"

"I have an enchanted weapon. You said yourself that counted."

"I said it sort of counted. Alaric, your brothers have trained as light wielders, and Nog defeated them without lifting a finger."

"Lina, I'm going to help. Whatever this magic is, however I'm wielding it, I will use it to protect you and get rid of that goblin."

Lina glared at the star.

"Alaric-"

"Don't argue."

"I wasn't going to argue. I was going to tell you this will be dangerous. You might be seriously hurt. You might die."

"I'm ready. Tell me what I need to do."

"You can't travel between the realms, so you'll attack Nog in the realm of light. He's pulled the realms together anyway, so it should be possible. You'll have to get close enough to stab him with the mirror. It won't be easy. I'll draw him away from the cave so you can get out. You'll need my diamond ring to unlock the door. Get ready and wait for my signal."

Alaric nodded. Lina shuddered as the diamond ring disappeared from her hand. She pushed the pea emerald ring back further on her finger to fill the empty spot. Below her, the goblin continued to dig at the rock.

"Hey, Nog!"

Lina wrapped the green light from the emeralds around her wrists. The gauntlets added power to her blows. She dropped from the sky. Nog tried to swat her away, but she was ready for him this time. She dodged and landed a blow on the goblin's right eye.

Nog grunted. Lina sent a burst of shadow magic into the blow and jumped back. Nog rubbed his eye and stood to his full height.

"Leave me to my work, goat girl. Go enjoy your last moments of life."

"You know what I would really enjoy? Punching you in the face again."

Nog laughed.

"You think you could land another such blow? You are nothing. A sorry excuse for a warrior. Without your gems, you are weaker than a goat."

Lina grinned at him.

"Is that a challenge? I accept."

Her heart beat fast as she pulled the magical gauntlets back into the emeralds.

"You and me," she said. "No fancy light magic. No enchanted gems. One shadow warrior against another."

Nog turned from the rock. He regarded Lina with his fierce red eyes.

"As if I would fall for that. You will lure me close and use the gems once I am within range. Not that they would hurt me."

Lina's heart sank. She had hoped he wouldn't realize that was a possibility. He definitely was smarter than most goblins. But she needed to keep up the front. If she could lead him just a little further from the cavern, Alaric could escape and join the fight.

Lina pulled the emerald ring off her finger. She put both peas in her palm and waved her hand. The gems disappeared. Nog raised a shaggy eyebrow.

"You really are a fool, goat girl."

"Well, can I help it if you're too scared to fight me when I have weapons?"

Nog grunted.

"I'm not scared of you."

"Prove it."

Lina raised her hands over her head. Her cape billowed behind her. She felt vulnerable. Exposed. She hadn't been in the realm of shadows without enchanted gems to protect her since she was a little girl.

Nog grinned. He stepped away from the door. Lina backed up the mountain. She pursed her lips as if she were nervous. As if she was having second thoughts.

Nog roared and rushed towards her. Lina sent a bolt of shadow magic to trip him and jumped further away. The magic brushed harmlessly against Nog's ankles. He turned and reached for Lina. She risked another blast of magic, and Nog's fist connected with her side. Something cracked. Her ribs again.

Lina jumped back. The cracked rib made breathing painful. Good thing she didn't need to breathe in the realm of shadows. She would deal with the consequences in the realm of light later.

Lina ran a few steps away. Please let him think she was retreating. Let him pursue her.

Nog pursued. He was almost far enough away from the door now. His eyes glowed red with the thrill of battle. Lina sent another blast of shadow magic. It blew past his face like a spring breeze. Nog's laughter filled the air.

"Foolish goat. I am a creature of darkness. I stand in both realms. Your shadow magic has no effect on me."

Lina made her eyes go wide. As if she hadn't known that. As if that hadn't been the problem all along. Nog was strong, but he underestimated her training. She jumped and landed on the next hillside up the mountain. Out of sight of the door. Nog followed. He was far enough away now. Lina turned to the glimmer of light by her side.

"Alaric," she whispered.

Nog reached the top of the hill. His eyes gleamed with fury.

"Nothing can save you now, shadow warrior. You are alone."

"Alaric," Lina whispered. "Go."

She gathered shadow magic around her fists and lunged at Nog.

❧ 43 ❧

Alaric searched the stone door for the keyhole. It shook as the goblin pounded from the outside. He watched Lina's face in the shard of mirror. She taunted the goblin. Tried to draw him away.

Something appeared in Alaric's hand. He jumped and examined it in the diamond's soft glow.

The emerald ring and Lina's gem.

Lina said these gave her power. Made her stronger. Why would she give them to him? He couldn't use them. He didn't know how.

Alaric slipped the ring onto his fingertip and put the gem in his pocket. He turned his attention back to the rock. There. A tiny opening near the bottom. He slipped the diamond into the keyhole. He would be ready whenever Lina gave him the signal.

The mirror showed Nog's fist slam into Lina's side. Pain flashed across her face. Alaric watched her agony and gritted his teeth. He couldn't stand this waiting.

They seemed to be covering ground. Moving away. The

scenery around Lina blurred as she retreated. Was Nog following her? Was it safe to open the door?

"Alaric."

Alaric stared at the mirror. Was that the signal? Was Lina ready?

"Alaric, go."

Alaric turned the ring. Something inside the stone clicked. He pushed the door open and stepped into the night. Rain pelted his face, and the goblin's stench washed over him. He pushed the stone shut and felt for the keyhole so he could lock the door.

Wherever it had been, it was gone now. Nog's scratches had destroyed the surface of the rock.

He would have to leave the cave unlocked. Leave Lina's body unguarded.

He needed to defeat the goblin quickly.

Alaric examined the mountain. He couldn't see much. The storm clouds blocked any light from the moon or stars, and the rain ran into his eyes.

Nog was nowhere in sight. Where had Lina led him? He looked at the mirror, searching for a clue.

"Follow the smell," Lina whispered.

Her face was a blur in the mirror. Whatever she was doing, she was moving fast. Her hair flew around her face, masking her expression. Alaric took a deep breath and gagged on the odor. He turned in a circle, sniffing.

There. It was stronger uphill. Flashes of lightning lit the mountain and showed a trail of muddy footprints. Alaric gripped the mirror tighter and ran.

The smell grew overpowering as he climbed the mountain. He heard the goblin before he saw him. Nog's footsteps shook the ground. His laughter filled the air.

"Foolish goat! Did you really think you could defeat me?"

Alaric paused. Nog waved his fists in the air. An aura of darkness surrounded the creature, but strangely it made him easier to see. This must be the goblin's magic. The rain slowed to a drizzle, although Alaric could still hear it pouring down around him. A wisp of shadow hovered around the goblin.

Lina.

She was a dim outline, but it was easier to see her here than in the mirror. She looked just like Alaric had always imagined she would. Well, minus the goat part. Her shadow clothes billowed around her. Her face was fierce. She was nimble and agile as she leaped around Nog. She landed blow after blow on his face, dodging his massive arms.

Alaric stepped towards them. The air chilled. His skin crawled. Something wasn't right. The air felt wrong somehow. That must be the effect of the goblin pulling light into shadow.

The goblin and Lina grew even clearer, and the mountainside grew dim. The rain stopped hitting him entirely, although he could still see ghostly silhouettes of drops falling.

"This is pointless," Nog growled. "I'm tired of your games, goat."

His hands glowed red. He hurled a wave of magic at Lina. It wasn't sophisticated like her magic. It was raw power and hatred wrapped in red light.

Lina jumped away, but the spell caught the edge of her cape. Lina's mouth opened in a silent scream as the fire consumed the fabric and burned around her. Alaric studied her face in the mirror. That was a clearer image, and it twisted his heart. Lina was in pain. Lina was in trouble.

Alaric circled around until he was at the goblin's back. Nog stared at Lina as she tried to extinguish the flames. She gathered shadow magic in her fists, but it had no effect on the red light. She collapsed on the ground and didn't move.

Nog walked toward her slowly, savoring the moment. His laughter shook the mountain.

This was his chance. The goblin was distracted. Alaric ran and jumped. He climbed Nog's back and stabbed him in the neck.

The goblin roared when the glass touched his skin. It cut through his hide as if it were made of paper. Nog regained his balance and threw Alaric off his back. Alaric crashed into a patch of snowbells. The fall knocked his breath out, but he jumped up and faced the goblin.

A shimmering scar marked the place he had cut Nog. The goblin reached his muscle bound arms up and scratched at it. He narrowed his eyes and turned his full attention to Alaric.

"Who are you?"

Alaric stood tall and tried not to look winded.

"I am Crown Prince Alaric of Aeonia."

Nog laughed.

"That's all? You have no magical title? No honor earned in battle? How is it that you are able to wield the light?"

Alaric glanced at the mirror. It glowed bright white. He wasn't exactly sure how it worked. The important thing was that it did. He raised the mirror above his head in what he hoped was a triumphant gesture.

"The light will be wielded by those who protect it."

He was pretty sure that was true. At least, it was a line from his play.

Nog laughed so hard he bent over to rest his hands on his knees.

"You are funny, prince without a title."

He kept laughing. Alaric glared at him. It wasn't that funny. It was a good line. Dramatic. Poignant. The audience had loved it.

No. This wasn't the time to feel self-conscious about that blasted play. Alaric looked at Lina. Maybe he could aid her while Nog laughed. He slid the diamond ring off his finger and threw it at her. He pulled the pea out of his pocket and threw that as well. They went through her and landed in the mud below her stomach.

Right, she wasn't really there. She was in another realm.

Nog frowned.

"What are you trying to do, wielder of nothing?"

"Nothing," Alaric said.

Nog looked from Alaric to Lina. She lay still on the ground. The flames had burned out and turned into a sick wisping smoke that hovered around her body. The goblin laughed.

"You are amusing at least. If you can't have a warrior, a clown will do. She must be desperate indeed. The shadow warrior cannot fight alone, but being alone might be better than working with a weakling like you. Run back to your castle, Prince Nothing. I seek only to free the darkness and devour the light. Perhaps you can find a safe corner of the world to hide. Perhaps you can survive."

Alaric shifted his weight into a fighting stance. It worried him that Lina was still down. That red magic had hurt her more than any of Nog's other attacks. The ring wasn't helping her.

It was up to him.

"Evangelina Shadow-Storm does not fight alone," he said. "I stand by her side."

Alaric raised the mirror above his head and ran towards the goblin.

44

Nog's magic devoured Lina's cape and crept across her skin. She pulled shadows around herself, trying to block the attack. The fire felt heavy. Was that how he was able to wield light? Had he mixed it with something else?

The magic's weight pulled her to the ground. She lay there, fighting pain as the red light attacked her shadows. Spots clouded her vision. This was it. Nog had her. She couldn't move enough to resist. A single blow would end the fight. He wouldn't even have to use magic. He could step on her.

She closed her eyes and waited for the end.

It didn't come. Lina opened her eyes. Nog wasn't looking at her. He hadn't moved towards her. He focused his attention on a faint glimmer of light.

Alaric.

Lina watched the light flit around Nog. She could just make out Alaric's shape. He was fighting Nog. Protecting her.

She winced as Nog punched Alaric's right shoulder. The prince switched the glass knife to his left hand and kept attacking.

He was doing it all wrong. Fighting angry and trying to manhandle the goblin. To defeat him with strength. No human was strong enough to defeat a goblin that way. If you couldn't outnumber them, your best chance was to outsmart them. Of course that strategy hadn't worked well against Nog so far.

Nog landed another blow on Alaric's side. He was just toying with him now. Alaric nicked Nog's arm with the glass, and the goblin's irritation rippled across the realm of shadows. He wouldn't toy with his prey much longer.

Lina's stomach itched. She reached her hand down and wrapped her fist around a familiar shape.

Her diamond ring.

She slipped it on her finger.

"Heal," she whispered.

Magic bathed her skin. The pain from her burns eased. She could breathe again.

She could move again.

Lina pushed herself to a seated position. The pea emerald sat on the ground beside her. She placed it in her headband. The emerald hastened the diamond's healing magic. She had strength now. Not much, but maybe it would be enough.

Alaric's attacks, however ineffectual, had distracted Nog. He didn't notice Lina's recovery. She stood and gathered her powers. She had enough energy for a single blast of shadow magic. Better make it count.

Nog turned his back to her. He raised his hands, ready to finish Alaric. Lina dove for the goblin. She aimed her shadow magic at the shimmering scar in his neck. A wound caused by light. If she added shadow to the injury, she might be able to defeat him.

The blow met its target. Nog roared and dropped to his knees. Shadow and green tendrils of light surrounded him.

They looped around him until he dropped to the ground. Lina leaned over and looked him in the eye.

"Who helped you?" she said. "Who let you out of the seal?"

Nog laughed.

"You did. Your awakening weakened the seal."

"I don't believe you. Someone taught you light magic. Who?"

"Is it so hard to believe that I learned it myself in a century of imprisonment?"

"Yes. You had help."

"Perhaps."

Nog's laughter turned to a roar of pain. Lina whirled around. The shimmering outline of Alaric stabbed Nog in the chest with the glass blade.

"Alaric, stop!"

Alaric raised the glass above his head for another blow. Lina grabbed his wrist. Their eyes met through the realms.

Then Alaric shook his arm loose and stabbed again.

Nog chuckled.

"Looks like you won't get any answers this time, goat girl."

"No!"

Lina wrapped her shadow magic around Nog and focused on his life force. He wasn't dead yet. There was time. She grabbed his arm and pulled him across the shadow realm to the seal. She ripped it open with her diamond ring and shoved the goblin through the hole. He watched her with dim red eyes. Lina gathered the magic in her ring and pushed the seal shut again.

Three stars appeared over her. With Nog sealed, there was nothing to keep them away.

"It's about time!" Lina said. "Help me shut this!"

The stars hovered around the seal and patched any weaknesses. Lina pulled the pea emerald out of her headband and held it against the seal. The gem crackled as the enchantment absorbed it. She hated to sacrifice the emerald, but it was the only way to mend the seal since she was so weak.

Nog crouched behind the shimmering curtain and glared at her.

"What have you done, shadow warrior?"

Lina focused the last of her energy and wove a truth spell into her shadow magic.

"Saved your life, goblin. You owe me. You will answer my questions."

Nog chuckled. The sound was so soft, Lina hardly heard it. She raised her hand to unleash the truth spell.

"You'll have to find me first," Nog whispered.

The goblin disappeared in a flash of red fire. Lina gasped and rested her hand against the seal. It had not been broken. Wherever the goblin had gone, he was still trapped behind the seal. The faint trace of his energy faded. Had he died? Or simply disappeared deep into the darkness?

Forming the truth spell had taken all Lina's strength. She staggered backwards and collapsed.

❧ 45 ❧

Alaric raised the mirror above his head. The goblin was weakening. He could tell. A few more blows would destroy the creature.

The faint silhouette of Lina grabbed his arm. She was trying to tell him something. Alaric didn't have time to listen. His strength was fading fast. His body ached and swayed. He knew he wouldn't be conscious for much longer. He had to finish this now.

Alaric shook his arm out of Lina's grip and brought the glass dagger down for a final blow.

Nog's body shivered and disappeared. The mirror plunged into a bed of crushed snowbells.

Alaric tried to pull it out of the ground, but his arms were too weak. He gasped for air and looked around.

He sat alone on the mountain. The air had cleared. The wrongness that surrounded Nog had disappeared. A gentle rain washed the smell away.

Alaric pushed himself up. Pain shot through his side, and he collapsed. Standing wasn't an option.

He left the mirror shard stuck in the dirt and crawled

down the mountain. He had to get back to the cave. Had to make sure that Lina was safe. He followed the goblin's muddy footprints as he crawled so he wouldn't get lost.

"Alaric?"

Alaric glanced towards the voice. He had to be dreaming. A lantern bobbed towards him in the darkness. Queen Marta and Henry rushed to his side.

"He's hurt," Marta said.

She placed her hand on Alaric's forehead.

"Heal."

Something cool tingled over Alaric's skin. His breathing eased. He sat up.

"Lina! She was in the realm of shadows! The goblin-"

"Save your strength," Marta said. "We know. Nog is back behind the seal. You're safe."

"What about Lina?"

Marta frowned. Alaric tried to stand but collapsed to the ground.

"What happened to her?"

"You're safe. She's safe. We need to get you all home."

Henry helped him stand. Alaric wrapped his arms around them. Together they hobbled down the mountain. Clouds parted, revealing patches of a starry sky.

The door to the cave was open. Alaric's heart plummeted.

"Did Nog-"

"No," Marta said. "We found her sleeping on the stone. Cael carried her to the carriage. Just a little further now."

Alaric kept walking. The healing magic eased his pain, and he refused to be carried away from the battlefield.

When he saw the carriage, he doubled his pace. Henry lifted him inside. Alaric froze.

Lina lay motionless across the seat. Her eyes were closed. Her face was swollen with cuts and bruises. Alaric sank into the seat across from her. He watched for her to breathe. Please, she couldn't be dead. Not now.

A shallow breath escaped her lips. Alaric leaned back against the cushion. Marta joined him.

"She healed the seal," Queen Marta said. "She put Nog behind it so she could question him, but he evaded her. It is possible that her injuries weakened her enough to put her back in the enchanted sleep."

"No," Alaric said. "No, I won't accept that. She saved us!"

Marta patted his shoulder.

"Yes. She is a true hero."

Alaric took a shuddering breath.

"I won't lose her," he said. "I love her."

Marta smiled sadly at him.

"I know. We'll take her back to the castle. There may be something in the vault that can heal her."

The carriage jolted to a start. Alaric reached his hand out to keep Lina from falling off the seat.

He watched her the whole ride back. There had to be a way to wake her. He was sure of it.

Luca had thought that too, he realized. Alaric wasn't the first to love Lina. He wasn't first to try to save her.

Alaric leaned across the carriage and took Lina's hand.

"Wake up," he whispered. "Please wake up, Lina."

He pulled the emerald ring from his hand and slipped it onto her finger.

❧ 46 ❧

L ina lay on the ground. She felt heavy. That wasn't right. She shouldn't feel heavy. You didn't feel heavy in the realm of shadows. She opened her eyes and stared into the empty sky. Why couldn't she move?

"You're close to death. That was foolish, trying to save Nog for questioning."

Lina took a deep breath. She knew that voice. She would know it anywhere.

"Luca?"

Her voice was raspy. Lina tried to sit up, but she lacked the strength. She turned her head and caught a flash of gold in the corner of her eye. The hazy outline of a star. She collapsed back to the ground.

"This is a dream."

Luca laughed.

"What else did you expect in the realm of shadows? So tell me, goat, why did you try to save the goblin?"

"It's good to see you, donkey breath. Or at least, it's good to hear you."

"Don't avoid the question. Why did you save Nog?"

"He has answers. He couldn't have escaped the seal alone. Someone helped him."

"He also had a century to figure out how to escape. Maybe he was working alone. Or maybe someone helped him decades ago. You can't know for sure."

Lina sighed. Luca was right. She had no proof. She had endangered everyone on a hunch. She should have let Alaric finish the goblin when she had the chance.

"He knew light magic," she said. "That's never happened before. Something has changed. Luca, there's more to this."

"Maybe. If someone helped him, it may be possible to find them and discover how they did it. It won't be easy though. It may take a long time. Will you be around for the quest?"

"What do you mean?"

Lina tried to turn her head. Tried to see him. He stayed just out of reach. A blur of light on the horizon.

"You're close to death. You slept a century, but did you rest? You could do so now. No one would blame you for it."

Lina swallowed.

"Or?"

"Or you can fight. You can search for answers. No guarantees, but it may still be possible to wake up."

"I always fight. You know that. But I can't this time. Luca, I don't have the strength."

"Then I'll see you soon. But don't give up too hastily. You have another chance at life, Lina. At least consider taking it. You've been alone long enough."

The light on the horizon disappeared. Lina stared at the sky above her. She saw nothing but endless darkness.

She closed her eyes. Even that small motion took a long time. Everything moved slowly.

Had Luca really been there? Or was she seeing things from her injuries? Projecting wishful thinking? Anything was possible in the realm of shadows.

Lina struggled for breath, but her lungs wouldn't work. It would be easy to sink back into sleep. So easy to slip into unconsciousness for another century.

Or permanently.

No. She couldn't. Aeonia needed her. Lina gasped and managed to inhale a bit of air. Her ribs ached, but it helped her focus her strength. She had little left. Lina tried to drag herself out of the trance, but it was like pulling an anchor up a mountain.

She couldn't do it. This was a fight she couldn't win.

A weight appeared on her hand. It tingled. Green light sparked over her skin. Lina turned her head and stared at her finger.

The pea emerald ring rested next to the diamond. She smiled. Alaric. He had given the ring back to her.

The pea's magic swirled across Lina's skin. She breathed again. And then again. The pain eased.

Lina closed her eyes. It would take time, but the pea would heal her. She would have the strength to fight after all.

Aeonia needed her.

Lina gathered a tiny bolt of shadow magic in her palm. She wrapped herself in it to intensify the effects of the pea's magic. Light from the gem swept over her body.

Lina tapped her finger impatiently. The motion was a triumph considering her condition a few moments ago, but she wasn't satisfied. She wanted to be healed! She was ready to wake up. Ready to live.

Evangelina Shadow-Storm had slept long enough.

47

Marta placed her hand on Alaric's shoulder.

"You should rest. You're injured."

Alaric shook his head. They had carried Lina through the secret passageway to her bedroom. She lay on her bed barely breathing. None of the potions or charms had helped her.

"I want to be here when she wakes up."

"Alaric–"

"No. I'm not leaving her."

Marta turned to Hilda.

"Bring in two mattresses. There should be plenty left from the mattress towers. And send someone to tell the king I'm back in the castle and taking care of the Princess Test."

Hilda nodded and left the room. Alaric raised an eyebrow.

"Two mattresses?"

"I'll stay with you. Lina means a great deal to me as well."

"Will you tell father about the goblin? About who you really are?"

"In time, after the kings have gone. I don't think it would be wise to mention a goblin to the Council. Revealing my true identity could cause problems. They might decide to trace the royal family's lineage and find another king. We don't need that sort of unrest right now. I had hoped Lina could be the one to tell everyone. It is her story more than anyone else's."

"What if the Council asks questions?"

"I issued an official report blaming our tardiness on the storm. The princesses are safe. Other than a hasty carriage ride down the mountain, they suffered no harm."

Alaric groaned.

"The princesses. Blast. I was supposed to announce my choice to the council tonight."

"It is too late for that now. Surely they've finished their meetings for the evening."

Alaric brushed a strand of hair off Lina's forehead.

"Tomorrow morning then."

"And if she isn't awake?"

Alaric didn't answer. He didn't want to think about that.

Hilda ran through the secret entrance. Bastien followed close behind her.

Hilda curtsied.

"Queen Marta, my husband is raving about something. I told him you were not to be bothered, but he insisted."

Bastien glared at his wife.

"Their Majesties need to know what is going on! The Council is in an uproar!"

Hilda guided her panting husband to a chair.

"Catch your breath, Bastien. What is this about?"

"The Council is still in session. Prince Stefan has sent messengers to every corner of the city searching for you! The King of Gaveron has demanded control of Aeonia if Prince Alaric does not choose a bride tonight as he promised!"

Queen Marta bristled.

"That's nonsense. He has several days to declare a winner."

"But he said he would do it tonight. Prince Stefan is stalling, but he is losing ground. The kings have voted to end the Princess Test if Alaric does not choose his bride tonight! They have all the girls waiting in the Council room."

Alaric stood and brushed his damp, tangled hair away from his face.

"I must go there immediately!"

Marta jogged after him and grabbed his arm.

"Alaric, what about Lina?"

Alaric glanced back at Lina's sleeping form.

"She would want me to protect our country. I cannot allow the King of Gaveron to make a formal motion for the rule of Aeonia."

"We could defend ourselves."

"It would mean war, Marta. You know that as well as I do."

Alaric ran out of the secret passage. His body ached from Nog's blows. He suspected he was almost as bruised as Lina.

Lina. She had kissed him. She had trusted him to fight by her side. He couldn't betray that trust now. He would save Aeonia, even if it meant marrying someone else.

Alaric's heart twisted. Blast it all! He didn't want someone else. He wanted her.

He didn't wait for the guards or trumpeters to announce him. Alaric pushed the doors open and stormed into the throne room.

The princesses stood in a line. Their hair was mussed from the mountain wind. Their clothes were wrinkled from the carriage ride. They whispered to each other as the Council debated.

No one noticed Alaric. He slipped into a corner to catch his breath. He was far too winded to speak at the moment.

"And that's the history of the three greatest storms in Aeonian history," Stefan said. "As the historical record shows, they blow in without warning. As we saw tonight, they can disappear just as suddenly. We had no way of knowing there would be bad weather tonight. But as you can see, the princesses were not harmed."

"I thought the carriage ride was rather thrilling," Marian of Fletcher said.

"That storm smelled like death," Fiora said. "That wasn't natural."

"Do the storms affect seagulls, Prince Stefan?" Carina said.

Everyone turned to stare at her. She gave them a bland smile. In spite of everything, Alaric chuckled to himself. She was devious, that one.

The King of Gaveron cleared his throat.

"We are satisfied with your account of the afternoon's events, Prince Stefan. The true cause for concern is Prince Alaric's disappearance. He said he would choose a bride tonight. If he does not, I must insist the Council consider my motion for Gaveron to-"

"Seagulls eat fish, you know," Carina said. "I thought all birds ate seeds, but seagulls eat fish."

The King of Gaveron glared at her.

"Shut your mouth, princess. No one cares about those blasted birds."

Carina's father stood.

"There is no need to speak to the princesses so disrespectfully."

The King of Gaveron nodded.

"Forgive me, King of Santelle. You are right, of course. I am not angry at these charming ladies. It is Prince Alaric who deserves our wrath. It is unforgivable that he disappeared in the middle of the Princess Test. Especially with such magnificent ladies to choose from. It shows a weakness of character I would expect from someone without noble blood. Now for my motion. I believe Aeonia would benefit from a ruler with a noble lineage. I propose-"

Alaric had heard enough. He stepped from the corner, working hard to hide his limp, and walked to the center of the throne room.

"Be careful of your words, King of Gaveron. The only weakness I have shown tonight is putting your daughter's safety above my own."

The words had an electrifying effect. Every king in the room turned to him. They didn't look happy. In other circumstances, Alaric would have found it intimidating, but these men were nowhere near as fierce as Nog.

"Explain yourself, son," King Noam said. "You look like you tripped and rolled down the mountain."

Alaric glanced down at his tunic. It was coated in mud and grass stains. And blood. Probably his. How had he not noticed? Even Bastien had been too flustered to insist that he change.

He brushed a clump of the mud off his tunic and nodded to the kings.

"One of the princesses had wandered away from the picnic to explore. I stayed behind to search for her so the other princesses could get back to the castle ahead of the storm."

"You spent time alone with her," Fiora said. "That means she'll have to be-"

"Disqualified," the King of Kell said in unison with her. "Exactly so."

Alaric bit his tongue. When he had time, he would reconsider Aeonia's trade agreements with Kell. They were insufferable! But that was not the battle he was here to fight. Lina would want him to protect Aeonia, not her place in the Princess Test.

"Is the girl alright?" King Noam asked.

Alaric nodded.

"She sprained her ankle on the journey down and cannot get out of bed."

Stefan raised his eyebrows at him. They both knew a sprained ankle wouldn't keep Lina in bed. Alaric shook his head at Stefan. His brother caught the message. Don't argue. Let them accept the lie.

The kings did just that. They nodded and whispered to each other.

"Are you ready to select a winner of the Princess Test?" King Noam asked. "The King of Gaveron has proposed several measures regarding your right to rule, but your choice of bride may render them null and void."

The King of Gaveron glowered at Alaric. So did several other members of the Council. Clearly they were not happy to see him.

Alaric ignored his aching heart and nodded.

"I am ready. I have made my choice."

"Then come forward, princesses," King Noam said. "You have had three days to prove your charms and win my son's heart. Let us see who has been successful."

The princesses stepped forward. They were a bedraggled group. Alaric's heart beat faster. He closed his eyes and took a deep breath.

He stepped towards Carina. She met his gaze and looked away. Emotion shone through her bland mask. Regret. Resignation.

Alaric hesitated. He understood those feelings all too well. Carina wanted this marriage even less than he did.

But she would do it for the people. For peace.

That wasn't fair. This wasn't her problem. It wasn't her fight. He thought of the Carina he had seen on the mountain. The one willing to charge at a goblin to save Lina.

She was brave. She was noble.

Carina deserved better than an arranged marriage to save another country.

But what other choice did he have?

Alaric's eyes swept the line of princesses. Fiora's bright red hair caught his eye. His mouth went dry. She noticed him watching her and smiled slightly.

Alaric's heart skipped a beat. Kell had the oldest royal family in Myora. The noblest lineage. He could choose Fiora. It would satisfy the King of Gaveron's claim.

His gaze darted from Carina to Fiora. He swallowed a few times and took another step forward.

❧ 48 ❧

"Lina! Evangelina, please wake up!"

Lina stared into the darkness. She was hearing voices again. The pea's healing magic made her groggy. She couldn't think straight.

Wake up. Yes, she was trying to wake up. That was her goal.

"Lina, can you hear me?"

The voice sounded familiar. She didn't know it as well as Luca's, but she had the vague impression she had met this person before.

Her sides ached. The magic had nearly mended her ribs. Just a few minutes more. She focused on breathing as the voices continued.

"Lina, please! Alaric needs you!"

Marta. That was the name that went with the voice. Who was she talking about?

"I don't think she can hear me, Hilda. What do we do?"

"You are certain they will make Alaric choose a bride?"

"If Bastien was correct, then yes."

A pause.

"We could set the throne room on fire."

"Hilda!"

"It would force the Council's retreat. It would buy us time."

"Could we do it without anyone seeing us?" Queen Marta asked. "We won't be able to get into the throne room without raising suspicion."

"I know a few servants who are crafty enough," another voice said.

A man's voice.

"Go fetch them," Queen Marta said. "Thank you, Bastien."

Hilda laughed.

"What is so funny?"

"You are, Your Highness. You pretend you don't care about these things, but you're the most meddlesome person in this castle."

"My son's happiness is on the line. Not to mention Lina's. I'll burn the whole castle down if I have to. Go fetch some torches, Hilda."

"Yes, My Lady."

Lina stirred. Torches. Fire. They were threatening the castle. Aeonia needed her protection.

She gathered all her strength and opened her eyes.

Light flooded her vision. She blinked. Even that motion hurt, but she was awake! The day's events flooded back to her. The fight with Nog. Kissing Alaric. A strange dream that the castle was on fire. She turned her head.

"Where's Alaric?"

Queen Marta and Hilda's jaws dropped.

"You're awake!" Queen Marta said. "How do you feel?"

"Not great. Are the princesses safe?"

"Yes. Drink this. We won't have to set the castle on fire after all!"

Apparently that part hadn't been a dream. Lina drank the vial of potion Queen Marta gave her.

"Why would you set the castle on fire?"

"The King of Gaveron is trying to take over Aeonia. He claims he has the right because Alaric didn't choose a bride in the Princess Test. Because he isn't noble. Alaric has gone to declare a winner to prevent the takeover."

And she wasn't there. Lina grimaced.

"Alaric's already made his choice. He'll choose Carina."

"He wants you, Lina."

Marta's serious expression caught her off guard. Lina winced.

"He doesn't. I kissed him on the mountain. He clearly wished I hadn't. I think it would be better if I left. He'll be happy with Carina once he gets to know her."

"Evangelina Shadow-Storm, you are going to the throne room to stop him even if I have to carry you."

Lina blinked. Hilda stepped forward.

"I'll help you carry her, Your Majesty. It will be much easier than starting a fire."

Lina turned to Hilda.

"Please, he doesn't want me. It would just be embarrassing."

"He only left your side to keep the King of Gaveron from taking over. He even brought in a mattress so he could sleep here and keep watch over you tonight."

She gestured to a mattress on the floor. Lina blinked. Maybe Alaric did feel something for her. Even if he didn't, she owed it to Aeonia to make sure the King of Gaveron did not succeed in his plot.

"I'll go," she said. "You might need to carry me after all, though. I'm not sure I can walk."

Hilda tucked her arms under Lina's shoulders. Marta grabbed her ankles. The women jogged through the corridor as fast as they could. There was no time to waste. They made a strange sight going down the hallway. Servants and nobility scuttled out of their way.

They stopped outside the throne room door.

"Put me down," Lina said. "I'll look stronger if I walk in. I need them to take me seriously."

"You won't look strong if you faint," Marta said.

"Please."

Marta lowered Lina's ankles to the ground. Hilda released her shoulders. Lina swayed but managed to stay upright. Marta nodded to the guards. They swung the doors open.

"Announce her with a trumpet blast," Marta said. "And Lina, I wouldn't mention the goblin if I were you. Or my true identity. The Council won't believe anything without proof."

The trumpeters raised their instruments to their lips and blew a long blast. Lina walked slowly into the throne room.

❧ 49 ❧

Alaric stepped towards Fiora. Carina didn't deserve to be trapped. If someone had to be miserable, it should be him. He was the one trying to prove his right to rule.

Fiora blinked in surprise. Then she smiled at him. Her fierce face softened. She reached for Alaric's hand.

The doors flew open. The trumpets blared.

Alaric winced. He hated those trumpets. Who was possibly coming in that needed to be announced by trumpets?

His heart skipped a beat. It was Lina. She walked slowly. Proudly. Her head held high.

Alaric turned away from Fiora. He rushed to Lina's side and helped her to the center of the room. She leaned against him with most of her weight.

"Will you marry me?" she whispered.

Alaric stumbled.

"What?"

"I have a plan. Are you willing to marry me if necessary? To save Aeonia?"

Yes! A thousand times yes! Alaric wanted to tell her he

loved her. Wanted to tell her he would fight a hundred goblins to protect her.

But the sound wouldn't come out. He opened and shut his mouth a few times. What was it about Lina that turned him into a babbling idiot?

He closed his mouth and nodded.

Lina squeezed his hand and stepped away from him. She faced the Council of Kings and looked straight at the King of Gaveron.

The king's face contorted into a sneer.

"I'm sorry, Princess. You've been disqualified from the Princess Test. Your little mountain adventure counts as spending time alone with the prince. What you did up there to gain those bruises, I can't imagine. But it doesn't matter. You broke the rules."

Lina nodded.

"I know the rules of the Princess Test. I did not come here to discuss them."

"She's my choice," Alaric said. "I chose her before that. See? I've already given her my ring."

He held Lina's hand up. The diamond and emerald rings on her finger glistened in the light. Fiora stepped back into the line of princesses and crossed her arms. The King of Kell glared at everyone around the room but said nothing.

"That doesn't matter," the King of Gaveron said. "She is still disqualified. This Princess Test has been a disaster from the start. My fellow kings, if Prince Alaric is incapable of choosing a bride, how will he rule a nation? Should we allow a goat herder and the descendants of murderers a place among us? I say we should not. I move for Gaveron to assume rule of Aeonia."

"I will not allow you to claim our land for yourself!" Alaric said.

The King of Gaveron smiled at him as if the outburst proved his point.

"I am not speaking for myself. There is someone with a far greater claim to this throne than you. He came to me for help, and I agreed to beseech the Council of Kings on his behalf. If Gaveron is given rule of Aeonia, I will see that he is given the throne at the proper time."

"The results of a Princess Test have never been used to prove the competence of a ruler," Lina said. "You are trying to turn the situation to your favor. But you are correct about one thing, King of Gaveron. There is someone in this room with a far greater claim to the Aeonian throne than Prince Alaric."

Alaric flinched. The King of Gaveron looked confused.

"I told you, I'm not speaking of myself. The one with a claim to the throne is not in this room. I have kept him secret to ensure his safety. He is-"

"Whatever impostor you've found doesn't matter, King of Gaveron. My name is Evangelina Shadow-Storm. I am a member of the royal family of Aeonia, born long before any of you. I slept for over a hundred years to save this land from a horde of dark creatures. I am the rightful heir to the throne of Aeonia, and I choose Prince Alaric as my consort to rule by my side. We will take care of the rule of Aeonia. Your interference is not necessary."

Lina swayed slightly. Alaric slipped his arm around her. They would stand together.

❧ 50 ❧

Lina leaned against Alaric's shoulder. She didn't have much strength left. That speech had exhausted most of it. Whatever she did, she needed to do it quickly.

The King of Gaveron's stunned silence turned into laughter. Most of the kings joined him.

"The girl is insane," he said. "She has fallen and injured her head. She thinks she is a fairy tale. The prince's play has made her delusional."

"Alaric, what is this?" King Noam said. "I know you've always believed in Evangelina Shadow-Storm, but she isn't real. There is no proof. This princess is obviously injured. She should be in bed."

Lina raised her hand. Her diamond flashed in the light.

"I have proof."

"A magic ring does not prove your identity," the King of Gaveron said. "It is a child's trick. An expensive trick, but a plaything nonetheless."

Lina grinned at him.

"The ring is not the proof. At least, not all of it. The royal family of Aeonia built secrets into this castle. They were carefully guarded. I doubt knowledge of them survived the war. Am I wrong, King of Aeonia?"

King Noam studied Lina. He shook his head.

"There are a few passages between rooms that could be called secret, but I know of nothing else. This castle has been renovated multiple times since the war. Any secrets it held would surely have been discovered."

"Why are we still speaking to her?" the King of Kell said. "She should be locked away. She is delusional. The prince must choose a bride!"

Alaric tensed. Lina patted his shoulder and winked at him.

"These are not secrets that carpenters could find. Only a member of the royal family with a magical signet ring may unlock them."

"It's a trick," the King of Gaveron said. "She's looked up some obscure architectural fact in the archives and will use it to deceive us all."

King Noam ignored the comments and kept his attention focused on Lina.

"My son trusts this young woman. Alaric, you believe her story?"

Alaric nodded.

"I do, father. I trust Evangelina Shadow-Storm with my life."

King Noam bowed to Lina.

"Then show us your proof, my dear. It is the Council's tradition to accept testimony if three pieces of evidence support it. You must show us three things that prove your identity. For all of our sakes, I hope your secrets are truly spectacular."

Lina grinned.

"Don't worry. They are."

She walked towards the King of Gaveron. He sat on the throne at the end of the room. Alaric walked with her. He was supporting most of her weight now. She would fall if he let go.

Lina stopped a few feet away from the throne.

"In addition to being a member of the royal family, I was a trusted agent of the Council of Kings in my time. An elite shadow warrior in charge of their protection. The King of Gaveron was the ceremonial head of the Council then as well."

The King of Gaveron bristled.

"My position is more than ceremonial. I am responsible for the wellbeing of all the countries in Myora. I take this responsibility seriously."

"Yes, you showed how seriously you take that responsibility when you aided Aeonia during their civil war."

"I did not interfere in the war."

"Exactly. King Noam ended the war with his marriage. Aeonia did not need your help then. We don't need it now. But that hasn't stopped you from sitting in the king's throne as if you had fulfilled your duties to perfection."

The King of Gaveron jumped to his feet.

"This is an outrage! I will not be insulted by a deranged girl."

Lina winked at him.

"Thank you for standing, Your Highness. If you would step to the side."

The King of Gaveron sputtered.

"Just do it," the King of Santelle said. "Let her present her evidence so we may put this matter to rest."

"I see you have made your allegiances clear, King of Santelle."

The King of Santelle shrugged.

"Santelle does not fear Gaveron. We don't fear anyone outside our borders."

The King of Gaveron glared at the King of Santelle, but he stepped to the side. Lina collapsed into the throne.

"Stand over there, Alaric. I don't want you to get hurt."

"Lina, what are you going to do?"

She waved her hand. Alaric took a few steps to the side.

Lina swept her gaze across the room, meeting the eyes of every king.

"Magic used to be an essential part of life in Aeonia. That was not a lifestyle without risks. More than once the king was attacked. He built protection into his throne."

She slipped her diamond into a small hole in the side of the arm rest and turned her hand. The latch clicked. A haze of pearly magic engulfed the throne.

Everyone gasped.

"It's a trap!" the King of Gaveron said. "She's tricking you! She's a witch!"

Lina pulled her ring from the throne. The shield around her disappeared.

"I present this secret of the Kings of Aeonia as my first piece of evidence: a protection spell unlocked with my signet ring. Does the Council accept this?"

Most of the kings nodded.

"You're fools," the King of Gaveron said. "So she knows one trick. That hardly counts as knowledge of castle secrets."

Lina bristled.

"I have more."

"Let her present the rest of her evidence," the King of Montaigne said. "She must present two more items."

He smiled at Lina. She smiled back. He was much younger than the other kings. About her own age. He could not have been ruling long. She curtsied to him.

"This throne room has other secrets if you still doubt me. The king who built this castle loved the night sky. He challenged his architects and enchanters to build a room that let him conduct official business under the stars."

She walked behind the throne and turned the latch with her ring. Sounds of grating stone filled the room. The domed ceiling opened to reveal a starry sky. The storm had faded completely.

Everyone stared at the sky above them. Lina stepped out from behind the throne and stumbled. Alaric caught her. He wrapped his arm around her waist and held her upright.

"Another secret of Aeonia for the Council," Lina said. "Do you accept this proof?"

Most of the kings were too busy staring at the sky to respond.

"May I see your ring?" King Noam said.

Lina pulled off the diamond ring and handed it to him.

"It is engraved with the royal seal of Aeonia," she said. "Don't try to deny it."

King Noam examined the ring.

"It is indeed," he said. "The evidence seems to support your claim."

"She can show you her temple," Alaric said. "The place where she slept for a century. The seal that holds the goblins even now."

Lina smiled at him. King Noam handed the ring to the King of Santelle.

"Examine this if you like. I am satisfied with her first two pieces of evidence. The secrets of the castle and this signet ring."

The King of Santelle turned the ring over in his hand.

"It seems authentic. It looks dwarf made. The King of Gaveron could confirm that better than I."

Everyone looked to the King of Gaveron. He glowered at them.

"The dwarfs of Gaveron no longer forge jewelry for humans."

"But they did a century ago," Alaric said. "They were the jewelers of choice for noble families of every country."

Other kings gathered around the King of Santelle to study the ring.

"It looks dwarf made to me," the King of Montaigne said. "You can compare it to mine if you like. This has been in our family for generations."

He held out his hand. The kings examined the two rings and nodded in agreement.

The King of Santelle handed the ring back to Lina. She slipped it on her finger.

"So you believe her?" Alaric said. "You will honor our engagement and Lina's claim to the throne?"

"Not so fast," the King of Kell said. "You must present another piece of evidence. A claim must be supported by three pieces."

"Surely the cave counts," Alaric said. "The temple where she slept."

The King of Gaveron sneered.

"Anyone could find a cave or a ring and claim to be the original owner. The third piece must be something more substantial. Perhaps this alleged shadow warrior could perform shadow magic for us?"

Lina's heart sank. She was exhausted. The King of Gaveron's sneer said that he knew it.

"Yes," the King of Kell scoffed. "Perhaps she could turn into a goat."

Lina stood tall. She stepped away from Alaric's embrace. Her anger boiled over. She had almost died to save their lives, and they wanted her to turn into a goat to prove her identity?

"I do not turn into a goat!"

Her anger flared into a burst of shadow magic. Dark lightning sparked around the room. It crawled along the marble. Her shadow cloak appeared behind her. The pea ring transformed into a spear.

Her magic faded before her anger did. She sank into Alaric's arms.

"A demonstration of a shadow warrior's abilities," Alaric said. "I present this to the kings as the third piece of evidence."

The kings stared back open mouthed. One by one they nodded.

"We accept this demonstration as evidence," the King of Montaigne said.

"It is a trick," the King of Gaveron said. "A parlor trick of a cheap magician!"

But he didn't sound convinced. His voice wavered a little as he said it.

The King of Santelle stood.

"The Council accepts Evangelina Shadow-Storm's three pieces of evidence: her knowledge of Aeonia's castle secrets, her dwarf-made signet ring, and her demonstration of shadow magic. We recognize her engagement to Prince Alaric and her claim to the throne of Aeonia."

King Noam nodded.

"I accept this evidence and support her. She may take the throne tonight if she wishes."

Lina shook her head.

"No, I will not overthrow you, King Noam. I wish this transition to be peaceful. You will rule as long as you like. Alaric and I will take the throne after you."

The kings nodded.

"That is a sensible solution," the King of Montaigne said. "I have no doubt that Aeonia will flourish under your rule."

"Her identity has been proved," the King of Gaveron said.

"But I do not accept her claim to the throne. There is one with a far greater right to rule Aeonia than this witch."

"I do not accept her engagement," the King of Kell said. "The prince agreed to choose a bride from one of our daughters."

The King of Eldria stepped forward.

"I fail to see how anyone could have a greater claim to the throne than a surviving member of the royal family of Aeonia. King of Gaveron, do you have three pieces of evidence with you to say otherwise?"

The King of Gaveron shook his head.

"There is evidence, but I did not bring it. I didn't think I would need it tonight."

"Then you cannot make your claim. As to the question of the Princess Test, their marriage provides a peaceful solution to the question of who will rule Aeonia. I propose that we honor her wishes."

The Council of Kings nodded in agreement.

"It is done then," the King of Santelle said. "Congratulations to Princess Evangelina, heir to the throne of Aeonia."

"And winner of the Princess Test!" Carina said.

Everyone turned to look at her.

"Well, she is, isn't she? The rest of us may go back to our rooms? We've had a long day."

The other princesses nodded. Fiora stepped forward as if to object, but thought better of it and stepped back into the line.

"Of course you may go," King Noam said. "Stefan, will you escort these ladies back to their rooms?"

Stefan nodded. He winked at Alaric as he passed.

"I'm glad all your research paid off."

The princesses filed out of the room. The King of Gaveron smiled at Lina. It wasn't a pleasant expression.

"Now that you are heir, you will of course attend the rest

of our council tonight. It will be an excellent chance to prove your strength. Your nobility."

Lina leaned against Alaric. She had spent her strength fighting Nog and the Council. She had nothing left.

Alaric held her close.

"Princess Evangelina has expressed her wish for King Noam to maintain his position for the time being. Surely he can handle any negotiations that are needed?"

Lina nodded.

"I support King Noam's decisions. He will remain the king."

King Noam hugged Lina and Alaric.

"I am happy for both of you," he said. "I do have one request before you go. Could you close the roof in case another storm blows in?"

"Of course."

King Noam watched Lina turn the latch with her ring. The roof slid shut.

"Marvelous," King Noam said. "Are there other secrets around the castle?"

"Hundreds."

"I do hope you'll show them to me sometime. Now go rest."

Alaric helped Lina out of the throne room before anyone could object. She stood tall until the doors closed behind them. Then she collapsed into his arms.

He picked her up and kissed her forehead.

"I'm sorry," she whispered. "Put me down. I'll try to walk."

"You've done more than enough tonight, Princess Evangelina Shadow-Storm. Let me help you."

Alaric held her close and carried her back to her room. Lina wrapped her arms around him and rested her head on his shoulder.

Alaric opened his eyes. He was stiff from sleeping on a mattress on the floor. He turned his head and searched for Lina. She lay on her bed staring at him. He smiled at her, but she looked away.

Alaric pulled himself to his feet and navigated the sea of mattresses and sleeping people on the floor. Marta had insisted on staying in the room with them. So had Carina. Hilda volunteered to be a chaperon for the night. Bastien had joined her.

And King Noam insisted on stationing guards inside the room just to be sure the new Princess of Aeonia stayed safe.

Alaric stepped over Marta's mattress and sat on Lina's bed. He took her hand. She tensed but did not pull back.

"How do you feel?" he asked.

"Better. A little."

Her voice was hoarse. Raspy. She was still bruised, but the swelling had gone down.

"It will take time," he said. "You will recover. I'll search that vault for every healing potion for you."

She smiled.

"Save some for yourself. You fought a goblin single handedly."

"No, I wasn't alone."

He squeezed her hand gently. Lina frowned.

"Alaric, I'm sorry."

"For what?"

"I know the idea of an arranged marriage bothers you. You've been miserable throughout the Princess Test. I didn't mean to trap you in an engagement with me. I should have found another way."

Alaric's mouth went dry. He had thought this was settled. Did she not want to marry him after all?

"Lina-"

Tears glistened in her eyes.

"You may be able to get out of it. Once the Council leaves, I can disappear. The world forgot about me once. They can do it again. You'll be free. You deserve to be free."

"Lina, I don't want to be free. Don't you dare disappear. I love you."

He raised her hand and brushed it against his lips. Lina shuddered.

"Don't say that. I saw your face after I kissed you. You don't have to pretend."

"Lina, I expected you to slap me or worse up there. I was too shocked to react. I thought you'd hate me for killing your family."

"Why would I hate you? You didn't kill them. You had no part in that."

"The Council of Kings blames me for my forefathers' actions. I thought you would as well."

She shook her head. A tiny gesture. Alaric wiped a tear from her cheek.

"If anything, I should apologize for trapping you," he said. "You're a hero. You sealed the darkness away twice.

You shouldn't have to marry me to save Aeonia from Gaveron."

The corner of Lina's mouth twitched up into a smile.

"I want to marry you."

"Why? Why would you want a second rate prince without noble blood?"

"Alaric, I haven't known you long, but I have seen your heart. You are the noblest person I've ever met. You are kind enough to share your breakfast with a complete stranger. Brave enough to attack a goblin with a piece of glass. Selfless enough to enter a completely miserable marriage to save your country. To choose the more miserable marriage to make sure you didn't bring unhappiness to another. I saw you were about to choose Fiora."

Alaric shrugged.

"If someone had to be miserable as a result of the Princess Test, it should be me. It was obvious Carina didn't want to marry me. And it was very obvious that Fiora did."

Lina laughed.

"That much is true. I'll have to watch my back. I think she might come after me."

"After spending so much time with the royal family of Kell, I'm seriously reconsidering our trade relationship with them."

Lina laughed.

"I can't blame you. It might be a good idea to put some distance between us while they cool off. You're sure this engagement doesn't bother you, Alaric?"

"Bother me? Lina, do you have any idea how magnificent you are? You sacrificed your whole life to save Aeonia. You worked to protect us when none of us believed in you. You're twice as brave as I am. Your story has been my inspiration since I was a child."

"I wouldn't trust that story too much."

"Then it's a good thing I loved you as Lina before I knew you were Evangelina Shadow-Storm."

She blinked.

"Truly?"

"I swear it. Ask Stefan or Marta. They knew it before I did. I love you, Lina. I want to marry you. I want to rule by your side. We'll protect Aeonia together."

Alaric bent over Lina and kissed her gently. She wrapped her arms around him.

"Ahem."

Alaric sat up. Hilda glared at them from a chair by the fire.

"As your chaperon, I cannot allow such behavior."

Alaric sighed.

"What sort of behavior can you allow, Hilda?"

She thought for a moment.

"You may hold hands."

They waited, but she didn't continue.

"And?" Lina asked.

"Anything more would be inappropriate. Be grateful I'm not regulating the time you spend in each other's company. When I was young, engaged couples were only allowed an hour of chaperoned time together each day."

Alaric looked at Lina.

"What about in your century?"

"I don't know. I was never engaged in my time."

She reached for his hand.

The sound of fabric ripping filled the room. Carina stood.

"Blast, I've torn my sleeve. Hilda, will you take me to have it fixed?"

Hilda narrowed her eyes.

"I'm not falling for that trick, Princess. I am not leaving them unchaperoned until the wedding."

Carina shrugged at Lina. The torn sleeve of her night-gown dangled around her wrist.

"I tried. You'd better invite me to the wedding."

Lina and Alaric smiled.

"Of course we will."

EPILOGUE

Queen Marta gripped Lina's arm as they exited the carriage. Moonlight bathed the archive in a soft glow, and the fresh scent of the ocean filled the air.

"Why are you so nervous?" Lina asked. "Do you think it is a mistake to tell them?"

Marta swallowed.

"No, but they'll be the first to discover the secret in over a century. That's enough to make anyone nervous."

Lina raised an eyebrow. Marta shook her head.

"I'm probably being silly, but what if Noam is angry that I lied? He thinks he married a goat herder. What if-"

"He doesn't love you when he discovers you're a member of the royal family that has been protecting Aeonia for a century? Marta, that makes you better, not worse."

Marta swallowed again.

"I know. I keep telling myself that. The other members of the Society weren't happy when I married him. They thought it was a mistake to get involved with the new royal family."

Lina stopped just in front of the archive door. She turned and met Marta's gaze.

"It will be alright. I told Alaric a far more fantastic tale, and he believed me. Noam will understand. If anyone in the Society objects to this, send them to me."

Marta smiled at Lina and knocked once on the archive door. Simon opened it.

"Thank goodness you are here! Everyone else arrived some time ago. I have had a hard time keeping them here without explaining what is happening."

Lina smiled.

"Thank you, Simon. We'll tell them right away."

Lina and Marta walked towards the group gathered at the front of the archive.

"But what is this about, Alaric?" King Noam said. "Why are we here?"

"Why, indeed?" Stefan said. "Dragging me here in the morning is one thing. Dragging me here in the middle of the night is something else entirely."

The rest of the princes ignored the conversation. Prince Marcus, Alaric's youngest brother, gazed around the moonlit archive. He stood taller than his father and had curly blond hair and a sprinkle of freckles across his face. He seemed completely content to study the patterns of moonlight on the mirrors.

Henry, Cael, and Benjamin stood in a group apart from the rest. They looked almost as nervous as their mother.

"Here," Alaric said. "Lina will explain everything."

Everyone turned to her. In spite of her reassurances to Marta, Lina's heart beat faster. This secret had been kept for a century. Luca had hidden their family well. But the King of Aeonia needed to know the truth.

Alaric wrapped his arm around her and smiled.

"Lina is not the only secret that was hidden away. She would like to tell you more about the past so that we can move into the future together."

King Noam glanced at Simon.

"This isn't a royal secret, is it? Everyone in the room can hear this?"

Simon bristled. Lina spoke before the archivist could.

"Simon already knows about this, Your Highness. He has kept this secret his whole career."

"Really?" Prince Marcus said. "Are there hidden scrolls somewhere? That would be marvelous."

"Yes, what a treasure," Stefan said. "More information."

Lina squeezed Alaric's hand and cleared her throat. It would be best to say it quickly. To get it over with. She didn't want to lose her nerve.

"Your Highness, this concerns the war. When your ancestors took over the rule of Aeonia."

The light faded from King Noam's eyes. Everyone grew serious.

"Go on," King Noam said. "I assume you have made yourself familiar with that incident even though you were asleep at the time?"

Lina nodded.

"Yes, but the story you know is not complete. My brother Luca was a court enchanter at that time. He opposed the king's actions and refused to aid him. He sheltered members of the royal family who did not wish to fight. Luca hid them as efficiently as he hid me. Those who fought died, but those who hid lived safely for the rest of their lives. Their descendants live still."

The princes turned to King Noam. He kept his face smooth and expressionless, but emotion wavered in his voice.

"You are sure about this, Lina? Not everyone died? They weren't killed?"

She nodded.

"Luca used his magic to hide every trace of them just as he did with me. He was surprisingly good at it."

"But you were asleep. Much easier to hide."

"Not necessarily. It took a lot of work to hide all traces of me. Luca had to erase records without being obvious. I think he even tried to make the wolf statue look older by wearing away the marble before burying it in moss. But he hid the royal family in plain sight. They became goat herders."

"Oh."

King Noam looked at Marta.

"Oh! So you mean-"

Marta nodded.

"I would have told you if I could. I'm sorry."

King Noam stared at her. Henry, Cael, and Benjamin were tense. Ready to run, Lina thought.

Then King Noam laughed. He took Marta's hands and kissed them.

"All this time I worried what you thought of me. How you could marry a man whose ancestors had such blood on their hands. But you were protecting us all along?"

Marta nodded. She laughed along with him.

"Yes! Your ancestors were simply bad at searching. And I suppose Luca was good at hiding."

"Luca was a master of pranks," Lina said. "And hiding that many people would be a sort of prank. He probably enjoyed the challenge. Most of the goat herders are descended from the royal family. Marta and I are distantly related."

Stefan gaped at his stepbrothers.

"You were princes this whole time?"

They nodded.

"That's it, then. No more goat herder excuses to get out of princely duties. I fully expect you to greet the next ten ambassadors who visit!"

Henry straightened his tunic.

"We weren't always looking after goats, you know. Most of

the time we left suddenly we were helping the Society of Evangelina."

"You're all part of the Society?" Marcus asked. "That's fantastic! Can I join? I've always wanted to, and they wouldn't let me!"

"The Society is an excuse for Luca's descendants to meet," Marta said. "We couldn't risk a member who was an outsider."

Marcus ducked his head.

"But now that you know, I see no reason you can't join."

"Really?"

Marcus beamed at Marta.

"When is the next meeting?"

She chuckled.

"I'm not sure. The Society's role will change now that Lina is awake. We have guarded her since Luca died, but I'm sure she'll need help in other ways now."

"Will you tell everyone?" Alaric asked. "Will we make a royal decree?"

Marta shook her head.

"No. Not now. This needs to remain a secret for the time being. The country needs time to accept Lina's return. The Society needs time to adjust to our new roles."

King Noam frowned.

"I would like to tell them sometime. It would ease my mind for everyone to know the truth about the royal family."

Marta smiled at him.

"Of course. Sometime soon, I hope. But not now."

He nodded.

"For now it is our secret," Lina said. "We're a family, and we'll need the resources Luca left behind to protect Aeonia. I still suspect someone helped Nog escape. I hope the magic in the vault will help me find out who did it."

Marcus's eyes lit up.

"Luca left magic behind?"

"Here we go," Stefan said. "You'll regret letting him into your club."

"Marcus has always loved magic," Alaric whispered to Lina. "He's been trying to teach himself enchantments since he was a child."

"I don't suppose you ever joined him?"

Alaric winked.

"I might have once or twice."

"Everyone must wear a smock in the vault!" Simon said. "The items Luca left are irreplaceable. I won't risk getting them dirty!"

He rushed around handing everyone white smocks. They slipped them over their clothes. The silver moonlight gleamed on the white cloth.

"I can't tell you how pleased I am to finally share this secret," Simon said. "The greatest resources in the Aeonian archive, and I've had to keep them hidden away!"

"They won't be for public display," Queen Marta said. "You know that, right? We're the only ones allowed in."

Simon bowed to the group.

"This is more than enough. And to have Evangelina Shadow-Storm to help us interpret the documents will be invaluable. I must apologize again for not recognizing you the first time you came into the archive."

Lina nodded to him. She was having trouble pulling her smock over her head. It had been a few weeks since her battle with Nog, but her arms were still stiff. Alaric took the smock from her hands and slipped it over her head and shoulders. She thanked him with a quick kiss.

Queen Marta and King Noam smiled and shared a kiss of their own.

"I am so glad you woke up, Lina," Marta said. "It is wonderful to have you here."

"It is wonderful to know the truth," King Noam said.

Stefan pulled his smock over his head and made a face.

"I was looking forward to not doing any more research. Is it really necessary for all of us to go to the vault?"

"Yes, it is," Marta said. "Together, we are the new royal family of Aeonia. We all need to understand what the previous one left behind."

Cael, Henry, and Benjamin ignored Stefan's protests and walked towards the center of the room. They gathered light magic in their hands and aimed it at the ceiling.

"Of course," Prince Marcus said. "The mirrors that reflect sunlight and moonlight also reflect light magic. Do you think you could teach me?"

King Noam laughed.

"Let them open the vault in peace, Marcus. If it is possible to teach you, I'm sure they will."

Marcus smiled at Lina.

"I found some scrolls at the school archive that might interest you," he said. "I could request to have them transferred here if you want to look at them."

She nodded.

"Yes, that would be helpful. Simon, how does the vault door work?"

The archive keeper shrugged.

"I'm not sure exactly. Light magic must be mixed with moonlight for the doors to open. It will take about an hour to activate the enchantment."

Stefan choked.

"An hour? We're going to sit here for an hour while they blast those mirrors with light?"

"Yes," Marta said. "We are. Be thankful all three of them are here. It takes much longer for one person to open it. This is why we weren't able to fetch enchanted gems quickly enough for Lina when she fought Nog. It took too long to open the doors."

"Moonlight," Lina said. "I wonder if the spell was originally meant to be aided by shadow magic. I can't imagine Luca having the patience to spend an hour opening a door."

She walked to the middle of the room and shot a blast of shadow magic towards the mirrors. The archive shuddered, and a section of the floor slid away to reveal a winding set of stairs.

"Remarkable!" Simon said.

"Thank goodness," Stefan said.

Simon led them down the stairs. Lina's heart pounded as she walked. It smelled like her old workshop. Like potions and gems and parchments. Like magic.

"All this time," Alaric said. "Proof was here this whole time. Do you know how many hours I searched scrolls for evidence of Evangelina? You could have given me a hint, Simon. Some encouragement."

Simon sniffed.

"I would not risk the safety of Lady Evangelina Shadow-Storm to satisfy the curiosity of a young prince."

"Or two princes," Marcus said. "I spend more time in the archives than you do, Alaric."

"I'm older. I started before you."

They reached the bottom of the staircase. A huge room supported by marble columns stretched as far as Lina could see in every direction. Enchanted gems in the ceiling illuminated the space.

"Oh," she said. "This is amazing! I had no idea it would be this big!"

"We don't know what half of it is," Marta said. "Luca's cataloging system isn't very organized."

Marcus ran to the nearest table and surveyed its contents.

"These are communication charms, right, Lina?"

Lina glanced at the table and nodded.

"Yes. How did you know that?"

Marcus smiled.

"I've spent a lot of time researching ancient magic. I recognize most of this. I could have helped Marta catalog it if she had told me."

"Well, you can help me," Lina said. "How would you like to be my research apprentice? I'll need a lot of help to take inventory of everything."

Marcus beamed at her.

"Truly? You would let me help you?"

"I'll need you to help me. Do you accept?"

"Yes! Of course!"

Marcus ran from table to table examining the magical objects.

"You've made him very happy," Alaric whispered.

"He'll be very useful. We can use this magic to protect Aeonia once we know what we have."

Alaric kissed the top of her head.

"I'm glad."

"I'm not helping," Stefan said. "I'm done with research for a decade at least."

Lina grinned at him.

"I won't ask for your assistance, then. From what Alaric has told me, you've already helped me quite a bit."

"More than you'll ever know. This oaf refused to acknowledge his feelings for you. He might have ended up with that bird brain Carina if not for me."

"She isn't really obsessed with seagulls," Lina said. "She was helping me. Distracting Alaric."

Stefan shrugged.

"So you keep saying. Ugh. The only one worse than her was Fiora."

"Stefan!" Marcus called. "Come look at this! I found armor and swords!"

"Excellent!"

Stefan bowed to Lina and rushed to join Marcus.

"Lina, come with me," Marta said. "I want to show you something."

Lina took Alaric's hand. Together they passed tables full of magical items. Marta paused in front of a small silver door.

"I think you'll want to look at these first."

Lina pushed the door open and gasped. Shelves of scrolls filled the room.

"Are these-?"

Marta nodded.

"Letters from Luca. He wrote to you every day. The earliest are over here."

She led Lina to a small shelf in the corner. Lina pulled out the bottom scroll and checked the date.

"He wrote this the day I fell asleep."

Tears gathered in her eyes. Alaric wrapped his arm around her.

"Do you want me to leave you alone?"

"No, please stay."

Lina unrolled the scroll. Her heart pounded as she read Luca's familiar scrawling script.

DEAR GOAT-FACE,

BLAST IT ALL, LINA. IT ISN'T ANY FUN CALLING YOU NAMES when you can't answer. I'm tempted to call myself donkey just so it feels like you're here.

From what I can tell, your enchantment was a success. At least, I haven't been ambushed by any goblins today. I reported as much to

King Dacian, and he seems pleased. I've been promoted, and he's agreed to give me whatever resources I need to make sure the seal holds.

I plan to use them to wake you. Don't worry. I won't do it unless I know the seal will hold without you. Well, I might do it if I know only a few goblins will slip through. We can deal with those.

I miss you, Lina. It has only been a few hours, but I miss you.

LINA LOWERED THE SCROLL. SHE COULDN'T SEE IT ANY more. Tears streamed down her face.

Alaric held her close while she cried. He stroked her hair.

"I miss him," Lina said. "I'm sorry, but I do."

"Don't be sorry. Of course you miss him. He was your brother. Your best friend."

Lina looked at the long line of shelves.

"He missed me for a lifetime," she said. "I've only been without him a few days. It feels so wrong. So strange to be out of sync. We did everything together."

"I can't imagine. Lina, I would make it right if I could."

"Make it right? No, Alaric. Don't think that way. Luca and I chose this. We made this sacrifice to keep Aeonia safe. I miss him, but I wouldn't change it."

"You are too perfect, you know. Too brave."

Lina rolled the scroll up and returned it to its place on the shelf. Her heart ached. She couldn't read any more right now.

It was too painful to have Luca's words and not Luca. She would read the letters later. A little at a time. She wanted to know Luca's story.

But she also wanted to discover her own.

Lina wrapped her arms around Alaric and pulled him into a kiss.

ABOUT THE AUTHOR

A.G. Marshall loves fairy tales and has been writing stories since she could hold a pencil. She is a professional pianist and perfected her storytelling by writing college papers about music (which is more similar to magic than you might think).

Want more stories? Find deleted scenes, blog posts, coloring pages, and writing playlists at my website! Sign up for my newsletter while you're there to get an exclusive short story for free!

Connect Here!
www.AngelaGMarshall.com
angelagmarshall@outlook.com

ACKNOWLEDGMENTS

Writing a book is both a solitary pursuit and a community effort. It would be impossible to thank everyone who helped me and influenced this novel, but here are a few special thanks.

To my parents, for always supporting me. Abby, for listening to many rambles about book related things and offering insight. Alex for being willing to talk about books in much more detail than most.

My beta readers, who always provide feedback that is both encouraging and cuts to the heart of the story. My mom, Aunt Cindy, and Kristin Stecklein provided a fabulous first round of comments.

I usually write at home, but large parts of this book were finished at other people's houses. Thanks to Stephanie. I finished my first round of edits while house-sitting for her. It was a marathon of editing! And to Audrey. I finished formatting while visiting her in Texas. Not the vacation most people would plan, but it was perfect for me.

Also thanks to Aunt Rebecca, who pitched my books to a stranger after texting a wrong number. I don't know who they are or if they ever read *Rook and Shadow*, but I do know my family will always have my back.

Calthyechild's wonderful brushes and map making tutorial made the map of Myora possible. Check her out on DeviantArt.

Made in the USA
Coppell, TX
19 April 2020

21050757R00196